DEAD MALLS

DEAD MALLS

a novel

DARBY HARN

FAIR
PLAY
BOOKS

For Kim

"All reality is a game."

– IAIN M. BANKS

DIANE

The sun rises early Thursday night.

Sam and Diane die with the TV. You think, *We didn't pay the bill again.* But your mother doesn't scream when you don't have enough money for the electricity. She cries sometimes, sure, but she doesn't stand at the living room window and stare in shock at the fire in the sky. She doesn't grab you and run down into the basement. You ask what's happening. *This isn't happening,* she says, and believe her.

This never happened.

Thanksgiving is still a week away. Christmas is coming. 1984. The world didn't just end in a hail of nuclear missiles. You're still sleeping in your bed, the brand-new department store Christmas catalog better than a toy in your arms, hoping this year is different. Read the entire catalog, over and over again. The items. The features. The prompts for tomorrow, the holiday, your happiness.

Endless possibilities await you this holiday season...
turn to the next page for details!

CHRISTMAS 1983

GIFTS FOR THE
ENTIRE FAMILY

WE'RE NEVER CLOSED!
SHOP TOLL-FREE ANYTIME!

SAM

BE KIND. PLEASE REWIND.

Perfect. Someone spray painted the food court again. Radiation yellow all across the mall directory. Not that an outdated map told you anything the overgrown weeds out in the parking lot didn't. This place is empty. Well. Theoretically, it is.

I thumb my radio. "Hey, Roger."

The radio crackles. "Go for Roger."

Least I can do is have fun with it. "Looks like The Joker left us another riddle down here in the food court."

I can already hear him running. "Code Blue."

"Pretty sure only somebody old can solve it."

Let's say trotting. "Hold position."

"So you'd better get down here."

"They could still be in the mall."

This will be the rest of the night. Going empty store to empty store through the entire mall to find out no one is in here but us. Check all the doors. Loading dock. Vents. Call the guy to come scrub the paint off. Pay him out of pocket so we don't have to file an incident report and the owners don't bounce us for another security outfit. Work for free tonight, because Roger underbid those other guys so much that I'm only getting paid out of pocket, too.

Theoretically.

"Clear," I say, and slide the security gate down behind me.

Roger holds his taser to his chin. "Let's move."

He draws in a breath, holds it, and then hustles to the next store on the main concourse. In his mind, I bet we're a special ops team dropped inside hostile territory in the dead of night.

May as well be.

The mall hums with wasted neon. Emergency flare red colors the main concourse. Aliens or robots could hide in the shadows, or at least I imagine they could whenever I'm bored.

So most of the time.

Roger likes to say the main concourse is longer than an airport runway, but the mall more or less forms a U shape. The old department store anchors the west side. Empty movie theater the east. The food court sits at the south entrance in the saggy center. The only remaining stores hold on the perimeter, leaving about half a million square feet split across two levels for someone to hide in. We clear the lower level and then move up the grand staircase.

Roger backs against the wall. "Draw your weapon, Sam."

"It's spray paint," I say.

"You don't know what it could be."

"Guess it could be mustard."

"Draw your weapon."

I draw my taser. Thing looks like some kind of *Star Trek* doo-dad. "This guy's going to be shocked when we find him."

"Call the Code Blue next time."

"I called you."

"Don't play around on the radio. Call it."

"I'm just trying to make it fun."

"I ever tell you about that guy at the bar?"

This is my own fault. "You told me."

"Slumped against the bar. Bartender's telling him he's got to go but he won't. I thought this was just some drunk, so I didn't give him a second look. Turns out he's packing a six-shooter in his belt. He came in to confront his girlfriend. I'm like, 'Reach for that piece, man, and you're going to end up on the news.'"

"Yeah."

"He was like, 'You're not a cop.' I said, 'I know. But I'm hired security. You have to be prepared for all contingencies.'"

"Right."

He goes to another vacant. "Check this one."

"The gate's secure."

"They can pick the locks."

"But they can't lock them from the inside. Roger. We should be checking the loading dock. It's the only way in."

"We need to clear the mall first."

"There's like three open stores left in here. Actually, I think the flower shop is gone. Have you seen them lately?"

"That's not the point. These YouTube guys come in here all the time. If they steal stuff, if they get killed doing their stunts on the property, that's on the company. Guess who they're going to pin that on? I don't know about you, but I can't afford a lawyer."

The YouTube thing is a real problem, especially when you have a mall as rundown as ours. How it stays open at all, I don't know. Twelve people work here now. Eleven? Back in the day, it was 2400. Guess it has to do with contracts and stuff Roger talks about but doesn't ever really explain. When I first started working security with him, I wanted to go store to store. I wanted to exhaust ten hours on my feet every single night. The less time I spent out there the better. I don't know. Guess I'm starting to feel as empty as this mall.

Roger peeks into another empty. "This one."

Fifty pounds of gear I'll never use nearly carries me over as I bend down to unlock another gate. I don't even know what half these stores used to be. Some still got their signs up. Claire's. Sears. Even when I was a kid, it was half empty, and we really only came out here to go to the movies. My Dad, though. He talks about this palace. This cathedral to the 1980s. Like I missed out on the best time to be alive.

I flash the dark. "Clear."

Roger finally breathes. "We might have lost them."

"They're getting in through the loading dock. They have to be. We either need to be there all the time, or we need another person."

"We just have to be more on our game."

"Our game?"

Roger shuffles to the old iron banister overlooking the lower level. He looks out over the main concourse below like it's some unprotected retail frontier. Jowly old cowboy. This is his domain. He's the last vanguard of a dying civilization. No one gets it but him.

"The Joker doesn't leave riddles," he says. "The Riddler does."

Oh, man. "Is that what you're mad about?"

"Maybe this is too boring for you. I can put you on the detail over at the nightclub. Tim will swap. He doesn't care."

I back into something. Something hard. My arms go up. Wait. I just bumped into the wall. "Roger, I like it here."

"This is a serious job."

"I know."

"People think you're playing pretend to guard a mall nobody goes to anymore. But you've got just as important a job as they do."

"Roger, I know."

"I know it's not a lot of money, Sam, but... I pay you."

"I'll do better."

He sighs. "At least move your car every once in a while."

He shuffles back toward the grand staircase. He flashes his light into empties on his way to the security office on the lower level. I should be lucky. I should be grateful. If it wasn't for Roger, I wouldn't have this job. I wouldn't have anything at all.

"Roger," I say. "Thank you."

His sniff echoes through the mall. "Check in every fifteen."

"Ok."

"Sam."

"Yeah?"

"Every fifteen minutes."

I set the timer on my watch. "Ok."

Time.

Why do I even think about my shift as starting or ending? I live here for all intents and purposes. I take my time checking all the places someone could hide. Loading docks. backrooms. Restrooms. Whoever our mystery graffiti artist is, they're long gone. Mall sounds like a wood shop with the guy running his paint stripper. A light flashes down the way. Is that him? This electric sound buzzes through the mall. Not him. Not the neon. Something else.

VAMMMMM

The hell is that? More light. North corridor. Six seconds. That's what it takes for me to run around from the south side to the north. Designing the mall with this big empty canyon in the middle probably made sense when you were forcing everyone to walk past every single store, but with less than ten-percent occupancy, it's just depressing. A shadow runs down the north corridor.

They're still in here.

"Hey," I say. "*Hey!*"

They beeline down the corridor. This crinkle sound behind them, like the wind going through that battered old tarp Dad pulled over the Monte Carlo in the driveway.

I thumb my radio. "Roger!"

The north corridor ends in what I think used to be the old toy store. Closed around 2010. Security gate is half up. The intruder ducks underneath it. Don't know why they're going in there.

This is a dead end.

I shine my light in the store. "Don't make me..."

Store is empty. Old fixtures. Big red and yellow signs saying

EVERYTHING MUST GO! I duck under the gate. They must have pried this up by hand. Great. Probably some meth head who doesn't know what they're doing. They could just freak on you and I'm never going through that again, so I draw my taser.

"Come out," I say. "Slow."

Small stock room in the back. I give it a once over. Nothing in there. Nobody. I check the door to the backrooms. Locked. They couldn't lock it behind them without a key. Where did they go?

The gate rattles.

I whirl around. "Freeze!"

Roger squeezes under the gate. "Hold your fire."

Jeez. "They're gone..."

He army crawls across the floor. "Check again."

"Maybe there wasn't anybody..."

He picks up some kind of book. "There was somebody."

"What's that?"

"Old Christmas catalog."

He passes me the book and pushes up to his feet. Dad mentioned the catalogs. He used to look forward to them because of all the toys, I guess. Department stores put these out every year back in the day. Some of them are worth money if they're in good condition. I don't think this thing is money, though. Pages are as yellow as the curtains in my grandma's house. Some are laminated. Glue wore off the spine. Looks like they kept it together with duct tape. It smells.

"Soot," I say.

Roger probes the store. "What?"

"Smells like soot... was there ever a fire in here?"

"Not that I'm aware of."

"You sure?"

"Some tweaker is probably burning pages for warmth."

"Roger... maybe I was seeing things. This thing has been in here for like a million years. It's older than you are."

He flashes the store room again. "Nice one."

"I try."

"Someone left that here."

"How?"

"That book wasn't here before. I'd know."

"We find old stuff in here all the time."

He tries to shimmy the security gate up higher. "Someone messed this gate up. Retrace your steps. Do another sweep."

"*"There's more for your life...*""

"What?"

This book. Cover must have torn off. Whoever left this here taped a fragment from it back on the first page. *There's More For Your Life*. Wouldn't that be nice?

"Hey," I say. "Can I keep this?"

Roger pries out through the gate. "It's evidence."

"I'll examine it."

Look at this thing. Thumbprints all down the sides of the page. Maybe someone did leave this here by accident. Who was this? They obsessed over this. Old mail as book marks. Postdates from 1983. Some kid like my Dad maybe back in the 80s, pouring over toys he couldn't afford. He had them in the pages, though. Whoever left this would be Roger's age. They didn't move like it.

They moved faster than light.

I sweep the mall again. There's more for your life.

Sunset like an atomic bomb.

Ugh. I'm becoming a vampire. I stagger out the security door to the back parking lot. I forget the Christmas catalog for a moment. If I don't, I'll fall down in one of these craters in the concrete and it will be tomorrow before Roger figures out he's replacing me.

Mail slides off the dashboard as soon as I close the car door. Don't know why I keep any of this. I don't open any of it. This only finds me because my Dad leaves it tucked under the windshield wiper every Friday. I'd feel better about it if he ever left a note, or a twenty, or anything that told me I could drive over there to get it instead. I set the laundry basket in the backseat next to the cooler and stretch my feet out a little. So tired. Man, am I tired.

But this book.

Sort of like someone scanned all of Amazon into a fashion magazine. They wrote it like those game books I read all the time as a kid, though. Pick your path, or whatever.

Your choice!

Everything for sale is a life choice. Happiness rests on what you decide. Fulfillment. Those books you made the wrong choice and died. Maybe you could in the catalog, too. This is back when kids were choking on little knick-knacks that came with toys.

Way to make everything grim, Sam.

Pages fall out. Whoa. Just the middle. Catalog index page. I set it back in there, but it keeps falling out. Guess it just wants to stay with me. I fold it up and tuck it in my journal with the other oddities from the job. Other pages are loose in the catalog, but they should hold. Every other page is some woman. Happy. Warm. Inside some ridiculous house you know is full of family and friends and food. No one tells them to leave and never come back. No one punches them in the ribs. Something behind me. My arms go up. Nothing out there but concrete. Cars and trucks hurry down the highway to where life takes them. Some ridiculous house. Family. Friends. Food. I'd be in a hurry, too. I lean the seat back a little. Settle in. The catalog is heavy.

I like how heavy it is in my arms.

DIANE

Ask to go back upstairs for some toys.

She won't let you. Wait three days for her to fall asleep. From the kitchen window, see dead birds in the ash out back. Dead squirrels. Get a few toys and go back down into the basement. When she wakes up, tell her not to worry. The volcano erupted again, you say.

That's all.

She nods with the same bleary confidence she's showed you in the checkout lane when it all rings up too much. *When things get better,* she always says, and you put back the candy bar or cheap plastic toy you wanted. Sometimes. Once there was this spaceship. Generic. White plastic. Bright red and yellow stickers.

You don't want it, she said, but you did.

You ran out of the store with the toy. A few minutes later, she tossed the groceries on top of you in the backseat and drove home. Never said a word. Don't voice this. Open the catalog. Crowd out your cold, your hunger, your fear with the future sure to come.

Seize the future by taking a journey into the past…

SAM

My radio squawks. "Sam."

God. I'm dreaming about work.

"Copy, Sam."

Sweet death. Deliver me.

Knock, knock. My eyes crack open. Man. Roger is knocking on the driver's side window. "Morning, sunshine."

The catalog slides down my lap under the driver's seat. I dig it out from the empty pop bottles and hurry up and get my crap together. I grab my gear, follow Roger into the mall security entrance, and I tuck the catalog in my locker with my lunch bag. Leftover pizza again. I'm so hungry for homemade pizza. I should call home. Tell Dad about the catalog. Maybe after my shift I'll drop by. He's usually out in the garage in the morning. Sometimes, I think he just sits out there to get away from her. I know he said to come by anytime, but if she sees me out there, it all starts again and maybe I'll call.

I'll try calling first.

Unlock the main mechanical room. Turn on the front lights. Canvas the mall. Make sure no one got in overnight. Inspect the food court. Not all the eateries have gates or doors and you can get into the kitchen by going over the counter. Roger found someone in the pizza place once with a stuffed panda bear.

He talks about it once a week.

Go back to mechanical. Turn on the back lights. Canvas again. This time, unlock the main doors. The mall walkers will be waiting for you to do this at 7AM, so don't be late.

The mall walkers are always waiting.

Same three people everyday. Every. Single. Day. Super skinny lady. Beer gut grandpa. Hairdresser before her shift starts. Find them at the door each morning. Waiting. Staring. Mannequins except they're set outside. No one says anything. All business.

10,000 steps to save your life.

Do a once around outside. Usually, it's just more mall walkers getting in early laps. In the winter, you see more homeless, especially near the exhaust vents. Open up the doors early on really cold days. Mop inside the main doors. Food court. Just enough to make it look good for the people walking through. Wipe down the tables. Surprise, you're the cleaning crew, too. Roger got this account because he underbid the other guys but threw in other things the owners don't really want to pay someone else for like janitorial. Sweep the bathrooms. Do this end of shift and start of shift, because panda bears.

Check the old department store. Exterior doors still open out to the parking lot, so theoretically, someone could get in. They'd make a lot of noise doing it. They'd make Roger really happy. Make a game of avoiding the rusted impressions shelves left in the linoleum. Clear the dressing rooms. Wipe off the toothpaste gunk you left on the sink in the employee bathroom and check your face. Crooked nose. You're always going to be broken. Whatever. 5AM blues.

Happens every day.

Switch the water on. Water is still connected to the mall mains, though the owners want all but one public restroom out in the mall disabled during the week to keep the bill low. Take a fast shower. Who knows why they put a shower stall in, but the mall used to be a palace. Everyone came here for everything, and they didn't walk away disappointed. Now it's a wasteland.

A homeless shelter.

Head out to the crossing escalators and walk up to the second floor. Nothing up here but the shelves, cases, and random stuff the department store left behind. Nowhere really to hide except the stock rooms. Clear. The backrooms got walled off when the store closed, so the only way in and out is through the access door back into the mall. Lock it behind you. Kill time looking at pictures of the mall from better days printed on the wall sealing off the old department store. Imagine going back in time. Go downstairs.

Start over from the beginning.

Roger spends his lunch on his phone shopping for guns. Ammo. Equipment. All the time. Early on, I thought he was talking to a girl-friend maybe, but all those pings are other dudes quoting him prices on guns and stuff he never buys. Whatever. Not exactly representing excellence in the romance department here.

"Got a 9 millimeter here," he says. "Good weapon for you."

I shake my head. "I'm good."

"Something smaller?"

"I hate them."

He sniffs. "Find anything out on the book?"

I flip through the wrinkled pages. "It's from 1983."

"You said there were prints."

"Thumbprints, yeah."

"Maybe we can get a partial."

Just about every page is thumbed. "Let me call CSI."

"Funny. We need to figure out where it came from."

Thumbprints all belong to the same person. I think. They over-lap, and some prints are bigger than others. If someone left this, they'll be back. They loved this thing. Took care of it, or at least tried to. Some pages I can't tell if it's mold or dirt or what. Water damage. But, man. They did everything to keep it together.

I turn the page. "Or we could call like Federal Mall Enforcement. You know. Agents from a super secret government program who got experimented on that was run out of empty malls."

"Sure," Roger says.

"Dude. We could make a TV show. Like a YouTube thing. Instead of people breaking into malls, it would be us protecting them. It would be cool. Don't you think?"

"Sure."

"I'd like to make something like that. Be creative."

"Cool."

"Actually, I kind of wrote something. I wrote a book."

He blubbers his lips. "Six hundred isn't bad."

The light blinks overhead. "Don't you have guns?"

"You never know what could happen."

"What could happen?"

"You never know."

"You're not one of these zombie apocalypse guys, are you?"

"All I'm saying is you can never have too many."

"If zombies come for the mall, they can have it."

He looks up. "Our job is to secure the mall."

"Well. The mall won't let you wear a gun, so..."

He shrugs. "We can wear them on other sites. I got the long gun out in the truck for the bar tomorrow night. Just in case."

"Why?"

"Had a guy shoot someone across the street last week."

"They never should have passed that open carry law."

"Constitutional carry."

"It's not like you're going to use it."

"People see a gun and they think twice."

"No one thinks with guns."

"You need to think about getting familiar with a sidearm that isn't a taser. I need you to work the festival in the summer. It's going to be people. It's going to be situations. I have to rely on you."

"I'm here every day, Roger."

"They pay me to keep the homeless out."

I close the catalog. "I'll get back to it."

He groans like a flat tire. "Sam."

I set the book in a box on top of the filing cabinet with the other lost and founds. "I'll case the old toy store again."

"I know it's easier to work a place you don't have to deal with people. Believe me. All I think about is that night in '99. So it's better I walk around here twenty times a night than work a door."

This again. "I don't want to hurt anybody."

"It's natural."

I put my lunch bag back in the fridge. "I'm not angry."

"It's ok if you are."

"I'm not."

"Someday, someone will get in here. You'll have to act. It's an ugly part of the job, but it's part of the job. You have to face it."

"Roger, do you want me to leave?"

"I want you to clock back in."

This guy. I mean, I'm grateful. If it wasn't for him, I'd probably still be in the ICU. He worked the door that night at the bar. I don't even remember being hit. What those guys said. What I said. I just woke up in the hospital and the doctor told me Roger pulled me out of there. After I got my feet under me, I really wanted to learn how to protect myself. He trained me in all his self-defense courses he does at the strip mall, but now it's guns. The mall is the Alamo, or Helm's Deep, whatever that is. We're the 300 or something.

I clock back in. Roger goes back to his phone. A message pings really loud. Echoes through the mall. The stalled horses on the merry-go-round and the abandoned mannequins all stand witness to the constant quotes from men selling guns online.

At least someone is talking to him.

I walk the mall. 3800 steps. Nothing and no one in the toy store.

Yesterday's dust. I peel off the scabbed tape off the floor the dealers left from the last comic book show. This is like a $25 fine for every little blue spot, but Roger always tells me not to report it. If we make the comic book guys mad, they won't come back. He likes the weekends they have the shows. Guys leave their tables up overnight. Some of those books are like ten grand each or something. All I know is I get a lot of steps in. Maybe the comic book guys left the catalog. They might sell something like this. Some of them sell toys. I'll ask Roger.

I walk down the east wing to the frozen escalator down into the food court. I pretzel up the west stairs back to the upper level, kind of like an 8-bit version of a spiral staircase. I cruise the old department store just to see the door to the employee restroom is still there, and the shower, and I'm still something like a human being.

VAMMMMM

That light again. That sound. Ratty tarp in a windstorm. I thumb my flashlight on and there they are. My shadow. Upper level. North corridor. Toy store. Again. This time I cool it on the radio. Keep quiet as much and as long as I can. If I can sneak up on them, I might be able to catch them. I creep up on the old toy store, moving slow down the corridor. My shadow crawls around in the dark on their hands and knees. Like they're looking for something.

I flash my light. "Hands."

Wow. Called the tarp. They're wearing a blue one you cover cars with in the winter. Old. Dirty. Frayed. Tied around their waist with some cheap rope. Must be homeless. Can't see their face. Back to me. Woman, I'm guessing, with all that long, wavy copper hair like the pipe Dad used to pull out of old houses.

"Hands," I say.

She doesn't move.

I draw my taser. "Right now."

Nothing. Don't be like this. Please.

"*Now.*"

Her hands grab some sky.

"Stand up. Turn around. Walk toward me."

She faces me. Whoa. She's pretty, in a kind of I'm an extra from *The Walking Dead* kind of way. Not sure if she's a zombie or a survivor though. I think those are shin guards for like a baseball catcher. Maybe the chest protector, too, underneath the tarp. Hard to tell. Some kind of protective guards on her arms. Might be for baseball also, but this stuff is old. This stuff is busted.

I thumb my radio. "Code Blue. Upper Level, north corridor."

She's not even blinking. I lower my flashlight a bit so it's not blinding her. Those eyes. Fast as lightning. Did she just size me up?

She totally did.

"No funny business," I say.

She's still as a mannequin. "Where did you get batteries?"

"What?"

"For the flashlight?"

"Is that what you're looking for? What are you doing in here? Wait a second. Are you looking for the Christmas catalog?"

Now she blinks. "Do you have it?"

"Maybe. Come out here. Nice and slow."

"Do you?"

"I said come out here. Now."

Her voice is so raspy. "Give it to me."

"You're not hearing me."

"I need it."

"My partner is coming. He's really going to want something to happen, so nothing's going to happen. Right?"

She ducks under the security gate. "I don't want any trouble."

"Good, that makes two of us. I'm going to escort you off the property. You're not going to come back, or we call the cops. Ok?"

She steps toward me. "I just want the book."

"What's the deal with that, anyway?"

"Where is it?"

"Hey. Stop there."

She doesn't stop. "It's mine."

"We all have to grow up eventually – "

My taser twists out of my hand. What? My legs go out from under me. My ass hits the floor and something sharp and cold and fricking huge presses into my neck.

"Please," I say.

I know that look. She's used that knife on someone before.

"Don't..."

She stares at me like I'm an alien or something. "You're..."

Her mouth opens in shock. She tenses up. Convulses. 55,000 volts. No mercy. The knife drops from her hand and she rattles to the floor. She doesn't cry out, though. Just that shock in her eyes. Hurt. She spasms as Roger drops his knee into her back.

"You were right," he says. "They were shocked we found them."

DIANE

The shock comes later.

One night, or morning, the difference is meaningless after, your mother wakes up screaming. This goes on a long time. Ask her what's wrong. Never get an answer, not in words. Read the catalog as she pounds her fists on the basement stairs, as she knocks over everything stacked in the corner, as she throttles you with a hug that is as violent as it is reassuring. Ask her when it's ok to go back upstairs.

Never get an answer.

Burn books for warmth, but refuse to give the catalog up. She slaps you. Run up the stairs. This smell everywhere. Dead mice behind the wall. Behind the houses. The mountains. The clouds dragging the ground like those old, musty curtains in the living room. She drags you back down into the basement, and you don't know why. There's no difference in the damp and cold up there, out there, everywhere.

Burning the catalog never comes up again.

Sometimes, shivering in the long winter, she asks you to read from it. Never use the flashlight, because you have it memorized. Her almost smile forms as you read the product descriptions, the features, and the promises. Pages yellow. Print comes away on your fingers.

Fear ruining your only warmth. Keep the catalog under your jacket, warm and safe, taking it out only for emergencies.

Keep a calendar as best you can.

The sun a memory. Summer. Life. Christmas. Christmas morning unwraps in the basement, the venue different, but the outcome is the same as always. This time there is nothing to open but a little piece of candy your mother has been saving.

I didn't get a chance to shop, she says.

She tries to explain, again, there might not be any shopping for a while. There was a war. A nuclear war. Questions like, *Is it over? Did we win?* pop in your head but they don't stick. The only thing you really want to know is *Did Dad get a chance to shop? When is he coming over again? When can we go back upstairs?*

She smiles, though it's more of a frown. That's your mom. A smile that's kind of a frown. Remember this, years later, when you have nothing to share with someone you love but hope.

Hope is what you covet most.

It's not so much the toys you want; it's the smiles on the faces of the children in the catalog, bright but never indulgent. Never ecstatic and there was no need. They knew. Young as they are forever in four colors, the catalog kids express this surety you recognize but never define. The book provides, in ways it was never meant to. The book contains, and in it you have everything.

(A) Never be in the dark with this durable flashlight. Comes in your choice of three distinct colors.

SAM

First big test.

Big fat F. Maybe Roger is right. I may not be cut out for this. He doesn't seem too disappointed, though. Actually, he seems thrilled. He drags the intruder into the security office and cuffs her to the rusty old radiator along the wall. She pulls at the cuffs, groggy, but she's still fritzing from all the lightning that flashed through her.

"Roger," I say. "We can't detain her."

He snaps a pic of her with his phone. "She attacked you with a deadly weapon. You bet your ass we can detain her."

I'm still fritzing, too. "It's against the law."

"So is breaking and entering."

"We need to call the cops."

Roger drops her knife on the desk. Knife doesn't begin to describe it. Some kind of iron stake duct taped to a broom handle.

"We call the cops," he says, "We have to file a report."

If the cops come here constantly, if the paint removal guy is here all the time, if we're replacing windows every week, then we're telling the owners we can't keep this place secure. Not that they care. They're fine with letting the rain get in. Insurance covers that. Not crap security. When the contract expires, they'll let us go and hire the other guys. They hire the other guys and I've got nowhere to go.

"So you're letting her go, Roger?"

He pulls out the chair at the desk. "We'll let her think about it."

I pull the other chair from the desk over to the radiator and set her up in it. "She probably needs an ambulance."

"She'll be fine."

"We need to make sure she's not injured, though."

"She's just a virgin is all."

"That's gross, Roger."

"With the taser."

"I know what you meant. Still gross."

"If you can't take a joke, how are you going to be able to take down a hostile intruder armed with... look at this thing." He traces a line down the knife's edge. "She sharpens it every day. She has to. See this on the handle? That's not varnish."

"What is it?"

He sighs. "How did she get the drop on you?"

"I don't know... she was just so fast."

"You had your taser drawn."

"It was dark."

"She disarmed you. I saw it."

"If you saw it, why are you asking me?"

"She put you on the ground and put a knife to your throat in one move. Textbook. She should be teaching self-defense courses."

"I did everything right."

"You can't hesitate. You have to act."

"I did."

"You were easy on her."

"The hell I was."

"She advances on you, you tase her. You never know who you're dealing with. For all we know, she's a serial killer."

"And you're not going to call the cops?"

He groans. "We're not filing a report. But we'll keep her on record if she comes back. Let me get some pictures."

Roger snaps a pic of the knife with his phone. Then he takes hers. The intruder moans with the flash. Starting to come around. Roger goes back to the knife, but I stay on her. Something strange about her.

Homeless, obviously. Knots in her hair. Cracked nails. Dirty hands. Callouses. Ugly scar on her right hand. No stitch line.

I nudge her arm. "Hey. Knife lady."

She blinks.

"How did you get out of the toy store the other night?"

She tugs on her cuffs.

"No point being hard on her now," Roger says. "Go canvas the mall. I'll get to the bottom of this."

I adjust her arm so the cuffs aren't digging into her. "I'll stay."

Roger scrapes his forehead. "You worried about me?"

"Yeah."

"She's not a serial killer, Sam. She's just a meth head."

"I don't think so."

"This could be a YouTube thing, actually."

I shake my head. "We didn't find any gear on her."

"Maybe she left it somewhere. Maybe there's someone else."

"Where would they be hiding?"

He shrugs. "Vents, maybe."

She's skinny, but ventilation shafts aren't as big as movies make them out to be. Where did she go from the toy store the other night? Where would she be hiding in the mall? Definitely not in the old department store. I'd notice if I had a neighbor.

"Roger, didn't you say there's an old fallout shelter here?"

He nods. "Basement. Still has supplies in it."

"Supplies?"

"Survival stuff. Green drums with water. Old medical kits."

I lean against the wall. "So someone could live down there?"

"Whatever food down there is fifty years old."

"It's not on our checklist."

"No reason to be."

"When was the last time anyone was in the basement?"

"Been awhile. You know what? I don't want you going down there by yourself. I'll check it out. Guard the prisoner."

I sigh. "We can't detain her..."

He places the knife inside the desk drawer and locks it. "Don't get soft on her. Whoever she is, she knows what she's doing."

"I wasn't soft on her, Roger."

Roger changes the cartridge on his taser. "Doors are 7AM."

"I know that."

He holsters the taser. "Not before."

He heads out of the security office. I don't have to ask him what he's saying this time. Cold days, I open the doors early for the homeless. Maybe I let her in. I would have remembered her.

Don't get soft.

I plop in the desk chair. "Man..."

Could use some aspirin right now. Coffee. The intruder stares at me. Maybe she needs some coffee. No. What am I thinking? I hand her a cup of hot coffee and she throws it back in my face.

I lean back a little. "Ever think you're not cut out for it?"

She shifts in her chair. "I wasn't going to cut you."

"I wasn't going to piss my pants, but I think I did."

She sniffs. "You didn't wet yourself."

"I just say things. Did you? Wet yourself?"

"No. Why?"

"People usually do their first time."

"What did he hurt me with?"

"The taser?"

"What's a taser?"

"You serious?"

"It was like being shocked. I remember touching clothes right out of the dryer and they would snap. Nothing snaps anymore."

Except maybe her. "We'll let you go in the morning. But don't come back. Don't murder anyone with the knife thing, ok?"

"I don't murder people."

"That's a relief."

"I only cut men."

"Oh. Ok."

"Men you cut without question."

"Why..."

"Because they only have one answer for you."

God. What has she been through? "Hey... we're not filing a report or anything, but Roger will ask. What's your name?"

"Will you let me go?"

"Look... we don't have to talk. We shouldn't. But there's a women's shelter on Fourth. I can give you the number."

"There aren't any shelters on Fourth."

"There is. I know, because... well. I sleep in my car."

"Cars aren't secure."

"It's just temporary. Until I save some money."

"Did you have to abandon your home?"

"My parents threw me out."

"Why?"

"Something came up. They found out I was... I was only back living with them because I dropped out after my first semester... my life sucks, basically. So. I understand life sucking. All I'm saying."

"Where is the book?"

"Good talk."

"Where?"

I glance at the box on top of the filing cabinet. When my eyes go back to her, the handcuffs are dangling from the radiator.

"Shit," I say and nearly fall out of the chair.

She tucks tweezers back in her hair. "I'm leaving."

We searched her. Damn it. I reach for my taser. Didn't exactly work out last time. "You're going to get me fired..."

"You're not good at your job."

"Wow. Ok."

"You're too kind."

"What?"

"You can't be kind and be expected to hurt people."

"I'm good at my job."

"Are you going to shoot me?"

We both know the answer. I take my hand off my taser. She pulls the Lost and Found box off the top of the filing cabinet. Takes the catalog out. Lost treasure. Who was that guy? Indiana Jones. Dad would laugh right now. This is some ancient ruin. The catalog is some ancient text. She's found the big secret.

"What's with the catalog?" I say. "I mean, I get it. You could sell it, but it's kind of beat up. I'm guessing you're not selling it, though."

She cradles the book against her chest. "It's everything."

"It's worthless."

"It's priceless."

"Why?"

She moves toward the door. "Will you call him?"

Roger could come back any second. "Look, just wait it out."

Back to a staring contest. "Will you?"

"If he runs into you out there... you can forget about the book. You can forget about anything that isn't a trip to the ER."

She's like a mannequin. "You'd be dead if I wanted it."

"Good to know."

"I'll leave."

"Man... go out the security entrance. Right down the hallway."

"There's nothing out there."

"I know it feels that way, but..."

"I'd prefer to stay in the mall."

"You can't stay... why am I even... I'm doing exactly what Roger told me not to. This is not what we train for. We're just supposed to run you guys off, but let's be honest, Roger is having too much fun and I know you're having a really bad time."

"You know? Do you remember me?"

"If I let you in, you'd think I would."

She seems disappointed. "I forget everything."

"Must be nice."

"You have to, or else... nothing can ever be new."

"You have to be gone or cuffed back up. Like right now."

She half-steps into the room off the office. "What's in here?"

I sigh. "Are you hearing me?"

She goes in. Like the mall, the security office had its heyday. This other room served as the nerve center back when there was a full-time squad. A bank of six black and white TVs line the operations desk. Janky VCRs roofed over each one of them. I don't know how many VHS tapes line shelves in the back corner. Every feed, every day, from the ninety days or so prior to when all this became overkill.

I step behind her. "You can't be in here."

She marvels at the VHS tapes. "You watch the mall?"

"Not really."

Security cameras dot the exterior, but none work. Owners won't pay for them. City has been on them for years, especially after that one guy died in the parking lot, but they still won't put them in. No cameras at any entrance or common area. There's just one working camera. Upper Level. West side. Right below the big old clock. You get the main concourse, more or less. Kind of a dashboard camera. Some YouTuber put it there for a live feed for their video, but we found it. Roger figured out how to link it to his tablet.

She touches a screen. Grid burn ghosts every TV in the office. Nine squares. Numbers identifying every feed. 3/47. 54/40. You can't really make out anything in them, except maybe the lines where the floor meets the wall in the corridor it's focused on.

She's fixated. "'Quick-start picture tube.'"

I stand in the door. "What?"

"Page five."

"Is that from the catalog?"

"Some TVs have these burns on them from when they died."

"Yeah, these are ancient."

"It was like the old world was trapped inside... trying to get out... when I was young, I thought all the TV shows were still going on. They were still making them. If I could get the TV to work, or find an outlet, then... I could just bring them back."

"What do you mean?"

"Do these TVs work?"

"No... I mean, I don't think so."

"Can I watch TV?"

"Roger is on his way back right now."

"I used to sit in the electronics department and watch TV while my mom shopped around the store."

"Is there somebody I should call?"

She turns around. "They're all gone."

I hold the door. "No one's looking for you?"

Pages press between her arms. "If there were someone... they'd come here looking for me. We came here a lot."

"So you're from around here, then?"

"We didn't have any money. But we came anyway. My mom... she just liked to look. She liked to imagine."

"You have family in town?"

She goes to the tapes. "We couldn't afford the VCR. They cost hundreds of dollars when they came out."

"Are you like a collector or something?"

"A collector?"

"You're into old stuff. I know VHS tapes because they're always at flea markets, but... is that why you like the catalog?"

"I've had it since I was a girl."

She's my age, I think. "You didn't find it here?"

"It came in the mail. The day before it happened."

"Time out. You got it in the mail?"

Her fingers browse the tapes. "November 9th. Wednesday."

"You ordered it off eBay or something?"

"The department store always sent them out."

"The store has been closed for... the book is from 1983."

"Yes."

"It's 2024."

She blinks. "I thought this was my mall still. I get confused. I've been alone so long. Everything is... sometimes, I think I'm..."

"What are you telling me? You grew up in 1983?"

"I was nine. I think I was nine."

Great. She's crazy. "There's help. We can get help. Ok?"

"I need help..."

"I'm going to help you."

"I want to stay... but if The Denomenon finds me here..."

"The what now?"

"I have to go back."

"Go back where?"

She turns back to me. "I get confused, sometimes. There are two malls. There are two worlds. It's like VHS and Betamax."

"It's like what?"

"My world ended in 1983. Yours will if he finds me."

I blink. "*What?*"

DIANE

Pages in your life stick together.

Remember going through the drive-thru in the same crease you do running for your life through the woods. Suckle from your mother's breast as a baby, as a child when all the food is gone in the basement and there is nothing but the rats nipping at your heels. Subsist from the memory when she is gone, milk is gone, the salt and taste of people is gone. Your first memory of the mall. The last time you were there, before the war. When you finally returned, after. Four years for two miles. Always come back to this moment.

Your birthday.

Before. Small cake from the bakery. Some plastic animals on it. A card your dad got at the gas station. Five bucks. A board game. Behind you, they argue. *You got her that game last time,* your mother says, but you don't care about that. Take the plastic animals off the cake. Lick their plastic pedals clean of frosting. Vanilla true.

It's all they had, your father says, his tone so heavy it should seal off the conversation but you get your indomitability from your mother. He gave up on this argument years ago, on a night a lot like this one, but she didn't and never does.

Every time I come here it's the same thing, he says.

Open the game. Let the cheap cellophane drop to the floor. Throw out the instructions. After all, you're an only child; you pretty much always made your own rules for everything.

Replace the game pieces with the plastic animals. *Dad.*
Nothing I ever do is good enough, he says.
You can't just show up and buy her off –
That stupid game cost me ten dollars –
You could have just bought groceries –
You could just get a job –
There aren't jobs –
Dad, you say.
The argument cuts out abruptly. He comes to the dining room table, smiling like everything's ok, and he kneels down beside you. He strokes your hair like he always does.
"What is it, button?"
Show him the new pieces. "It's ok. I changed the game."

You make the rules now!
Choose your style from the available options.

SAM

Dad told me once there are two kinds of people.

Some people ding and some people dent. Dings buff out. Dents take more work. You go in the shop. Garage. If you don't have the tools, if you don't have the means, then you stay there. You sit up on blocks or under a tarp and maybe you tinker a little every day. Give yourself something to do. But you don't move. You never move.

I step back from the door into Mission Control. "What do you mean your world ended in 1983?"

She takes a VHS tape off the shelf. Opens the case. "They dropped the bombs. Everything died. Everyone."

"Bombs... like nuclear bombs?"

She takes the tape out. "Yes."

"You really think you were in a nuclear war?"

"Yes."

Mom said her mom went catatonic after she lost a baby. *What does catatonic mean?* I said. My mom yelled at me, because she says things and I ask questions and she can't stand answers. Dad told me later. Catatonic means switched off. Light's on. No one's home.

That's this woman here with me now.

"I'm not trying to be smart... but let's go outside," I say. "I know the parking lot doesn't look like it, but the world didn't end."

She opens the top flap on the VHS cassette. She pinches the tape reel inside and lets the whole thing drop to the floor.

"It will," she says. "If The Denomenon finds me."

"And he's... some sort of post-apocalyptic warlord?"

"He protected me, but then... I wanted to leave."

I don't even want to know. Can't be good if she's disassociating into a nuclear holocaust. "Look... there are meds. You can get help."

She cradles the book. "Meds?"

"You know. Anti-depressants. More advanced stuff. I took some pills for anxiety until I went off my parent's insurance. It helped."

"You don't need it now?"

"Nowadays, I punch stuff."

"People?"

I'm not Roger. I didn't take this job to maybe luck out one night and get to beat the crap out of someone. Take out all my frustration and anger and pain on some random because whoever hurt me in the first place is long gone or untouchable. I took this job so no one would ever hurt me again. So for an hour every day, I lift tomato cans in grocery bags to get little rocks on my arms.

"Punching bags," I say. "Walls, sometimes."

The staring freaks me out. "That helps?"

"Yeah. A little. Not really."

"You're not an angry person."

"No."

"You're afraid."

"Should I be?"

"Yes... but not of me."

"Because of this Denominator? Who I'm guessing rules the wasteland back in 1983 where you come from?"

"It's not 1983 anymore. I think it's been ten years."

"How did you even get here?"

She looks at me like I'm glitching. "The toy store."

"How is the toy store – actually, you know what? It doesn't matter. Why am I asking you this? You're... I'm not going to do that, either. My parents freaked out on me and called me crazy and tried to shrink me, and I just want to help you. I think the best way to do that is for me to maybe call someone. I know you don't want that, and Roger doesn't want that, but I think you need help."

"Do you have any medicine?"

Maybe she's glitching. "Like I said, I'm off the pills. I think you need maybe more... weapons grade stuff, just keeping it real."

"I've gone through everything left in my mall... I rationed everything, but... I had to pull a tooth out last year and it still hurts."

"You pulled your own tooth out?"

She moves into the door. "I think I did it wrong."

My hand goes to my taser. Reflex. "We gotta come to an agreement, ok? You're trespassing. You're armed and dangerous."

"My knife is in the desk drawer."

"If Roger comes in here and you're walking around..."

"Do you have any medicine?"

"I might have some painkillers in the car... actually, I have some aspirin on me. I forgot because I mostly rock the hard stuff these days. I'm going to reach for it on my belt. Don't freak out."

I open a pouch on my belt. Med-kit. This thing has it all. Never thought I'd use any of it. Let's see. Shears. Gauze. Pads. Bandages. Wipes. Tweezers. Burn cream. Lighter. Syringe. Spare charger for a cell phone I don't have because I can't afford one right now. Tourniquet. Rubber gloves. Super glue. Stuff works. There they are. Aspirin. Shifts run long. Breaks vanish. You're on your feet all the damn time and sometimes you've got to have back up.

I should have back up.

"I don't have anything to drink," I say, and hand her the pills.

She holds the aspirin packet in her hand like it's a butterfly.

"You open it. Here."

I tear the packet open. If she's mental, I don't know, but she acts like she has legit never seen travel size anything before.

She swallows the pills. "Why do you take pain killers?"

I take an itty step back. "You're welcome."

She winces a bit. "Are you injured?"

I don't want to talk about this. I can't really be talking to her, and yet I just do. "Broken ribs. They haven't really healed right."

"I have that, too."

"Oh."

"It hurts when I breathe."

"Yeah..."

"You were in a fight?"

"Some guys beat the crap out of me."

"You killed them."

"No. What? Roger broke it up."

"He protects you."

"He's a good guy. He came to see me in the hospital. He runs these self-defense courses, and he helped me out."

"Self-defense?"

"I train. I box. I just really got into it. It keeps me focused. It keeps me contained. I appreciate that. If I didn't have that after, I don't know what I would have... Roger helped me a lot. So, it would be cool if you were either gone or back in the chair when he shows up. Honestly... I don't know which is worse."

"Being gone."

"I'm getting such a migraine right now. I just give you my aspirin. I probably should have split that with you."

"Do you want them back?"

"No."

"How do you keep contained?"

"Is this for your tooth? Or..."

"Can you show me?"

"I feel like you're pretty locked down."

"Sometimes... things get away from me."

"Like thoughts, or..."

"Yes. Thoughts."

"I get it. I do. Some days are bad. I do my job, I go a few rounds with the punching bag, or I lift cans for an hour, but sometimes things get past you. And if you're not healthy and on your game, then I get it. I get how a person might suffer."

"I play a game."

"Ok."

"It helps me. It helped me. It doesn't help anymore."

"That's ok. You know that. We're being honest and not judgmental. So, you know you have a problem."

"It's a very dangerous problem."

"Do you want to go to the shelter? I'll take you."

"There's nothing else out there."

"There is. I know it doesn't seem like it sometimes... sometimes, it's easier to stay put... so. I'm here a lot. All the time. But there is a world outside the mall. I know there is. I will take you to the shelter. I would be happy to take you. Anywhere but jail."

"I want to..."

"Sometimes, there isn't a bed at the shelter. Setting expectations. But if we're lucky and we work on our presentation – hint, no knives – maybe we can get you in tonight. I'll have to explain to Roger, but... it will be ok. No one has to get hurt. You don't have to be afraid. You're not afraid of me, right?"

Right now, she seems afraid. "Your name is Sam."

"You heard Roger. You know I'm not like him."

"My mom called me Diane."

"Diane... it's nice to meet – "

The lights blink. Man. Don't tell me it's the breakers again.

Diane clings to the book. "It's him..."

I flip the light switch to make sure it's working. "Him who?"

"The Denomenon."

"It's just the breakers. They're junk. Don't worry."

"I should go back..."

"Go back?"

"It's a game."

I hit my radio. "Roger, I've got blinkers in the office."

Static.

"Roger, go up to six."

Diane shakes her head. "Your radios won't work."

"What? Why?"

"The Denomenon's steed emits a natural electromagnetic pulse."

"His what does what?"

"It interferes with electronics."

I thumb the radio again. "Roger."

Nothing.

"Give me my knife back," Diane says.

I step toward the office door. "I told you. It's the breakers."

"I need it."

"Diane. There's no electro-mutant thing chasing you. That was a really crummy straight to VHS movie you watched, ok?"

"Open the drawer."

I get where I can reach the office door handle. "Sure, why not? Do you want some more aspirin? Bottle of water? Anything else I can get you? McDonald's? Massage?"

"Massage?"

"Work out some tension, maybe? I feel like there's some."

"What's tension?"

"Right here between your eyes."

"That's my brain."

"Right, my entire brain is *tension*. You're not getting it. You're not going to get it. It's not your fault. You're clearly suffering from some mental health issues, and I sympathize, I really, *really* do. Also, you're stupid hot in your own very DIY way, and I have a history of doing *literally* anything for stupid hot girls."

"I'm not stupid."

"I mean, you kind of are in a way that's just this side of adorable. Which makes this extra sucky, because there is no way I'm getting the knife and oh my God, you're unlocking the drawer."

She tucks her tweezer pick back in her hair. "Let me go."

I palm the door handle. "Diane... let's be cool."

"What are you doing?"

"I'm sorry. I'll let you walk. But not all over me. Ok?"

And I thought she was upset about the catalog. "Don't."

I need this job. The mall is home for me right now. I can't afford for Roger to box me and then be alone with nowhere to go. Or become an accessory to his murder. Not sure which would be worse.

Probably the murder.

"I'm sorry," I say and hurry up and back out of the door.

I slam it in her face. Hurry. I hold the handle while trying to find the key. C'mon, c'mon, c'mon. She twists the handle. God. How is she so strong with those chicken arms? I find the key on my ring and lock the office door. Diane pounds against it.

Dum, dum, dum.

Her scream muffles behind steel. Pretty sure that wrenching sound is the knife. I doubt she can get through two inches of 12 gauge steel. But then again, she got out of her cuffs and into the desk drawer with tweezers, so what do I know?

VAMMMMM

Sick yellow light flickers down the corridor. Mist rolls through the concourse beyond. Breakers must really be on the fritz this time. *Dum, dum, dum.* Any second now a cover band will start playing some Journey. Shadows flash on the floor. Trees in a lightning storm. Moving. Something is moving.

I thumb my radio. "Roger, is that you?"

There's something down there. Big. Really big.

My hand falls to my taser again. "Roger?"

Dum, dum, dum.

I draw my weapon. Light swirls out in the mall, like someone is holding a lightsaber except this one is kind of bendy like a snake and just really big. Like my car big. Something bangs against a kiosk in the concourse. The kiosk rolls down the corridor at me.

Dum, dum, dum.

The kiosk crashes into the wall. I advance past it down the corridor. Gears shred against each other as the security gate shielding the old shoe store pancakes into the ceiling. Something is trying to get in. Something is inside the shoe store.

Dum, dum, dum.

Don't be soft. "Hands!"

Toxic yellow slithers out of the shoe store and this dragon-serpent thing stands like a cobra before me. A burly guy who looks like he mixed up his cosplays for *Star Wars* and *Lord of the Rings* rides on its back. He points a very serious sword at me.

A hiss presses out of his mask. "Shall we play a game?"

DIANE

Play store to pass the time.

Make a game of it. Set up the dwindling food. Hunger is the same after as it was before. Every month, it's the same stretching the last week into the first, making dinners of stale English muffins, packs of crackers and powdered milk from the food bank.

Shop for hours.

Put things in the cart. Set them back. Save things for later. Later becomes more and more important as the days go on, the weeks, and understand without your mother having to tell you that the TV isn't coming back on. Dad isn't coming by Friday or maybe Saturday with twenty bucks to get through the weekend. Christmas, if there is another, will be the gift of your survival.

Play store all night and day, taking things back to have full shelves tomorrow. She shakes her head, though she's always shaking now. She only stops shaking when she thinks she hears people outside. Sometimes, there are people outside. Dogs.

Other things.

She makes a knife from a hand trowel and a broom handle she breaks the end off of. Go over it again. Never go upstairs. Never answer the door. If anyone comes down, hide in the laundry chute. If something happens to me, run. If anything happens.

Just run.

Ask questions like, *What if it's Dad?* She smiles like it's a frown, and says if he could come, he would have come. Push back on this, because you're nine years old and still don't know better. Your mother explains politely, calmly, respectfully, no one is coming. She tells you this like she told you they were getting a divorce. These things happen. It's hard. You have each other.

You have the catalog. Some toys. A runny nose all the time. You have the laundry chute, which lets you get back upstairs in the night, though you're not supposed to be upstairs. A downstairs drain you go potty in, but the plumbing hasn't worked since that night. The smell stings your eyes, but mostly don't think about the smell. The cold. The scratching at the kitchen door.

Play the game.

(3) *Provide greater and more satisfying challenges for those who have mastered the game...*

SAM

"Code blue!"

I don't know if I even hit the button on the radio but no time. Situation. Face it. I fire my taser at this armored Japanese robot guy. The taser darts stick in his armor. 50,000 volts.

He just sits there on his glowing dragon. "Trifles and trinkets."

"What the actual – "

Before I can shock him again, he sweeps his big chonky sword through the copper wires attaching the darts to the gun. Wires go limp and I go numb. His sword cocks back again and I dive into the pit that used to be the kiddie playpen. Worn brick slaps me in the face. My head pounds like my heart. This guy is real.

I thumb the radio. "Roger! CODE BLUE!!!"

No answer.

I move up to channel six. "Gary! Anyone! Help!"

Nothing. Get up. Hurry. The snake-dragon thing inches into the pit toward me like a snail or something.

The armored guy points his sword at me. "Where is she?"

Get up. "What do you want with... what are you..."

"And what are you? Guardian? Sentry? Rook or pawn?"

"Mall security... you're trespassing."

"Forgive me. I'm not acquainted with the rules here. This place is so much like hers. Defended by its own emptiness."

I extend my baton. "Stay away."

"Ah. The rules are largely the same."

"Is this a YouTube thing?"

He pulls on the reins. "No. It's not a 'YouTube thing.'"

An eerie firefly glow brightens in the snake's mouth and I hit it hard as I can in his short, stubby nose. Yeah. Shouldn't have done that. Yellow, glowing spit flies at me and my baton bubbles away. I jump behind an empty kiosk. Laminated plywood dissolves in acid. Security office. Get back to the security office and lock yourself inside and down the corridor, Diane pries the door open.

I'm so going to die.

Yellow light flickers in her eyes. "He's here..."

"The security entrance," I say, running down the corridor.

Diane races toward me. "The toy store!"

Our heads bounce off each other. Ow. Man. This isn't happening. On the floor again. Has to be a record. Diane's on the tile with me, too. Blinking like a railroad crossing. The knife. The knife is on the ground. She lunges for it and I put my arms up, expecting to get killed this time, and she's dragging me down the corridor.

"What are you – "

The lights blink. No. That's the dragon-snake thing. It squeezes down the corridor at us. My boots squeak across the floor as I try to get up on my feet and Diane tries to drag me wherever we're going.

"Outside," I say and she cuts down the pass to main maintenance. "What are you doing? Diane, you have to go back – "

Diane opens the unmarked door to the backrooms and pretty much throws me through it. She barricades the door behind her with one of the big department store clothing racks that's just been sitting back here for years with the forgotten Christmas displays.

She runs past me down the hallway. "Hurry!"

I slap my hands on the floor. "What the hell?"

Her voice thunders back to me. "*Hurry!*"

How does she even know this is back here? Most people don't. This hallway links every store on the lower level with the loading docks up on the north end. No one uses this space anymore. Mostly, it's just where tenants left the things they didn't want to carry out. Mannequins. Racks. Shelves. Cheap plastic Santas.

"Diane," I say. "Where are you going?"

Something crashes into the door behind me. Old Santas melt in radioactive spit. What is that thing? What is this? Maybe I hit my head. Could be. Or I'm just disassociating. Big time. She pulled that knife on me. I bailed on reality. Classic Sam.

I catch up to Diane. "What the actual – "

She holsters the catalog in this leather satchel on her hip. "Shh."

"Tell me where we're going."

"The toy store."

"Toy store? Why?"

"I have to get back."

"To 1983? How can you do that through the toy store? How can you do that at all? Have I asked about the snake thing?"

"C'mon."

"The toy store is upstairs."

"We'll go through the department store. Up the escalators."

"It's walled off."

She stops dead. "What?"

"That's all walled off. They closed. Years ago."

"We can't get there?"

"I mean... I know a way in, but we'll have to go back out – "

Radioactive loogies hock down the corridor and the dragon-snake thing pushes through the clustered clothing racks behind us. If we stay in here, we'll get trapped in the dead end down at the department store. I cut down another pass back out to the food court.

"This isn't right," Diane says.

I leg it for the security entrance. "Let's go!"

The door rattles in its frame behind us. Too small for that dragon-snake thing to get through. Small favors. I tug on her hand and she pulls back in the opposite direction. There's no going back.

My turn to drag her. "What are you doing?"

Diane tears away from me. "It's the only way – "

The metal gate on the Chinese place explodes out of its frame. The dragon-snake thing slithers over the counter after us and chases Diane deeper into the food court. The rider swings his sword. What did Diane call it? The Denomitron?

"Diane," I say. "What is – "

The grommets in her tarp slap against the door closing behind her down the hall. What is she doing? What am I doing? You're going after her. This is your job. Do your job.

Ok.

Taser is shot. Security baton is melted. What do I got? Mace. Pepper spray. Flashlight. I could use that maybe. But really I need to get Diane and get out of here. Where did she go? I've lost her.

He's lost her.

Chairs slide into each other as the dragon-snake thing worms through the food court. All the vendors and tables and chairs are offset in a way that makes the court a giant maze. Should slow you down, but The Denomination just hacks through it with his sword.

Whoa.

Halved plastic furniture friezes like old TV screens. Prismatic color slops off the tables and chairs, like it's gooey cheese off a slice of pizza. Light worms across the floor, feeling out, reaching out to each other. All the ruin he leaves behind warps back together, except it seethes with these gleaming eggshell cracks and lines.

What. The. Hell.

I sneak through the food court. Keep off the glowing cracks frosting across the floor. Peek over the counter into the kitchen every vendor hides in the back. She's not in them. Where is she?

"You cannot win," the armored guy says.

A little voice whispers back. "I don't want to play anymore."

"You don't want to play? How rich. The game is all there is. You cannot escape it. You can only win... or lose. You've lost."

"No..."

"This world is no escape. Only a dead end. Give me the book."

Book? The catalog? What does he want the Christmas catalog

for? Should tell him he can find one online. A decent one might set him back, but it's going to cost way less than the court costs. Solid idea, Sam. Find Diane. Get back to the security office. Browse eBay.

Diane sounds so tired. "It's mine."

He pulls back the reins on his mount. "Is it?"

"I just want to be left alone."

"Yes, I'm sure you do. As I wanted only my peace and ignorance of this reality. But you didn't afford me that, did you?"

"Please..."

"Nothing is free, Diane. You see it, even in this world. You imagine only gifts. But nothing is given. Everything is purchased. The toll for a child's innocence is steep. You remain in arrears."

"I just want to stop hurting..."

"I hear you, Diane. I can hear you..."

He turns back into the food court and so do I. I scramble under a table as the dragon-snake thing blinks past. Whatever it is, it doesn't have much of a nose. That, or I broke it.

Let's go with I broke it.

The dragon-snake thing blinks like the bad neon farther down the concourse. Shadows flicker on the floor behind. Diane. She's behind a pillar on the north side. Must have doubled back. I crawl over to her. Tears streak the grime on her face. I don't know if any of this is real. Her anguish is. Fatigue. I hold my finger to my lips.

Shh.

Ok. Think. Where are we? Close to the south entrance. I don't think I can crack a door without it sounding like thunder in here right now. What's his name blocks the way back into the concourse and the security office. Guess we're doubling back. I grip Diane's hand and go back to the mall Chinese. I climb over the counter and then back through the little kitchen into the backrooms.

I ease the door shut behind us. "Ok. Ok. We're ok."

Diane tugs on my hand. "I have to go back."

"Shh," I say. "Shh."

She holds the catalog like it's a life preserver. "I have to."

"Diane," I whisper. "What is this thing?"

"The Denomenon."

"But what is it? Like a radioactive mutant or something?"

"No…"

"Whatever this is, it doesn't matter. We'll get out. Call the cops. FBI. National Guard. X-Files. Wait. Is this an X-Files thing?"

She blinks.

Of course, she doesn't know what that is. 1983. Seriously? If she's lying, if she's mental, then she's really committed to the bit. The Denomatrix seems real. His dragon thing. No way this is a Halloween prank. No one has the budget for this, not even YouTubers who travel from one dead mall to the next filming their adventures. This is real. Her fear. Her scars. Her broken teeth.

I put my hand on hers. "Diane. I can help you."

She stares at my hand like she did the pills.

"I mean, I want to. I don't know what's going on. Maybe tell me what's going on. Maybe do that while we go find Roger. Ok?"

"Ok," she says.

"Wait. For real?"

"Ok."

Expected the knife or the tweezers again. She gets it. If we're getting out of this, we need to work together. All of us. Roger will know what to do. He'll have a plan. This kind of thing is all he ever thinks about. Well. Not exactly an armored guy riding a radioactive snake, but some major drama. This qualifies. He's one of those guys whose grandad was in World War II or something, and they fought at one of the big battles, and it's all he talks about. He's been waiting for this and Roger is in the basement scrolling through his phone.

"Is this what you do when I'm on rounds?" I say.

Roger stops scrolling. "You let her go?"

"Didn't you hear the commotion?"

"What commotion?"

"This isn't happening…"

"You're right, it's not. You better have a good reason for why she's not cuffed to the radiator in the security office, Sam."

Diane reaches inside her poncho.

I grab her wrist. "Hey! *Hey!* Just chill out. He's cool."

She eyes all his gear. "He's armed."

"He's not going to hurt you. Are you, Roger?"

"Sam," he says. "Did you give her the knife back?"

"*Are you?*"

"Did you?"

"Things are complicated."

His hand falls to his taser. "Uncomplicate it."

"You chained her to a radiator against company policy and also against the law and then you disappeared on me."

"Hey."

"You did."

"Ok, calm down. What's going on?"

"Roger, is your radio working?"

"Should be." He hits the button. "Comm check."

Static. No infinite echo.

"Radio check, copy?"

"It's not working," I say. "None of them work."

He tried again. "Why not?"

Diane stares back at the door. "The Falken emits an EMP."

"I thought he was The Denomino?"

"The Denomenon. The Falken is his steed."

Roger snorts. "Did you breathe in some of the smoke?"

"There's something in the mall." Severed wire dangles from the end of my taser. "There's something following her."

"What do you mean, 'something?'"

He swipes at his phone and taps the app that links to the live feed from the action camera the YouTuber left out in the mall.

He taps the screen. "What in the Sam H..."

Grainy green night vision streams on the phone. The Falken blends right in, making it seem like The Demonster or whatever he's called is riding around on nothing in the food court. Roger expands the picture with his thumb and finger.

His jaw hangs as low as his pants. "This is a prank."

"It's not," I say.

"The radios don't work, but the camera does?"

My head hurts. "I don't know..."

Diane blinks. "Is the camera plugged in?"

"No, you charge it. It's like the phone. Small."

"If it's small, and not connected to any outlet, it may not be affected by the local distortion field. Some things worked after."

Roger tapes the screen again. "After what?"

"The war."

"What war?"

No time for this. "Roger... what are we going to do?"

"I'm going out there."

I grab his arm. "The taser doesn't work on him."

"What do you mean?"

"He's wearing armor."

"I'll call the other guys."

"Just call the cops."

He thumbs his radio. "Gary, move up to six."

"It won't work."

No answer. "This is Roger over at Crossroads Mall, copy?"

Diane eyes the corridor. "Who is Gary?"

"He works the casino," I say. "Roger has a couple different contracts around town. We use a few channels on the radio."

Roger groans. "Let me try him on the cell."

He swipes away another gun auction. Calls Gary. No ringtone.

"There's no one," Diane says.

His frustration builds. "What did she do to the comms, Sam?"

I eye her hand. "I told you. It's not her. It's that thing. She can explain in the car while we drive out of here, ok?"

Roger stows his cell. "We're not leaving."

"What?"

"We have a job to do."

"There's no way we can take this thing. We're mall security."

"Exactly."

"It spits acid."

"Sure it does."

"Look what it did in the food court, Roger."

Wormy light spreads across his phone. "What is this?"

I turn to Diane. "Yeah, what is it?"

Diane seems way more into the phone than she does the food court cracking in light. "The Denomenon breaks things."

"Sounds bad."

"Then he makes them his."

"What do you mean?"

"I have to go back. Now."

"You guys stay here," Roger says. "I'll be right back."

I'm still catching up. "Where are you going?"

He pushes past me. "To get something from the truck."

"No, Roger. C'mon."

"Stay here. Get in the shelter. Lock the door."

"Can we please just get her out of here? She's in danger."

"She's in trouble. Stay put."

"We're all in danger. Roger. Are you listening?"

He scopes the hallway, and then heads down it toward the back-rooms with his taser drawn. This isn't happening. Musty air breathes on us as I open the door to the old fallout shelter. Cobwebs deny us. Last thing I want is to lock myself in a dark, dank, scary place, but what choice do we have? I close the shelter door soft as I can and pull an old green drum in front of it.

Pretty sure that won't keep the sword guy out.

DIANE

Spring comes without the sun.

The sheriff comes door to door on horseback. He asks where your father is. Your mother shrugs. Learn your father had been arrested once for something called drunk and disorderly. This isn't the sheriff's concern. His concern is how many people are still alive in town and how many are still able. Some think there could be a harvest in the fall if there are enough workers and the clouds lift. The clouds never lift. There is not another harvest in America.

Go with some other kids through the shops downtown, breaking down anything wood. Breath rattling in their throats like the crackle of Geiger counters. In the Ben Franklin, find a case of *Return of the Jedi* figures in the storeroom. Forty-eight altogether. Unopened. Unpunched. Pristine. Cry to the confusion of the other boys.

You're not a boy.

You're not a child, not really. What are you crying for? Break down the cardboard box. Tear the figures from their packages and toss the cardbacks into a pile for kindle. Take the figures home and play store. Collect them all. Create an expectation of happiness.

Boy's toys, your mother says. *I'll never understand.*

She never understands. Do you? You just like them. Army men. Star warriors. Knights in armor defending castles. Imagine them not in the mythologies they embody, but ones you invent in the ash after. *Play with your dolls*, she says, but dolls jus sit there on your dresser. They will remain there long after people are gone from the valley.

Never think about this.

Never think much about anything, especially that which just comes natural. Boy things make more sense. Toys. Clothes. Games they play with each other and other girls. Keep your hair long and wild, though, because that's how your mother keeps it. Think of her wild. Free. Tumbling from one disaster to another, but moving.

Always moving.

Doug Johnson uses the last of his diesel to ferry people into town on his tractor. All they have there is disease. The sheriff presses you and your mother into service burying bodies. Blackened skin slides off bone in your hand lowering them in, like the plastic wrapping from the catalog. Count 1,138 dead in the high school football field. Ask your mother if the two of you will be buried there.

They're going to make us do other things, she says, caressing your long hair, faster and faster, harder and harder. Ask her what, but never get an answer. She holds you close, crying a little bit, and when you tell her *It's ok*, she kisses you for the last time.

(17) *Space Figure Collector's Case holds 24 figures (sold separately). Not licensed by Lucas Film Ltd.*

SAM

"Well," I say. "You're probably used to this."

Dust and who knows what else snows through my flashlight beam. I set it on its end on top of a rusted green metal drum. A dozen crowd the fallout shelter, stacked three high. DRINKING WATER. 17 1/2 gallons. Cardboard boxes wall off the back. SURVIVAL SUPPLIES furnished by Office of Civil Defense.

Cobwebs strand her hair. "This was gone before I got here."

I park it on top of a drum. "Before?"

"We were in our basement the first winter."

"Your family, you mean?"

"Mom and I."

"What, um..."

Diane faces me, but looks away. "How do I see the camera?"

Shouldn't have sat down. Now I hurt. My side. Ribs. A chair hits me. Something hard. Metal. Behind me. I can't see behind me. They're surrounding me. Pushing me. Shouting at me all at once.

What did you say?

Get up. If I sit here too long, it will all come back to me. I'll go back into my head and I go to the door like I'm going to walk the mall at first light. I can't go out there. We're not going anywhere unless Roger comes back, and then maybe TBD on that front.

My head is killing me. "What did you say?"

Diane taps my shoulder. "Are you injured?"

"I'm... in shock, mostly. I'm fine. How are you?"

"What?"

"You're not hurt, are you?"

Am I making sense? She doesn't think so. "No."

"Ok. Good."

"How do I watch the camera?"

"Um... Roger has the app on his phone."

"The phone is a TV?"

"Are you really from 1983?"

"I think it's 1994 now."

"You know what I mean."

"Yes."

"That thing. Out in the mall. He's not from 1983."

She blinks. "Not really."

"Where is he from? Who is he? What does he want?"

"We had a portable black and white TV in the house. It ran on batteries, so we could use it until they went bad."

"*Diane.*"

"The screen was tiny." She cups her hands together. "It was like a crack in the wall. Another room. Another world."

"You said there are two."

"Yes."

"And the Nom-Nom-Nom will destroy mine?"

"The Denomenon. Yes."

"So he's just an asshole or something?"

"He's... a guardian."

"Of what? Oh. Ok. Like no one is supposed to pass between worlds or something? That's some gatekeeping junk. But that's always the way, though. Right? Bad enough you have to deal with a nuclear holocaust, and then this guy shows up?"

She stares at the stacked boxes.

"Diane," I say. "Did you hear me?"

She examines the stacked boxes. No one has touched this place in a long time. A real long time. Doesn't make sense. The world ending.

Her world. Its survival stored under a dead mall.

"Hey... I know this must be... I don't know. You don't have to explain. Well. Right away. I feel like there's going to be questioning."

"I don't know how to explain," she says.

"It's ok. Stuff is hard. How... how did you get here?"

She shimmies a box out labeled MEDICAL KIT. *This unit contains no narcotics.* "Where there are people... life... and then it's all rotted and wasted... the tissue gets soft. Bad fruit."

"Ok... and the mall is one of those soft spots."

She knifes open the box. "Yes."

"And the guy or whatever, he guards these soft spots?"

Diane rummages through the box. Baby gold scissors. Giant sort of flask of isopropyl alcohol. Pectin powder. Bottle of aspirin. She pockets the bottle. Bandages. Syringes.

I clear my throat. "Diane?"

Another box opens. Ok. Usually, I go walk the mall when I'm frustrated, but I can't exactly do that right now. Diane pockets more supplies, leaves others, and searches another box.

"You know what all this stuff is," I say.

Diane nods. "Yes."

"But this was all gone in your mall."

"I went to the library. The post office."

Oh, God, the woman says. *I think I'm going to die.*

Can't. I can't sit down here like this. Hanging out down here with all these boxes is like hiding down in the basement in my head. There's a reason all this stuff hasn't been touched in years. My chest hurts. I can't breathe. I need to do something.

A box caves in beneath my fist. "Sorry."

Diane blinks. "I'm telling the truth."

"No, I know. I mean. I'm not angry with you. I'm..."

I pry my hand from the box. An instruction slip sticks between my fingers. Look at this. Who did they think they were kidding?

This kit consists of medical items to care for the day-to-day common ailments of fifty persons during confinement in the restricted environment of a shelter for fourteen days in the absence of specifically trained personnel.

"Fourteen days," I say. "Sure."

She plucks the instructions from my hand and tucks them in with the catalog. "You can make them last longer."

Other things stick out from the catalog's middle. Old pictures. Mail. Postdated from 1983. "That guy. Super Dimension Border Patrol out there. He said he wanted the book. Why?"

"Our TV was a radio also."

Does she have PTSD or ADHD? Place your bets.

I rub my head. "Probably wasn't anything on, right?"

"For a while there was a college radio station. KLCC. They reported rad counts. Any news that they came by. But then they stopped transmitting. There wasn't radio after that."

I thumb my radio. "Roger, how about now?"

Nothing.

Diane sits on the drum beside me. "It won't come back."

"Ever?"

"Nothing comes back. How do I watch TV?"

I sigh. "Maybe when Roger gets back you can watch some YouTube or something on his phone. I don't know. Five minutes of that and maybe you'll be happy the world ended."

"I'm not happy."

"I didn't mean... hey, I'm sorry. I'm just... banged up, and confused, and scared. So I get smart. You know?"

"Smart?"

"That's what my Dad says. Gets me in all kinds of trouble. But you know what's weird? I'm more scared about losing my job than I am that thing killing me. Why is that? That's messed up, right?"

"Your self-worth is connected to your production."

"That's... pretty advanced for someone who I'm guessing didn't finish high school. Not judging. Just saying."

"A person's industry is all that matters in my world. If you can't work, then... there isn't food for people who can't work."

"What kind of work is there?"

"They tried to plant crops. But the sun never came back. The soil was bad. There weren't enough of us. A few years after... you were a hunter, or you were hunted. I'd like to watch TV."

All I want to do is ask her more about this crazy world she's telling me about. And then I don't want to antagonize her. She may be cold as ice, but I know. I know that flinch in people when their trauma balls its fist. Squeezes their heart. Last thing I want to do is think about what I don't want to think about.

"I don't own a TV," I say. "You don't really miss it."

She sort of looks at me. "I miss it."

"What was your favorite show?"

"I liked Saturday morning cartoons."

"Name one."

"*Dungeons and Dragons.*"

"Isn't that a game?"

"Yes."

"Actually... I just read. And write. I wrote a book."

"You wrote a book?"

"Kills time."

"What's it about?"

"It's like... well. You might remember them. The Pick Your Path books? You know? You choose which way to go."

Her brows arch. "You wrote one?"

"It's stupid."

"Can I read it?"

"Well..." I reach inside my jacket. The cardboard cover takes a beating carrying it around like this, but I like to have it on me. Sometimes, I just have to start writing. "I read yours, so."

Diane opens my journal and starts reading.

THE LOST CHILDREN

1,347 children just disappeared in the United States.

Director Packard pulls you out of storage down in Unexplained Cases because those kids didn't sneak out the back door, hide under their beds, or paint themselves the same color as the walls in their bedrooms. They just vanished. All at once. All over America.

Poof.

Nothing connects these kids, except they were all there one moment and gone the next. Blink. Miss the chaos of children. Miss chocolate milk shakes made with chocolate ice cream, Saturday morning cartoons, or going to the mall on the weekend. *Oh, God,* she says, but this isn't the time to think about that.

Focus.

The Director picked you for this case because you like this weird stuff and without a doubt, you're the most dispassionate agent in the bureau. Nothing rattles you.

"You can figure this out," The Director says. "Right?"

If you can, turn to page 131.
If you can't, because let's be real, turn to page 62.
Go back to the basement.

DIANE

Everything is in the index.

All your possibilities. All your options. You've been looking for something this entire time. Another door. Another way. Is it in Sam's book? Or just Sam? Sam holds so much. If Sam could open to you; if you could pass through another's heart, into peace.

Open the door, turn the page.

Stay in the basement, keep reading. See how long you can shelter from the world you don't want to go back to. The agony between all these pages. Pages of your life stick together. Thursday night. Tomorrow morning. The day you got back to the mall. Four years. Two miles. A few pages. Flip back to the first page of the story.

1,347 children just disappeared in the United States.

Make a different choice this time.

Or turn the page.

You'll be right back here, eventually.

Right?

Step Into The Future

SAM

"I like it," Diane says.

Head-on collision in my brain. "What? You do?"

She skips through the pages. "I like going back."

I sniff. So damp down here in the basement. Musty. Ancient boxes all labeled with upside down triangles. Diane must feel like she's always going back to where she came from.

I tug my sleeve down and wipe my nose. "You like going back? But your world is like a wasteland or something, right?"

She keeps reading. "There are places I feel safe."

"So... like these soft spots? Wait. Have you been here before? You were. You lost the catalog here. But like before that?"

She blinks. "I've been here before."

"Hey, it's ok. You're not doing anything wrong. You're safe here. You know that, right? You're safe with me. Well. I'd feel safer off-premises, but one thing at a time."

"I'm not doing anything wrong."

"No."

"Sometimes..." Diane looks at me like she's known me for years. "I think I'm scared. That's why I keep going back to... I should go forward, but that would mean letting go, and..."

I get it.

I go back and forth in my story. The books I grew up on all sort of branched in different directions as they went on, but I like this idea of circling back. Every day is lapping the mall over and over. Start of my shift no different from the end. Sunset. Sunrise. I'm going out, I'm coming back in, eventually I'm seeing myself.

That's me, isn't it?

Across the concourse. Rounding the food court again. I've walked so many circles around this mall I've gone back on myself. That's me right now, ahead of me, though I'm ahead of her. Days loop on each other. Months. Years, maybe. How would you know?

How would you know when you were? Where? Who?

Am I the person I was when I started working here? Or am I the person when I leave? Do I ever leave? Why do I feel like I never get out of this basement? I've never been down here.

I take the book from her. "I like to go back, too. I mean, I don't, but... it keeps your mind off things. You know?"

Diane eyes me flipping the pages. I feel her eyes on me, like I'm a movie screen, like I'm a movie she knows backwards and forwards.

"I like your book," she says. "It's... cool."

She says 'cool' like she hasn't said it ten years. She says it like she's just now remembering talking like teenagers.

"It's not finished," I say.

"You never finish these kinds of books."

"Even though you mess up, you die, you can still go back."

"Yes."

"And not back the same way. A different way. Some things you never want to go back to. You know all this."

"Yes."

My tongue gets heavy. Everything I want to say starts to sound stupid in my head. For some reason, I can just blurt out whatever to a girl when I'm not really thinking or I don't care.

I must care.

"It's lonely," I say. "Isn't it?"

She blinks. "Yes."

"You get desperate, and then you maybe get involved with the wrong person, or you just sort of get dusty, you know? Like all the empty shelves in the mall. Sometimes, they have these impressions on them, where something sat for so long even the dust avoids it."

"Yes."

"Diane... do you really want to go back?"

She looks down at the book. "I want to find the right path."

"I want to help you."

"I haven't told you everything."

"For real, but... it's ok. You're... it's ok."

"I want to tell you."

"You can."

"I don't go back to places I've been before that don't work, but... sometimes, I miss things. I think I missed something here."

"Your catalog, you mean?"

"Can I read more of your book?"

"Well... like I said, it's not finished, but..."

"You never finish these kinds of books."

"Roger will be back soon. If he sees me with this, he'll wonder what I'm doing all shift. I think he already does."

Her finger sinks between the pages of my book. "Choose."

"What do you mean?"

"Should I keep reading... or should we answer when Roger knocks on the door?"

Someone knocks on the door. Useless copper wires flail from the end of my taser. Roger's voice muffles from outside. *It's me.*

"If you answer," Diane says, "We should turn the page."

I shake my head. "If?"

"But if you keep reading..." Pages brush her thumb. "We should go back. Deeper into the basement."

I peek through the boxes. "Deeper... why?"

"I think there's something down here."

"A way out?"

Diane smiles, like she's just remembering how. "It's like a game."

What do you know? My book's come to life. Or I'm in my book.

Some days, it's hard to tell. Some days, it feels like you're just a character in someone else's story. A game piece.

"Choose," she says.

I unlock the door. Roger emptied his trunk, I guess. Besides the shotgun, he's rocking a shotgun, his Glock, and something else tucked in his belt. A bandolier studded with clips strains against his paunch.

He cocks the shotgun. "People see a gun, and they think twice."

Didn't expect to die this way.

If I ever thought about it, I figured I'd die of boredom from my Dad and his brothers arguing about whether or not *Die Hard* was a Christmas movie. Goes without saying. But we're pretty much guaranteed to eat it now Roger has decided to level up on this Denomenon. For some reason, I don't think a shotgun is going to intimidate a dude carrying a giant airplane propeller for a sword while he's riding a dragon-snake thing that spits radioactive waste.

Just a theory.

Roger studies the mall directory on the wall in the backroom hallway. "We're taking back the food court."

I shake my head. "Taking it back?"

"You come from the west. I come from the east. Classic pincer."

"Shouldn't we just get back to the office?"

We're in the backrooms on the southwest side near the loading docks. Security entrance is north side, Parking lot B, tucked in this little corner where the north face meets the west wing. Basically, it's directly across from us, through the food court.

Roger taps the map. "I'll get the high ground on him."

"You're going upstairs?"

He traces his course on the directory. Down the backrooms. Left to the escalator. Right across the upper level to the stairs overlooking the food court. After a while, it wasn't worth it to pay for printing a new directory, so PayLess, B.Dalton Booksellers, and Sam Goody promise something between Roger and his destination. Really, it's just empty spaces all sealed off from one another.

Diane gazes at the directory. "The mall has changed."

"They remodeled in the 90s," I say.

"Remodeled..."

Roger sighs. "Is she going to be a problem?"

I throw up my hands. "Both."

"What?"

"She has both. PTSD. ADHD."

Diane blinks. "What are those?"

"Me being smart. I'm sorry. This whole thing is a problem."

"Which is why we're solving it," Roger says, and takes out his phone. "This is going to work. He seems distracted enough."

The live feed blips on. The Denomenon snakes around the food court, not so much searching for Diane, but building something. His dragon – The Falken, Diane called it – slithers between the damaged chairs and tables, piling them at the west end. The bigger the pile gets, the more cracks vine from it into the mall.

I expand the image. "What's it doing..."

Diane takes the phone from Roger. "He's building his throne."

"His what?"

"How do I watch TV?"

Roger groans. "You weren't kidding."

I nudge him down the hall a bit while she discovers streaming for the first time. "I think we should stay in the shelter."

"Stay? Down here?"

"She knows this thing. It's just waiting for us out there. So we wait until morning. Mall walkers will come. We won't be there to open the doors. They'll call someone. Someone will come."

"Sam, we have a job."

I keep my voice low. "She's like... I know she seems crazy and she's got issues... but you can see what's going on out there, Roger."

He shrugs. "We need a better look."

"He's riding a dragon-snake thing."

"We can't hide, Sam."

"This is strategic. Strategically not being found."

"I told you. Situations come up. You've got to face them."

"This isn't facing them."

"No one's going to come for you."

"What if we went to the casino to get Gary?"

"They got their own problems out there."

"I feel like they're different problems."

"You can't always call for help."

"And you can't go nuclear on every break-in. Sorry, Diane."

She blinks. "For what?"

"Well – I don't know. I guess you just cut people, so..."

"Yes."

"But we're not doing that. Ok? And we're not shooting, Roger. If you start shooting in here, there will be a report."

"Extraordinary circumstances," he says.

Can't argue with that. "We could lose our jobs."

"If we run out on our duty, we're done."

"Extraordinary circumstances. Right?"

"Whatever this is... it picked the wrong mall."

"Roger."

He hands me his Glock. "Take this."

"What? No."

"Shoot only if I say."

"I'm not doing that."

"Conventional arms are useless against The Denomenon," Diane says, swiping through the phone. "This won't work."

So much for whispering. "He wants the catalog, right? Which, maybe now might be a good time to explain why?"

"I'm not giving him the book."

I rub my head. "Look, I know it's important to you,I get that, but we can get another one. There has to be one on eBay. Right, Roger?"

"We're not giving this guy anything," he says.

"She just said nothing can hurt him."

"Doesn't matter what kind of Kevlar he's got on. He takes a shotgun blast to the chest, he'll be doing what I tell him."

"I'm going back," Diane says and cuffs snap around her wrist.

Before I know it, they cuff around mine. "Roger!"

"You're not going anywhere, little lady." Roger takes the phone back. "We still need to question you when this is done."

I sigh. "Roger, I told you..."

"She broke in. She's doing something with our radios. Whatever she told you, she can tell me. Later. First things first."

Diane gives him that same look she did before. I shake my head as vigorously as I can. Don't. Please don't. I'll clean up anything in here. Graffiti. Garbage. God knows what on the bathroom floor. Not blood.

She tugs on the cuffs so hard she pulls me into her. "Let me go."

"Just wait," I say.

She reaches in her poncho. "*Now.*"

"*Wait*, Diane. Ok?"

Her eyes dart from me to Roger. His every last weapon. Ammo. Vest. Knee brace. She games out something in her head. I can tell. If she waits, if she lets Roger run off to be a hero, then she plucks the pick from her hair and undoes the cuffs. Again.

Diane's hand falls to her side. "Ok."

Breathe. "Roger, let's think about this."

Roger shakes his head. "You want the job? This is the job."

"Our job is to make sure nothing happens."

"You guys stay down here on the lower level. Things go sideways, exit through the loading docks. Contact the authorities."

"Cool plan, let's do that right now."

He rests the shotgun against his shoulder and heads down the dark corridor past the locked doors and closed gates.

"Let's roll," Roger says.

DIANE

Don't eat today, your mother says, more than once. *That way we can keep on shopping.*

She enjoys the game more than she ever did actually going to the store. *We have to*, she always said, like she resented it. Sometimes, think she resented you because you enjoyed it so much. All your fights were about the store. What had to be left behind.

Fear that you are forever left behind.

The day it happened, you had gone to the supermarket in Roseburg in the afternoon. No money, never any money, but you had to. Your mother stood in the checkout line, calculating, as you browsed through the *TV Guide*. Somewhere in the middle there was an advertisement for an upcoming television movie on ABC. Forget the title, but never the ad, a two-page spread, black and white, dark and ominous. A woman stood on her farm, framed by large pine trees. Behind her, missiles pillared the air with their exhaust.

Your mother rolled her eyes. *That's all it is now.*

On the way home, you asked her if it would ever happen. Not that you knew what a nuclear war happening meant, other than everyone talked about it a lot right before. Your father did. *You need to be ready*, he told your mother, in some fight that was about the future and the past. At school, teachers asked each other if they should go through the duck and cover again. Some of them laughed.

They all died.

The news talked about it. Movies showed it. She took you to the drive-in that summer. Second feature. Last movie you ever saw that wasn't on TV. What was it called? They played a game. Joshua. The world ended and ended, but in the end, it was only a game.

Let's play, your mother says in the stillborn spring.

Remember her saying this. Not so much the other things. Not the drive home from Roseburg into the last clean sunset you would ever see. *If it happens, it happens*, your mother said, one hand barely on the steering wheel, eyes not quite on the road short and dark ahead.

(4) *Strike first in this revolutionary new video game!*

SAM

Roger grimaces as he kneels at the junction between the backrooms and the main concourse. "This is it."

This isn't happening. Stop saying that. Something like this was always going to happen. Maybe not a girl time traveling forward from a nuclear holocaust and followed by a Whatever That Is Out There™, but something. For a while, the police department used one of the old anchor stores for their training facility. They walled up a maze and turned some mannequins into targets. After they left a few years ago, Roger used the course for himself. And then the cops showed up because someone reported there was a mall shooting.

I tug Diane with me. "Roger. Can we talk about this?"

He peeks around the wall toward the food court, making like he understands any of this. "Nothing to talk about."

"Look, we're outmatched."

"After that night in '99, I swore I never would be again."

Every single time something happens in here, it's not about doing our job, filing a report, moving on. Somehow, every break-in or tweaker who runs their mouth at us on their way across the parking lot has to be about 'that night in '99.' I don't even know what actually happened, because as much as Roger talks about it, he doesn't really talk about it. Best I can tell from all the classes, sparring sessions, and laps around the mall, someone beat him up. Just like me. After that, he got right with guns. Started quoting scripture from 2nd Amendment blogs. Went into security defending America's soft underbelly. Then, he took on disciples. Some more willing than others.

"This isn't about that," I say. "Not everything is about that."

Roger goes as blank as Diane. "I thought you understood."

"I don't. I'm sorry."

"I'm starting to get that."

"C'mon, Roger."

"Didn't I train you better than this?"

"You didn't train me for whatever this is."

"I trained you to keep your guard up."

"My guard is always up, Roger."

"No one is taking these guns away from me."

"Oh, c'mon."

"No one is pushing me around."

This isn't about doing our job. Definitely not about me not doing mine. Roger wants something to happen. He cuffed Diane to the radiator. He went for the shotgun. He won't call the cops.

"Roger," I say. "No one is pushing you around."

Roger cocks the shotgun. *Ch-chk.* "That's what I just said."

"I don't think I can go along with this."

"This is your job."

"My job is call the cops when things go sideways."

"Cops won't do a damn thing. Never do."

"Roger, it was twenty years ago."

"All these guys. Same guys, Sam. Same as your guys. Like it's their world. You're trespassing. Well. Now they're trespassing."

"What happened to me was completely different than what happened to you, Roger. Wasn't it?"

"You can't run. If you don't go out there and face this thing... if you just stay in this mall and hide away from what hurt you... then all the training, all the energy, all the effort, it was for nothing."

I don't know who he's talking to. "Not if you've helped people."

Disappointment creases his face. "What does that get you?"

"Roger... it's not about making someone pay."

"Everybody pays," Roger says. "This loser picked the wrong mall. We're not getting fired, Sam. We're getting raises."

This isn't happening. "Roger..."

"Follow the plan. Wait for my mark."

"What's your mark?"

"You'll know it. Maintain radio silence."

"The radios don't work."

"Break," he says, and runs down the hallway into the east wing.

I need to be moving. I just sit there. Spinning.

The cuff dangles from my wrist. "Oh, man."

Diane sheaths her pick in her hair. "You can't help anyone."

"What?"

"All you can do is... save yourself. Any way you can."

"I don't believe that."

"I've known people like you."

"Noting the past tense."

"You don't have to follow him, Sam."

"He's my boss."

"He's only protecting his insecurity."

"You've known people like him, too?"

"Yes."

"Gun guys probably do pretty well in the apocalypse."

"No."

"Why not?"

"In the beginning... people with guns and ammunition... they were frightening. They were in control. But it didn't matter if they killed you, because you were going to starve anyway. You were going to die of thirst. And then the bullets were all used up."

Her knife. Stained. Sharp. No question. "We have bullets."

"None of them will help you tonight."

"I have to help Roger."

"You don't."

"I don't have anywhere else to go."

She tugs on my dangling cuff. "I want to be free, too."

"Diane... what are you..."

"The Denomenon will follow me."

"You don't need to go back. We'll figure something out."

"He'll destroy this place."

"We'll find a way out of this."

It's like she's looking right through you. "For a long time... I had this fantasy. Someone would come and rescue me. A hero. Sometimes... I still imagine someone will..."

"I'll get you out of this. Diane, I promise."

"No one can save you," she says and runs into the dark.

Hopefully, she remembers she has to go back out in the mall to get upstairs. Hopefully, she remembers to wait until the fireworks start. I wish she'd wait. But I can't stop her. Can't bail on Roger.

He's right.

I have a job to do. If she gets back to the toy store while we shoot it out with The Denomenon, then maybe all this ends. No one's going to believe this. I don't believe it. You have experience with not believing things. Wake up in a hospital bed. Can't move. Broken ribs. Nose. Couldn't believe it, but it happened. This happened.

This is happening.

I hurry down the backrooms west. My head running back with Diane. Not so much because I'm attracted to her – she's about 75% tarp – but there's something about her. Like I understand her. She understands me. Get it together.

Get ready.

I exit the backrooms through the old candy store. Still smells like peppermint, kind of. Someone sawed through this gate last year because they needed that sugar or something, and now I can just walk out onto the concourse without a sound. The food court hisses. I hide behind a support pillar. Broken tables and chairs pile at the north end, kind of where they used to set up Santa Claus during Christmas. Glowing cracks splinter through them, into the floor, into other debris scattered in the food court. What am I supposed to do?

Just don't get hit again. Stay on your feet. Bail if you have to.

Running has its place. I'm sure Diane can speak to that. She's probably down to the west stairs by now. Probably, she can see me.

I wonder if she sees me.

The Denomenon hunches forward on The Falken's back, like some cowboy in an old Western. "What game do we play now?"

Does he see me?

His voice echoes around the food court. "None you can win."

Don't move. Don't breathe.

"You can never win. Can you, Sam? It's frustrating, isn't it? All you want is what other people have. A car. A girlfriend. A home."

Don't.

"Why can't you have them? You've paid for them. You've paid for them in blood and shame. You imagine it, don't you? So quickly. So... certainly. You see yourself, in a large house perfect in its bounty, clinging to Diane under a blanket by the fire."

How does he know that?

"You're all so quick to imagine. Imagining it is the best part. For you... all of you... winning is not the object, is it? Only playing. So long as you have the promise, you feel rewarded. Validated. Vindicated, even, when vindication is always the shell under the cup, moving around, and around, and around."

Two hands. Hold fast. "She's gone... so just leave."

"There you are. Excellent form, Sam."

"I'll shoot. I swear."

"Is an oath required to fire it?"

"I'm warning you."

"Tell me, Sam. I've always wondered. What use is a warning?"

"It doesn't have to be like this."

"Those with power and the will to use it do not need to communicate their strength. Where is she?"

"I told you. She's gone."

"She took the catalog with her?"

"Look, if that's important to you, we can go on eBay right now. We can find you one. We'll pay for the expedited shipping."

"If any other book would do, Diane would not have come back for hers. She shouldn't have been so careless with it, either, but she is long bored with this game. She seeks a new challenge."

Cracks spread across the floor. "What do you seek?"

"Power, Sam. The same as you."

"I just want..."

"You want what they all want. To 'win' at life. You're not winning now, are you, Sam? You cannot win the game... anymore than I can. But while validation and vindication remain impossible for me... I take great reward in preventing you from yours."

"Why..."

"Because I desire it."

A shotgun cocks in the dark. "*Freeze, dirtbag!*"

Roger stands on the upper level, where the grand escalators used to deliver people straight from the food court. The owners took them out to open more space downstairs, but really it was just to force people to walk the entire mall to get around.

The glow stick stands on its tail and The Denomenon holds his sword up high. "Another player... and one who came to play."

Roger aims the shotgun at him. "Drop the hockey stick!"

The Denomenon considers his sword. "You mean this?"

"You attacked a security officer and I have every authorization to use deadly force if you do not cease and desist right now."

"You all insist on explaining the rules to me."

"I will fire."

"This is how you tolerate a game you cannot win. You think you know the rules. You think you're in control."

"Drop. It. Now."

"You're not," The Denomenon says and throws his sword.

Glass and plaster rain down on the food court. Half the floor up there. Roger. Shit, shit, shit. I'm shouting. I'm shooting. I empty the clip and The Denomenon is still sitting on his dragon. He's still looking at me like I'm an ant on a picnic table.

The Denomenon dismounts The Falken into the ruin of the food court. "I'm disappointed in you, Sam."

I fumble a new clip into the Glock. "Stay away..."

He clangs through the rubble. "Unlike your partner, you have insight. But you lack his will. Imagine if you could harness your perception... truly harness it... then I would pose no threat to you at all. But all you can imagine is what is fostered upon you. A car. A girlfriend. A home. The fantasy you are all sold."

"Don't come any closer!"

"The same is true of Diane, though one must acknowledge her persistence. You see, Diane comes from a world where everything was taken from her. She doesn't know how to give. She expects only gifts. She is a child in that way. You must be firm with children..." He tears his sword from the rubble. "Or else they become spoiled tyrants whose expectations can never be met."

"I'm warning you..."

He turns toward me. "You have seen it already, Sam."

Sweat slicks my Glock. "*Stop!*"

"You do your duty... and she abandons you."

Every bullet flattens against his armor. "Please..."

"You needn't worry. I suspect you will see her again, though you're unlikely to hold any grudges against her. A grudge has no place in a game, you see... unless, of course, you want to win."

"Please – "

He raises his sword. "I offer you no quarter, Sam, After all, any worthy player should have a pocketful of their own – "

Thunder. Shells crash into the Denomenon's back. I find my ON switch and run behind a support pillar. Roger cocks his shotgun again. Fires. Staggers through the food court covered in dust and blood and The Denomenon slumps to his knee.

Roger presses the shotgun to The Denomenon's head. "I warned you what would happen."

"We both know the rules," The Denomenon says, and sweeps his sword through Roger so fast his scream dies before he does.

DIANE

Some men break into the house after dark.

Quick. Determined. Practiced. Your mother is as well. She stabs one in the leg. He bleeds out on the basement floor, twitching while the other fights her for the gun. She makes a sound, like people do when they're so insulted they can't speak. A gasp of indignation. She pancakes to the floor and doesn't move again. *Now she's useless*, the man says, and drags you out of the house, screaming. He hurts you like you've never been hurt. He threatens to kill you, but he doesn't. After a few weeks with him, moving from house to house, town to town in search of food, realize you are never going home again.

Can't make it home for the holidays?
Show them you care by shipping any item!

SAM

Shells fall to the floor.

Half a shotgun. Cut strap. Roger's radio chops with static, fritzing like the tables and chairs. A chair hits me. Something hard. Metal. Behind me. I can't see behind me. They're surrounding me.

What's happening?

What did I say? Drunk. Stupid. *Hey. You're hot.* I think that's all I said to her. This guy who got everything in XL except his brain follows me into the bathroom at the nightclub. Pushes me into the stall. Whatever nerve I had out in the bar flushes right out of me so fast my knees rattle. His buddies follow him in. *What did you say?* I push back. That's me. Little Dog. Dad always said.

You don't know how small you are.

The guy slams his fist into the wall beside my face and I duck under his arm, already imagining myself out the door, and someone clocks me in the temple. Floor is spinning. I'm on the floor. Arms and legs. They're kicking me. Punching me. Spitting on me. Hey.

Hey!

The guys tear away. Hands up. Laughing like someone farted. *What's the problem?* Roger shoves in between them. XL is too far into kicking me to death, so he doesn't stop. Roger punches him in the kidney and this little hurt squeal breaks the spitting and shouting. Everything goes white. Numb. Cold. I'm screaming.

I think I'm screaming.

Roger. His pieces lie all over the food court. Baton. Cuffs. Cell phone. Something in my brain lunges for the phone even though I know it doesn't work and The Denomenon swings his sword again. Half the pillar I hide behind comes away and I hit the floor.

The Denomenon points the sword at me. "Game over, Sam."

I roll over to crawl for my life I guess and shadows flicker on the floor. Long. Wild. Still, at the same time.

"Diane..."

She stands behind me, the catalog in her hands. "I'll do it."

The Denomenon hesitates. "You and I both know you won't."

Her fingers crimp into an open page. "I will."

If there's a face behind that mask, I can't tell. But I can tell no doubt The Denomenon is furious. "For this one? Why?"

Diane stares at him. "We both understand the rules."

She grabs my hand. Pulls me along. Drags me across the floor like I'm some kid throwing a tantrum over a toy they can't have. That thing killed Roger. Roger is dead. Diane drags me toward the escalator. We're going back up. The Falken coils around a support beam and he's on the upper level in a flash. We've only got one way up now and we're not going to get to there before it does.

"This way," I say, and now I'm the one pulling her.

My keys fumble out of my hand to the floor.

C'mon. Get it together, Sam. I scoop them up, unlock the access door hidden in the wall closing off the old department store, and close it behind me soft as I can. C'mon, c'mon, c'mon.

Diane's voice echoes into the dark. "This was Sears..."

50,000 square feet. A vast concrete frontier interrupted by customer service desks. Makeup kiosks. Naked mannequins. Signs they left hanging: CHECK OUT HERE. I pull Diane along the far wall past the dressing rooms, through the office, into the employee restroom. Diane pumps the brakes at the shower stall. I only take a shower on Saturdays when the traffic's higher in the mall and I can disguise the water usage. Maybe Roger knows. Could be why he's pushing me so hard to leave. Roger is upset.

Roger is dead.

I brace against the sink. "He's dead…"

Diane cradles the catalog in the mirror. "You're injured."

"Huh?"

Stuffing foams out of my jacket. Sword must have grazed me. I tear the jacket off. Blood oozes from the Standard Security patch on my shoulder. Wow. Just got me. Didn't even notice. Now I notice.

I slump against the sink. "Ow…"

Diane sheaths the catalog. "Take your shirt off."

"What?"

She reaches inside her poncho. "Take off your shirt."

She pulls out this old vinyl see-through pencil case. Little lunch money coin pocket on the front. She digs through pens and pencils for the ancient, yellowed medical supplies she nicked from the fallout shelter along with a more suspect needle and thread.

I hold my arm. "You're going to stitch me up?"

"Yes," she says.

That scar on her hand gets uglier every time I see it. "I appreciate the thought, but… maybe we'll leave this to the professionals."

"The Denomenon won't let us leave."

"What?"

"He wants the catalog. He's not going to let me leave with it through the toy store or out the security entrance."

"Why does he want it?"

Diane stares at me in the mirror. "It's a game."

"What game? What was that? Back in the food court. You were going to tear out a page out of the catalog. He was almost scared."

"It's important to treat your wound fast to avoid infection."

This is beyond frustrating. "I don't know sometimes if you're not understanding me or you're just ignoring me."

"The alcohol is old, but it will clean the wound."

"Diane. Roger is dead."

"The Denomenon can only use broken things."

"What does that mean?"

"You've saw in the food court. He changes things. He uses them. The catalog... there's power in it."

"I don't understand."

"The world in the catalog doesn't exist anymore."

"Well. Maybe it never did."

She blinks. "It did."

"I just mean... you know. It's all a fantasy."

"It existed."

"Ok. I'm just trying to understand. What are his powers? How does he do the crack thing? What happens if he does it to the book?"

She opens the rubbing alcohol. "We need to treat your wound."

"Just use water," I say and turn on the faucet.

I may as well have landed in a spaceship in front of her. Diane fixates on the sink like she does her catalog. She holds her hand out, wanting. She holds her hand under the water slow but sure and she flinches. Hot. Surprise. She almost smiles.

"Diane," I say. "This is for real? Right?"

Water pools in her hands. "Take your shirt off."

Not a fan, but I guess I don't have a choice. Diane cuts some thread for the stitch with her teeth. She guides it through this needle which I'm looking at hard to make sure isn't rusty. But she's not rusty. Every move is clean. Quick. Sure. She's done this before.

Diane swabs my shoulder again. "What's your favorite thing?"

What have I got to lose? "I like your hair."

Zero reaction. "Why?"

"I just do."

"What do you like about it?"

"Just... everything and OWWWWWW you're doing this..."

She laces the thread through my shoulder. "I like your hair."

Don't look. "Really?"

"Yes."

"Diane... why did you come back for me?"

"Be still."

"You're sort of one step forward, two steps back, you know."

"Is that a game?"

"It's called life."

"In Life, you can be sent back numerous spaces."

"Yeah... true."

"I didn't like that game. You don't make the rules."

"Who doesn't want to make the rules? I don't want to play games... I'm glad you came back for me... I'm trying to process that along with everything else, so it's slow coming. I'm sorry."

"You're sorry I came back?"

"No. No. You saved my life. Why did you?"

She pulls the thread taut. "Be still."

Got it. "You've probably been alone for a long time. You forget how to talk to people. I get that. I'm not really wired for an empty mall, you know? But sometimes, it's just easier being here."

"It is."

"Don't you get lonely, though? Don't you..."

"I've been alone for five years. I think it's five years."

"Five years... there's no one else?"

"Not in a long time."

"Everybody died? Like everybody, *everybody*?"

"We didn't get as much fallout as other places. Some thought that meant the war wasn't bad. The spring after, they put together the diesel we had left to try and reach other towns. A few came back on foot. Everything beyond Boise was asphalt."

I can't even imagine. "Who did it?"

"Russians. The radio said."

"Why... why did they do it?"

"I don't know."

"Did we bomb the Russians back?"

"I don't know."

"No one's tried to rebuild, or..."

"I don't know."

"It's like a movie..."

My shoulder is all she cares about. "I miss movies."

"What's, um... what's your favorite?"

"*Somewhere In Time*."

"I don't know that one."

She bites off the thread. "Superman fell in love with Solitaire."

"No clue."

Diane peels a government-issue bandage from the 60s. "He sees her picture. He goes back in time. They fall in love. It's sad."

"Hold up, I've got all that." I take the med kit from my belt. Take out some less-ancient gauze and pads. Athletic tape. "Only thing I don't have is the needle and thread."

The way she looks at things. Blank screen. Like she can't even process it. Maybe she can't. Probably hasn't seen a med kit, let alone a medicine cabinet, this stocked in years.

"You can have it," I say. "Hopefully, we won't need it again."

She just nods.

"We won't need it, Diane. It will be ok."

Diane slips a pad from the kit. "You're a hopeful person."

"I guess so. I mean, you are, too. Right?"

She peels out the pad. "We didn't get much fallout... people thought it wasn't that bad. There were people at first. We used up the food. Diesel went bad after six months. Gasoline. All the batteries died after a few years. People became... less."

That word. *Less.* Holds everything she thinks about people. It's not much from the sound of it.

Diane applies the pad to my arm. "You'll be ok."

I reach for her hand. "Diane..."

She kisses my arm. "Makes it better."

My arm still hurts. Roger is still dead. I'm still probably losing this job, if not my life. But I'm not as terrified as I was when I woke up in the hospital. For the first time in a long time, I'm not scared.

Is that a smile?

Shy. Girly. God. Diane's like another person right now. She's so close to me. So strange. Wild. But contained. She's got a vacuum seal on her emotions. I can tell, though. Everything in her wants to stay. Be free. Live her life. She's my age, I think. Maybe a little older, but that could be just living in the apocalypse. Diane has been alone for most of her life. I used to freak out staying home Saturday night. I couldn't do it. I don't know how anyone could do it.

How do you keep human?

Is that why she came back for me? Some hope. Humanity. I was kind to her. I was fair with her. Nobody has been that with Diane for a really long time. This catalog. Coping mechanism. Remnant. Reminder. Normal life. Christmas. Toys. Kid stuff. You're not supposed to fend for yourself in the apocalypse. But she has. She's survived for years and it's left her wild. All this hair. Down to her waist. Frizzy copper. Hard, but soft. Like all of her.

I sniff her hair. "Soot..."

Diane flinches. "What?"

"Your hair smells like soot. The catalog."

"Everything does."

"You were in a nuclear war..."

She's from another world where there was a nuclear war in 1983. Everything died, and all the suck made her world soft, which let her pass into mine, where the suck is hard. Now some video game boss is going to destroy my world because we exist, I guess. I hug her. Adrenaline. Fear. Grief. I can't help it. Diane tenses. She hardens, but then softens. Her head eases to my shoulder. Heavy.

"You don't have to go back," I say.

She blinks. "I don't want to, but..."

I grip her hand. "We can hide here in the department store."

"Hide?"

"I was telling Roger. The mall walkers will come. They won't be able to get in. They freak out if they can't get in right away. Seriously. They'll call Roger and complain – "

Wait. Do I have his cell? I have his cell. Takes a minute, but I work out Roger's passcode from the thumbprints on the screen. I try to call Gary. *We're sorry. You've reached a number that has been disconnected or is no longer in service. If you feel this is in error, please check the number dialed, and please try again.*

Maybe the phone got damaged when The Denomenon killed Roger. "The mall walkers will call, Diane. Roger won't answer. So they'll call Gary. Management. The cops. Someone will come. We'll figure this out. We'll figure it out together."

Her voice is soft now, too. "Together..."

"I promise."

She slips away from me. "If I stay... you've seen what The Denomenon can do. You've suffered it. All your weapons... all your soldiers... they're just toys to him."

Roger is dead.

She reaches for me but claws her hand back. "I don't want anyone else to... I don't want you to... stay. I'll go to the toy store."

My job is to protect this mall, but there's nothing here. I'm only protecting some private equity firm's bottom line. I'm protecting this idea I have any future here, when I know I don't. If I let Diane go back to God knows what just to save my own ass, then what kind of person am I? What kind of person would I become?

I'd just be Roger. Angry at myself.

I claw her hand. I hold on until I get it out. "You came back for me. Give me a chance, Diane. Give me until dawn."

She stares into herself. "Nothing changes with the dawn."

"Plenty has changed already. Please."

A war plays out in her eyes. Her expression is so stoic, so forced in its emptiness that it could just snap.

"Ok," she says.

DIANE

Thumbprints fringe page 48, where you spend more and more time. The woman on page 48 is on page 76, too, in a long blue nightgown with two other women, reading a book. The caption reads *Beautiful evenings*. She's on a lot of pages, wearing different outfits, her auburn hair sometimes worn long, sometimes braided, sometimes cascading over in a wave down her cheek your fingers long to surf. She reads, she smiles, she shares a knowing, almost secret look with the other women. Sometimes, she's looking off to the side. Imagine she's looking at you. Imagine what it would be like to touch her hair; kiss her mouth; sleep in her arms and wake up warm.

Romance is back this holiday season with this sheer gown (colors and sizes vary, see table).

SAM

My watch must be broken.

Still the same time it was before. I have never wanted for another boring night at work so bad. I've never wanted to just go home so bad. No way I'm sleeping in the parking lot after this. If I even survive.

Roger is dead.

I try to call out again on his phone. *We're sorry.* You're sorry? I walk toward the far end of the employee bathroom, hoping to find a signal. No joy. Diane watches me like this hawk who hangs out in the parking lot. He perches on a lamppost and every time I walk to and from the car, he stares me down, like this is his space.

I'm the trespasser.

I scroll through Roger's contacts. I don't know. Who would I call? Who did he have? He never talked about anybody. I swear, all he did was talk, but it was just about working the job.

What was he working for?

Buying more guns? Do they keep better company? Probably didn't even think about it. I never think about the future or what I don't have. I don't want to think about it. You want something, you give something of yourself to the world, and the world punches you in the mouth. Kicks you in the ribs. Why would you ever want to put yourself out there like that? Why ever take the risk?

We're taking a risk.

Thunder rattles through the mall. Tiny earthquakes. Probably

The Denomenon and his dragon choo-chooing through the kiosks or tearing open security gates looking for us. Hold on. I tap the app streaming the camera feed from the main concourse. Downstairs is like a lit swimming pool thanks to the TV tube kintsugi growing in the food court. Best I can tell, The Denomenon isn't there.

Where is he?

Metal rattles. Glass shatters. What I think are gumballs spill from the janky old machines in the west wing. The Denomenon is in the west wing. Coming our way. I can't tell from this feed, but they must be going store to store. Eventually, they'll bash their way in here. Mostly, the department store is empty space, so the only places to search are the dressing rooms. Stock rooms. Bathrooms.

"We're not going to be able to stay in here," I say.

Diane gazes into the phone. "He knows this place."

"From your mall?"

"Yes."

"But you've managed to hide from him? How?"

She blinks. "The secret room."

"The what?"

Hard to imagine how Diane stays hidden with that tarp flapping like it does. She sounds like someone eating a bag of chips as we move through the department store's dark. First chance we get, we're ditching it for something more stealth. We come to the escalators in the middle. Classic crossing pattern. Pitch dark up there. I know it's empty, but all I see is Roger on the floor and I give the rubber handrail a love tap. Too bad there's not a gym still in the mall. I could use some quality time with a punching bag right about now.

I aim my flashlight up the escalator. "The room's up here?"

Diane stares off into the dark.

"Hey," I say. "You ok?"

She nods. "The store is... different. The ceiling. The paint."

"Is this room still going to be there?"

"I hope so."

Me, too, otherwise we're going to end up stuck out in the open. "They've changed a lot in the mall since... well."

"I couldn't have imagined..."

"What is yours like?"

She winces. "The roof caved in a few years ago. Snow got in. Rain. Everything is... mold now."

"Probably as empty."

"The shelves and fixtures are still there. The signs. I left the things people didn't loot. I played store."

My laugh echoes back to me. "You played store?"

"Didn't you?"

"I mean, I guess. Dad hated to shop, so I did, too. But Mom loved it, so... I guess I did, too. I never wanted things. Honestly. Sure, sometimes it sucked when you knew you were going to be about two or three models behind, but... I think I just wanted this vibe people had. You know? You ever meet people, and they're just so... together? Comfortable? I don't know... happy."

"Yes."

"I always felt like I had to be a few things at once. I'm always walking this high wire. I'm good at it, but... it's not natural."

"You seem natural to me."

"Was it the screaming?"

"You don't want anything from me."

"Some answers. Maybe."

She blinks.

"Sorry... I'm just trying to keep it light. Things aren't light. I know you're doing your best. We're doing our best."

"You've helped me from the beginning."

"Anybody would."

"No. They wouldn't."

I shrug. "I got picked on a lot growing up."

"Why?"

"Look at me."

She does. "Why?"

"I guess I look like I fit in, but... I don't."

"Kids at school would ask me where I was from, and I said 'From here.' They called me... names... and pulled my hair. To see if it was real. It couldn't be real, they said, because Chinese don't have red hair. I'm not Chinese. My mother was from South Korea."

"Diane, I'm sorry."

She nods.

"I would have beat up those kids. For real."

"I buried most of them."

"I regret my words."

"I regret..." She touches the catalog, hanging from her hip in its leather satchel like some magic book. "Sometimes, I think it would have been better if I had died, too."

"Don't say that."

"Sometimes, I think I did. This is all... after. The mall is..."

"Limbo."

"Yes."

"All evidence aside, I'm still questioning stuff. But you're here. You survived. Don't feel bad about that. I'm sure your mom..."

She steps onto the escalator. "I know the way to the room."

I walk up past her, searching the upper level with my flashlight. "Diane... you're not doing anything wrong by staying."

She stops on the dead stairs. "My father was in the Navy. She said he was in the Navy. My uncle said he was in the CIA."

"CIA? He was a spy?"

"I don't know. My uncle would say the craziest things. My father was part of experiments. Cold War psy-ops."

"Psy-what?"

"I don't know what that is. My parents fought. All the time. He drank. He told me he was a coward. Cowards prefer guilt."

"He told you that? You were a kid..."

"Guilt is safe. Guilt is comfortable. Guilt costs you nothing."

"I don't know about that."

"It's living you have to pay for. It's facing your reality."

I rub my side. "What if you did? What if reality kicked you in the ribs? Kicked you out of your parents' house because you hit on a girl? What are you supposed to do, then?"

"Survive."

Diane marches up the dead escalator like she's done it a hundred times before. Probably has. Alone for years. Playing store. This is her store. Her world. She makes the rules, I guess.

Mostly, the upper level was the women's department. A few more dressing rooms hide inside the walls, but I don't think Diane is talking about these. She goes into the east corner, back where the shoes used to be, straight toward a tall, skinny mirror on the wall. She peels it right back from the plaster to a little cubby room.

Two-way mirror.

Wow. You can look out into the store through here. A clipboard sits on the floor next to a coffee mug I'm pretty sure hasn't been touched in a million years. Dates and times written on the yellowed paper. Initials next to each.

"This is a security room," I say.

Diane nods. "I found it by accident."

Makes sense. Back when the mall first opened in the 70s, there wouldn't have been security cameras all over the place. Security would have parked it in here and watched people through the mirror. Air vents. I bet there are rooms like this all over the store.

I shine my flashlight around. "Wow…"

Not much space, but it will do. I slip my jacket off. Too warm in here for that thing. I'm sweating buckets, anyway. I toss it on the floor and take a seat. May as well settle in for the night.

"Diane... The Denomenon doesn't know about this room?"

She sits across from me. "No."

"Is this where you... live? In your mall?"

"Yes."

"Does this connect to anything?"

"Connect?"

"Storeroom... backrooms... toy store?"

"No."

We're quiet for a long time. I want to talk, though. I need to do something, or I'm just going to sit here and think about Roger and that's like she said. Bad fruit. Soft tissue. Thoughts mush into other thoughts. Bathroom. Nightclub. *Oh. God. I think I'm going to die.*

"Hey," I say. "How does it work?"

Diane blinks. "How does what work?"

"Going back and forth. Is it like a portal?"

"You just do."

"No word or phrase or anything? No magic trick?"

"No."

"Just asking."

"Yes."

"I want to talk to you. I don't want to upset you."

"Are you?"

"What?"

"Upset?"

"Why would I be... oh. Roger. I'm trying not to be."

"Yes."

"What do you do? Like... what's your day like?"

"It's like this."

"No heat, though. No electricity."

"I'm used to the cold."

Here in the dark, close, I hear this wheeze in her. Every breath. Her chest swells. Tarp wrinkles. Tragic nails. Dirty hands. She sees me looking at them and I don't think she's looked at them in forever.

She ducks her hands inside her tarp. "I'm used to it."

"Must be lonely," I say.

"I don't think about it."

"There's no one else? Like, in particular?"

"I have the book."

"Do you have a favorite part?"

"Page 48."

"What's on page 48? Can I see?"

She shakes her head.

"It's ok."

"You've looked through it."

"When I found it the other night... I know what you see in it. Your world ended. When I went through what I went through... I wanted to do some retail therapy, too. Like hardcore shopping."

"Retail therapy?"

"Takes the sting off, I guess. Roger wants me to... he wanted me to buy these guns, and that's not my scene, but... when you're browsing, you're scrolling, you're not thinking about anything else."

Diane stares at the floor. "You can't think about it."

"I don't think you're thinking about anything. Not the past, which is a positive, but not the future, either. You're just thinking about how to fill this cavity you've fallen into. You just don't want to think about the space, you know. There's so much... emptiness... and I don't know why. I don't know why."

Something creaks downstairs. This whine. Is that a door? No. It's The Falken. Sounds like a hungry dog. He can't get up the escalators. Too narrow for him. Maybe we'll be ok.

She starts a yawning contest. I snort. She doesn't know why.

"Get some rest," I say. "I'll keep watch."

"I never sleep."

"You don't feel safe."

She shakes her head.

"I know it's scary, Diane. I'm scared. But I'm safe."

Diane reaches inside her poncho. Not a great history here. The knife comes out and this little obituary flashes through my head. Sam.

College dropout. Mall security guard. Dead in a closet. LOL. She passes me the knife. She squeezes my hand around it, and then she leans back into the corner, eyeing me like the hawk.

If I wasn't wired before.

I bring up the live feed on Roger's phone. Won't do me a lot of good, but I just like having an eye on things. Funny. The Falken is worming down the west wing back into the food court.

There's still something banging around downstairs.

The Denomenon? Can't tell from the video. Crappy resolution. Must be him. That or this place is falling apart. Whatever it is, it's not as intense as before. Maybe they're giving up.

Please let them be giving up.

Bang-bang-bang.

Oh, God. I fell asleep. How did I fall asleep? I grip the knife. Roger's phone fumbles out of my hand. The live feed spins on the floor inside the security room and *bang-bang-bang.*

I kick Diane's foot. "Hey."

She opens her eyes, startled. "What's wrong?"

Bang-bang-bang.

"Those are the exterior doors." I minimize the live feed and check the time on Roger's phone. 8:19 A.M. "It's the mall walkers."

Diane blinks. "It's morning?"

"They're probably calling Gary right now."

"Was I sleeping?"

"It's going to be ok."

"Their phones won't work, either."

"Why not?"

"EMP field."

I calmly hand the knife back to her. "This didn't come up last night when we were talking strategy, because…"

She stows the knife. "I wasn't thinking."

"It's... ok. I didn't remember, either. We have to get to them."

"The mall walkers?"

"We've got to let them know what's going on in here, or we're never leaving. We have to get to them before they do."

Of course, they stop banging as soon as I say that. Relax. They're probably going back around to another entrance. That's what they do. Get their steps in. They'll come to the security entrance. We can't get there without going through the food court.

"We need to create a diversion," I say.

I bang on the hidden entrance into the department store as hard as I can and then I run back to the escalator. The Falken is halfway down the west wing in the live feed before I'm to the top and then Diane and I bolt through the upstairs access door into the mall.

Wow.

Diane runs any faster she'll take off through the ceiling. I stop myself from shouting for her to wait up. She's in the east wing before I'm even to center court. Doesn't matter. Just stick to the plan. She winds down the east stairs and then into the old photo place like I told her. I follow her into the backrooms and finally, I catch up to her where they intersect the corridor leading to the security entrance.

I rub my side. "Hold up."

She wheezes. "Ok."

I grip her hand. "You good?"

"Good."

"Hey... why does the Wi-Fi work if there's an EMP?"

She shrugs. "What's Wi-Fi?"

Maybe they're different. "What was it like without the internet?"

"What's the internet?"

Right. "You'd be like my dad's age now."

"What's your dad's name? Maybe I went to school with him."

"Didn't you say everybody died?"

"Yes."

"Let's..." I peek down the corridor. "We're in business."

Shadows lurk outside the security entrance. They're not knocking now. Probably trying to call someone. Cops could already be on their way. I creep down the corridor, never so happy to see the same three people every single day. Super skinny lady. Beer gut grandpa. Hairdresser before her shift starts. Mannequins except they're set outside. All business. 10,000 steps to save your life.

Ch-chk.

What's that sound? I turn around into Diane. She draws her knife as Roger slouches out of the security office behind us, late-night TV light cracked through his broken and pasted body.

"You let your guard down," he says.

DIANE

The man targets grocery stores.

Not because they have food, but because the people left think they do. Your mother talked about the supermarket sometimes in the basement after. The meat counter. Piles of oranges and apples and pears. Potato chips that had this weird green edge to them that you picked off. *Eat it,* she said. *It's fine.* This want in her voice, and this shame, but you didn't know what it was then. Why would there be shame in wanting, and how did it take so long for you to discover it? Shame introduces itself to you, again and again, every day on the road with him, like a beggar who's forgotten he already asked you.

Forget the years.

The bloody nights. The horror of the burnt world. Remember the skirmishes, the fits, and the battles over something you wanted and she couldn't afford and feel sick now that she is dead, for having embarrassed her like that when all she had was her pride.

The whole way upriver, keep hoping to come across a girl like Page 48, but there aren't any girls like Page 48, even in Kettle Falls. There aren't any girls or boys or people at all.

Those girls are just cut like girls, the man says between spitting black. *Real girls are pressed like records.*

No idea what he means.

No idea if you are a real girl. If you are cut or pressed. Try cutting yourself. Search for robbers and looters to do the deed for you but your persistence in life keeps moving, and keep moving through days of only night and gray snow, through long, disfiguring years into the empty land, propelled forward by a cruel hope.

When things get better, she said.

The man dies, just as the air warms.

A fast, pitiless cancer thieves your carefully manicured plot to slit his throat in the middle of the night. Resent this, but later, be grateful you didn't become the thing that hurt you. Give thanks that among the catalog, scraps of food, and improvised weapons, you carry a little bit of your humanity still. Still. Leave him to whatever scavengers are left in the valley. Do what you always do.

Go back to the beginning.

First the cords went... now the size goes too!

SAM

Back when I was seven or eight we had all these problems with the neighbors behind the alley. I don't know. They were loud, that's all I remember. One night, I was in my room reading and something bounced off the window. Next thing I know orange is flashing outside. Smoke is rising. Shadows are prancing on the garage and my mom is screaming. I ran downstairs, outside, where Dad was already spraying down the fire with the garden hose. Neighbor kid threw a Molotov cocktail at the house. Bounced off my window. Right then, seven years old, my little life flashed before my eyes.

Just like it does right now.

Roger is supposed to be dead. But he's here, blocking the way down the corridor into the mall, glued back together wrong.

"Roger... what happened to you..."

Ch-chk. "I saw the light, Sam."

Diane pulls on my hand. "Run."

I'm stuck here like he is. "Roger..."

"*Run!*"

Brick clouds the corridor. My ears ring. I trip over what's left of the fire extinguisher cabinet that Roger just blasted off the wall and I crash in the glass. Glass grinds my hands as I scramble to get up. Glass sparkles. Light worms from Roger's boot across the tile, through the debris. Broken shards clot back together in light.

The Denomenon makes use of broken things.

Diane's hand slicks through mine. She says something. I can't hear her. She looks down the corridor. Roger pumps the shotgun. He's out. He searches his belt for extra shells, but the belt is put together backwards. I grab the little hammer chained to the cabinet. I tear the extinguisher out from what's left of the cabinet and I throw it at Roger. The shotgun spins on the floor and get it.

You have to get it.

I slip on glass. Roger lurches for the shotgun. Slow and broken as he is, he's video game fast. Not going to get there. I kick the gun out of his hands, between his legs, down the corridor behind him.

Even Roger's voice is cracked. "You really don't like guns."

"Roger," I say. "This isn't you, this is..."

Diane tugs on my sleeve. "Why are you talking to it?"

"He's not an it. He's my friend."

"Your friend is gone. You can't save him."

"Why not?"

"You can't save anyone."

Roger groans. "Little lady has a point, Sam."

Diane pulls me back. I can't leave him like this.

Roger's voice cracks. "Some people can't be saved... most are just forgotten. Who will miss us, Sam? Who will care?"

"I care," I say.

"The Denomenon knows what it's like to be forgotten. He knows what it's like to be discarded. To be used."

"What are you talking about?"

"The game demands soldiers. Knights. It uses them. Exhausts them in defense. They are never tallied in the final score. Only the games that are won or lost. We are uncounted, Sam."

"You're not uncounted. You matter."

He lurches toward me. "To you?"

"Roger, I know you're in there."

"I helped you, Sam. I taught you everything I know. Gave you a place to work and live. And I'm a joke to you."

"No..."

"I didn't see it before... but now I do. You don't respect me, Sam. You talk back. You disobey orders. You disregard protocol."

"In fairness to me, I didn't know it was all about you."

"You've got a lot of lip, Sam."

"That's how you wound up with me, right?"

"Lucky for you."

"Did you want to help me that night at the bar, Roger, or did I just give you an excuse to beat up those guys?"

"What do you think?"

I think the mall walkers should be in here at the security entrance by now. They should be knocking down the door.

Roger vines in light. "All he wants is the book, Sam."

Nothing's more busted than Diane's catalog. The Denomenon can use it. Make something from it, like he has Roger. The mess in the food court. But what can he make from old, rotting paper?

"If I give it to you," I say, "You'll... what?"

Diane's eyes plead with me to run.

"Give me the book," Roger says. "I'll let you go."

Sure he will. "What about Diane?"

"Doubt it."

"What about you? Is he going to let you go, Roger?"

"I'm not going anywhere. I'm doing my job."

"Given the circumstances, we'll pass."

Ch-chk. "Wrong answer."

Diane yanks me toward the backrooms but I bolt for the security entrance. We can't stay in here. I can't be in here with this craziness. I push on the door handle. No click. The door flies open. The mall walkers face toward the parking lot, twitching like trees in a thunderstorm. I know they keep a schedule, but man.

"Guys, run – "

The mall walkers jerk around. This winter blue glow cracks through them like it does Roger. I pull the door shut. The door doesn't lock. The lock is busted. Someone broke the lock.

"Doors are 7 AM," Roger says behind me.

Shadows creep toward us. "What did you do…"

Diane pulls on my hand. "Sam."

"What did you…"

"*Sam!*"

Super Skinny Lady speed walks right into a launching kick and I I'm back in the corridor. When I look up her fist is hammering down on me. I slide out from under the hit. Diane drags me across the floor as tile craters beside my head. Super Skinny Lady springs up like she drank all the punch at the raver and she swings at me wild and fast.

Ok.

She folds over when Diane knees her in the groin. Damn. Beer Gut Grandpa charges at us. Diane steps aside and trips him. He rockets past me onto the floor and get up.

You have to get up.

Get out of this corridor. How? The mall walkers pin us between them and Roger ambling back for the shotgun. Beer Gut Grandpa gets back on his feet and barrels at me for round two.

"Don't let them touch you," Diane says as the hairdresser goes after her with a pair of giant shears.

Sure. Don't let them touch you. There's just zero room to move in here and Beer Gut Grandpa watches way too much wrestling I'm guessing. Training. Remember your training. I deflect his momentum past me best I can and he takes out Super Skinny Lady.

Diane duels The Hairdresser with the knife. The Hairdresser chop-chops at Diane's long hair but Diane holds her own. Beer Gut Grandpa barrels into another attack run and knocks Diane off her feet. The Hairdresser grabs at her tarp, trying to pull it away, and the armguard Diane wears comes off instead. All that baseball stuff. Catcher's gear. That's what it's for.

This.

TV screen zombies. Super Skinny Lady comes at me again. Nowhere to move. Don't touch her. Don't box her. Defend. Deflect. I block her hands with my arms and then I sweep my leg behind hers.

Her head bounces off the tile.

Ch-chk. "Nice form, Sam."

He closes on me. Gun pointed at my chest. If he pulls the trigger, they'll have to ID me from DNA. Roger won't hurt me. He loves his guns, but he helped me before and he'll help me now.

I reach for him. "Roger…"

Maybe I can help him. Or maybe Diane can sew him back together. His hand pixels. Light crackles from it. Cracks form in the steps under his feet, snaking into the tile and the brick, deforming it like the tables in the food court, like Roger, like the mall walkers.

Diane pulls me back. "Don't touch him!"

I stumble back on my heels. "But – "

"Don't touch him!"

I whirl around to the backroom's entrance and Super Skinny Lady fast-walks at us with the scissors in her chest. Looks like I missed an update. Her hands chop-chop through the air. Cracked hands lunge at me. Beer Gut Grandpa lowers his head for another attack run. The Hairdresser rips the scissors from Super Skinny Lady and impales Diane's tarp to the wall.

"Diane," I say, with the shadows closing in on us.

Diane rips free. The Hairdresser chases her down the backrooms. I try to follow but the others back me into the security office. I can't get stuck in here. Only one way out. They're on me. Tapes fall. I block and kick and something hits me. Something hard. Metal.

Behind me.

I can't see behind me. They're surrounding me. They're tearing at me. I'm cracking. Go numb. Wait for it to be over. Maybe you'll wake back up in the hospital. Maybe someone will pull you free.

DIANE

Her death never becomes a reality.

Imagine her where you left her, wanting. Alive. Hopeful. Imagine you are back at the mall, both of you, and though you cannot afford anything there but your shame, you are rich. You share in all this neon splendor, same as anyone visiting a great museum, gazing upon the priceless, the profound, the human, and you leave only with the joy in sharing your mutual treasure.

Go back to the mall.

Go back, over and over, as you did before. Each return a chance to discover something new. Every door a portal to a new world. Start from the same place, every time. The movie theater. Posters for movies promised in 1984 still in the lobby. Some from that last summer. Stare at them for a long time, remembering, and for the ones you never saw, imagining.

Will she have the power... to survive?

Empty popcorn buckets tower behind the concession stand. Take one into the main theater. Sit there in front of the vandalized screen. Pretend. Watch a movie in your head. Speak the lines. Hum the music. When the movie ends, sit there like you did once or twice really young, and in about fifteen minutes, the movie starts again. Every fifteen minutes or so after that, a yellow circle blinks in the upper right-hand corner of the screen. A phantom eclipse. It blinks once and then point at the screen as it does again.

It's a game.

After the cholera, the famine, the endless winter, there is no one to fear but yourself. Still. Check every store. The food court. The bookstore with all its choices. Public restrooms. Empty the basement of its last supply. There's little left to sustain you there.

Isn't there?

Save the toy store for later. The department store provided the catalog, but if you're being honest, the toy store was the best part of the mall, the cherry on top, the sweet that held on your tongue as you left for home empty-handed. Enter the department store. Play store with the board games, baby clothes, and other useless things. Play days away in the cold and dark, thinking this is still enough to sustain you but get bored.

Want for something else.

Keep returning to a mannequin on a pedestal in the center aisle. 80s color on her cheeks. Certainty in her eyes. Softness in her lips, despite her rigor. You like those things in girls. Hardness and softness at the same time. Hold the mannequin's hand.

On your way to the toy store, look down the long corridor to the mall security office. Police died with everyone else. The myth of safety. Save yourself, but imagine someone. A guard. A protector. A hero. Think of them coming to your rescue. Think of them like you do Page 48, the mannequin, the ghosts burnt into dead TV screens, their lips locked in magnesium shadows for all time.

Think about rescuing them.

Rewind to yesteryear! Start over in the basement.

Want to fast foward your life? Turn the page.

SAM

Floor is spinning.

I'm on the floor. Streaking blood. Someone pulls me by my leg into the backrooms headed east. Diane. She came back. Oh, wow. Wait. We need to go west. Back to the department store.

"Hey," I say.

She drops my leg. "Run!"

"*Hey!*"

Mall walkers frenzy after us like coked up zombies. No going back now. Fast as Super Skinny Lady is, she's got nothing on Diane. Diane runs down the hallway behind all the stores in the east wing. Tarp flapping like mad. I thought she tore it back there against The Hairdresser. Could have sworn she tore it.

I can't breathe.

I slump against the wall. Heart pounding. Here they come. Diane flaps back to me. She drags me with her, but I'm dead weight. Here they come. Go. Get out of here. Diane pulls the keys off my belt and unlocks a door deep in the east wing. She locks it soft behind us and then tugs me into the dark with her. Something big and plastic wobbles when I bump into it. Dominos teeter all around me.

Nutcrackers.

This is the old furniture store. Management stored all the big mall Christmas decorations in here since it's closest to where we set up Santa's chair. Six-foot-tall nutcrackers form ranks on either side of the store. Two and three rows deep. Plastic jewels in gold crowns glint in faded neon from out in the mall. Half-moon eyes stare into each other. Diane leads us deep behind their line.

Blood runs down my arms. "Jeez..."

Diane pulls out her catalog. "Did he touch you?"

"What are you..."

She flips through the pages. "He didn't touch you, did he?"

"No... why? What happened to him?"

"The Denomenon."

The Denomenon can only use broken things. "What does that mean, Diane? Roger is a zombie?"

"What's a zombie?"

"Can we help Roger? Can he come back?"

"You can't start over once you're broken."

I squeeze my hands. Glass digs deeper into my palms. I pick out little fragments stuck to me like wet sand and Diane stares at me blank as all the red and black nutcrackers standing at attention.

"Diane," I say. "He can do this everybody?"

She blinks. "Everything."

"There's nothing we can do? There has to be something we can – what are you looking for in the catalog?"

"What?"

"Is there something in there we can use?"

A page sticks to her in blood. "I was..."

Compensating. Avoiding. Didn't even think about it. Diane never thinks about it. Here comes an obstacle she couldn't negotiate and she did what she's done since she was nine years old.

She turned the page.

I take her hand. "Diane... we have to leave. We have to warn people. Get help. All the help."

"The Denomenon will do the same to them. Everything he touches... everything they touch... I have to go back."

"Back to where, 1983?"

"1994. I think."

"Diane, you can't go back."

She squeezes my hand. "I went back for you."

She didn't have to. "You want to stay. Right?"

"Sometimes, you have to go back to go forward."

"What?"

Trainers squeak as Super Skinny Lady blazes down the backrooms. The mall walkers pound on every door. Jerk every handle. Commotion. Dogs finding a possum. They hammer on a door down the hall. Maybe the one Diane touched my hand to? Guessing from the way she's looking at me, it was. Take the bait.

C'mon.

Keys jangle. Crap. Roger still has his keys. The pounding becomes more pitched and then the door springs open down there. Doesn't take the mall walkers long to figure out we're not in that store, because they're back out in the hall quick. Light buzzes like the old neon in the gap between the door and the frame.

Roger.

Diane pries loose from me. Wait. Don't go. Ok. I'm just cutting off the circulation in her fingers. Get it together, Sam. She's breathing hard. Really hard. I almost shush her, but this isn't fear. Fear only operates on low-end frequencies with her. This is something else. Hoarse. Ragged. Pained.

I take her hand again.

She clutches her chest. Diane braces against the nutcracker. This is like an asthma attack or something. What has she been breathing for ten years? Soot? Mold? God knows what chemicals are in the air. Asbestos from two skyscrapers scarred the lungs of all those police and firemen on 9/11. In her world, every building in every city went up in the stratosphere. We need an inhaler.

One thing I don't have in my kit.

A snort rumbles down the backrooms. "Still hiding, Sam?"

My shock must have run out with all this blood. Now I'm just pissed. Really pissed. Diane shakes her head. *Don't say anything.* Takes everything I have to fight everything I am.

Smart.

I don't feel so smart now. My hands shake. My legs. The nutcracker I lean against wobbles with me. The door handle jiggles. Please. Keep going. Don't come in here. If he does, I don't know what we'll do. Well. Diane is going to cut him. No questions.

"I can hear you," Roger says.

Please.

"She makes a lot of noise for someone who can't afford to. She must be pretty alone, Sam... or have really good protection."

Diane squeezes my hand.

I mouth our next move. *Get ready to run.*

Roger taps the shotgun barrel on the door. "Are you decent?"

Little Dog. I don't even think. I just react. "I thought you were."

He kicks the door. "They're in here. Go around the other side."

Shoes screech down the hall. Great. Now the mall walkers are going to be coming through the furniture store's security gate. We're pinned in here, just like we were back at the security entrance. They're wounded. Lurchy. We might have a couple minutes. Well. It's Super Skinny Lady we're dealing with here.

Let's say we've got a minute.

"Help me move the drums," I say.

Diane blinks. "The what?"

I hurry down the line out from behind the nutcrackers to their drums stacked in the corner. Each one is like garbage can-sized. They set them out in the mall during the holidays and some you could put donations in or coins or something. Changed every year. I start pushing them in front of the security gate and Diane does, too. Pretty quick we've got a wall three drums high at the gate.

Roger snorts. "I can hear you..."

I point to the backrooms' door. Diane muscles a drum in front of it and I go down the line plucking drumsticks from the nutcracker's hands. Nothing major, but it's wood, and like a nightstick. I stuff a couple in my belt and help Diane move more drums.

"Too bad those aren't real soldiers in there," Roger says.

I stack another drum in front of the backrooms' door. "Too bad there aren't any out there, either."

Ch-chk. "I am combat-ready."

"You're empty."

"And you're smart."

I shove another drum behind the others. It will take some real muscle to move these. Light bristles in the crack in the door. How can I tell if this is really Roger or some warped version of him? What does it matter if he's cracked now? We're all cracked.

God knows I am.

Roger rams into the door. I brace against the drums. Roger shoves his foot in the crack, but he stops trying to push his way in.

Light smears off him. "All he wants is the book."

Roger has to be careful. Down in the food court, Diane made like she was going to tear a page out and The Denomenon pumped the brakes. They want this thing clean as they can get it.

I clutch a drumstick. "Diane, tear a page out."

Diane stares at me blank as all the nutcrackers bunched around us. She's terrified. The way she holds the catalog, she seems as afraid of me getting a hold of it as anyone else.

"Diane," I say.

A shadow falls over us. Perfect. I've spent too much time yapping and now the mall walkers have got in on us. Those aren't worn-out sneakers, though. Wood. Painted wood. A nutcracker splinters his leg from his base. Light cracked through his uniform. His blank expression. His dead eyes, blinking like a bad TV.

"Um... Diane..."

Nutcrackers Frankenstein-stomp off their wooden pedestals. They lumber at us, crowding us toward the backrooms and we just barricaded ourselves in here with living murder nutcrackers.

Oh, man.

Drumsticks missile at us. Crooked arms bash us not like hard but really inconsiderate and Diane sweeps her knife through a nutcracker's legs. It halves to the floor. Another stumbles over it, falling on me and it has to weigh fifty pounds. Get off.

Get off me.

I try to push the nutcracker off and something pinches my collar. Something is gnawing at me. Little white teeth gnash on my neck and oh my God this nutcracker is trying to crack me.

"Diane!"

Her boot shatters the nutcracker's mouth. She pulls it still twitching off me. The entire store creeps toward me. These nutcrackers don't have much reach but they do pack a punch. I block their attacks with my drumsticks and kick them back.

I stab a drumstick into one. He chomps it in half. So much for that. We're being swarmed by living dead nutcrackers and Diane leaves her knife impaled in one. It pushes her away.

What do I got?

C'mon. No taser. No bullets. Baton is wasted. Drumsticks are breadsticks to these guys. Pepper spray. I still got the pepper spray. I charge at the nutcrackers ganging up on Diane.

I spray the can in their faces. "Take that!"

Blank mustached faces stare back at me. Should have thought that one through. I take a swing, but I'm trying to not touch these things, either. I end up doing a whole lot of nothing.

Nutcrackers surround us. They push drums away from the back-rooms door. They topple the wall we built before the security gate and then one of them finds the access panel on the wall for the overhead manual pull chain. The security gate ratchets up.

Traitor.

Mall walkers shimmy outside. No way out. I bump into Diane. Our hands find each other. Nutcrackers reach for us, wormy light slithering from their closed sculpted fists toward us.

"I'm sorry," Diane says.

"Wait a second." I pop open my med kit. Dig out my spare lighter. "Totally forgot about this."

"Do you smoke?"

I shake the pepper spray. "Someone always needs a light."

I flick the lighter and spray the nutcrackers again. Tough to scream when you don't have a mouth that works. Wood goes up in flames. Plastic melts. Nutcrackers blaze like burning trees in a windstorm, keeping the mall walkers out in the concourse and opening an escape path for us out through the store room. No thinking. No debate. I pull Diane with me through the inferno.

Roger blocks the backrooms door. "We want the same things."

All my disgust sinks into my shoulder and I lead into him with it. We crash through the door into the corridor connecting the backrooms. Smoke alarms screaming. The shotgun spins across the floor. Random bits of gear. Roger cracks a smile.

"I knew you had it in you," he says.

I never wanted what other people wanted. That's why I've got ribs that won't heal right. Same is true for Roger. I know it. He wanted what he wanted, and then someone beat it out of him. Now he tries to beat it out of other people by teaching them how to be good little soldiers who fit perfect back in their cases when they're done.

Forget that.

Tarp scratches past me. My hand hooks with Diane's. Wait. I dive for the shotgun. I smash it against the wall. Anger erupts behind me. Eerie, uncanny screams. Wood blisters and pops. Flames spit into the corridor. Roger staggers for main maintenance.

That's right.

Sprinklers aren't active everywhere in the mall. Just the common areas people still frequent. If he doesn't reach them on in a hurry, this place will go up in flames. Maybe the catalog will, too. At the very least, the cops will show up, and that will be one hell of a report. He's going to have to double time to main maintenance.

He's going to have to forget us for now.

DIANE

You've been here before.

The toy store the end of your journey, always. Looters hit the mall hard after like they did everywhere else, but only took what they could use. Toys from 1983 remain exactly where they were on the shelves five years later. G.I. Joe figures. Atari 5200 consoles. Barbies galore. An empty island out front holds only a sign:

Cabbage-Patch Kids SOLD OUT.

Walk past them all.

Harvest every animatronic doll you can for batteries. Talking teddy bears. Electronic games. Remote-control cars. Take the batteries out of all the Glo Worm dolls. Pile them on the floor beside you in the narrow aisle. Sit among the culled toys, dead but alive with the press of a button. Cling to a Glo Worm, your purpose in coming here fulfilled, but not the emptiness within you.

(8) Glimmer with happiness... shine with joy!

SAM

Flames light up the lock on the false door into the old department store enough for me not to waste time feeling it out. I close the door soft and then stand guard inside with my empty pepper spray and lighter. One Mississippi. Two. No one followed us.

Stiff tarp crinkles against me when I run into Diane. "Go."

Diane frets beside me. "We have to…"

"Go!"

We're quiet as mice to the employee restroom. I wish there was a lock. Feels like there should be with a shower in there. Nothing really to barricade the door with, not that it's been a solid strategy for us so far. We should get out of here. Or maybe I can dismantle the stalls. I've got a screwdriver on my Swiss Army Knife. A little work and I can reassemble the walls into… something. The Denomenon can make use of broken things. Why shouldn't I be able to?

Diane weeps at the sink.

"Hey…" I touch her arm. "Hey, it's ok. It will be ok."

"I got pepper spray in my eyes," she says.

"Oh. Sorry."

"It's ok."

"We'll wash it out," I say, and run the faucet.

She holds her hands under the water. Just lets them fill. Grime runs off her hands. Blood. Shoot. I'm covered in blood. Glass. Roger is dead. He isn't dead. He's something else now. What is he? What's happening? How do you know if you're losing your mind? Is it when you feel like there's no way out? I don't know the way out.

Tears and water run down Diane's cheek. "Sam."

I'm still here. "Huh?"

"You have tweezers in your kit? Mine are old. Rusty."

"Yeah... why?"

She guides my hands under the faucet. "You were brave."

"I don't feel brave."

"You can't be brave in my world. Brave gets you killed."

"You are."

"I go back on myself. I'm afraid. I'm a coward."

"Hey, whatever your Dad said... and I'm not trying to psycho-analyze you, but it's kind of what we do in my world... you know what, forget it. I have no idea what I'm talking about half the time."

She inspects my hands. "The tweezers."

I let her dig around in the med kit for them. Ow. She picks little glass out of my palm and drops it in the sink. Expert. Efficient.

"You've done this before," I say.

She blinks. "Yes. Your shoulder."

My shoulder starts throbbing. "I almost forgot..."

"You'll be ok. These are minor wounds."

"You're kind of like Buffy."

"Buffy?"

"She was a vampire slayer. Cheerleader. So she was a little girly but totally badass at the same time. She liked to shop."

"There are vampires here?"

"It was a TV show. I can find it online."

"Online?"

I take Roger's phone out of my back pocket. I tap the app streaming the camera feed from the main concourse. Mall walkers circuit through the upper and lower levels, searching for us. Smoke. Flashing lights. Sprinklers. The Denomenon on his throne.

Waiting in the rain.

What are we going to do? We can't hide in here watching old

reruns forever. Maybe the fire department shows up. Police. Or maybe they get cracked, too. *He can only make use of broken things.* Too bad there's nothing in the mall that works. We could try to get to the car. Not that driving down the highway chased by a dragon-snake thing spitting toxic venom motivates me. The Denomenon chops through traffic. Broken cars and trucks fuse together.

The world ends, a little bit at a time.

"We can't stay here," I say. "We can't leave. He'll go looking for us everywhere. But we can stop The Denomenon. Right? You were going to tear a page out of the book. Let's just tear out the page."

She finds me in the mirror. "You don't understand."

"I get that. I don't know the deal with the catalog, but I know we have to do something. We have to do something soon."

She plucks glass from my hand. "I need to go back."

Blood runs down my wrist. "Diane..."

"He'll follow me."

"But..."

"It will be like... none of this ever happened."

"Let's think for a second."

"It's the only way."

"I mean... the catalog is important to you, but... your life is more important. Your health is. You know. The world."

"I don't know what the world is. It was the mall, and then people said everything beyond it was gone. I never knew anything else."

"You can. You want to."

"After wasn't that different than before. We didn't have food. Electricity, sometimes. She wouldn't have anyone over. Dad would come over. He'd bring something, and she'd be mad at him. They always wanted something and then when they got it..."

"They wanted something else."

"I was always trying to be somewhere else. Another world. The catalog was like this... portal. It took me away. It's all I have."

"It's not all you have, Diane."

Glass clinks in the sink. "If I stay, you'll end up like Roger."

"I can take a beating."

"You make fun."

"I... I have to do something. We all deal with stuff how we deal with it. I know you want to go back. And I know it's because you're worried about me, which means everything. No one worries about me, Diane. I got beat up and tossed out on the street. You feel like trash. Worthless. Like you shouldn't even exist."

"You do... you're real."

"I feel real. You make me... it's been a long time since I felt part of anything, you know? Since I mattered to someone."

"You matter."

I catch myself before I say something clever. Before I kiss her. I shouldn't just kiss her. I don't know if anyone ever has. I do know no one has taken care of her in a long time.

I can do something about that.

"Diane... I'll go back with you."

She blinks. "What?"

Every instinct tells me to stay here. Wait it out. Figure it out, somehow. But Roger didn't train me to run the other way from my problems, even if that's what both of us have been doing here all this time. If the only way I can do my job is to see Diane back through to the apocalypse, then I guess that's what I've got to do.

"I'm going with you," I say.

She shakes her head. "You can't."

"I don't have anything here. I don't have anyone."

"Sam..."

"If you think that the only way to protect my world is to go back to yours, then I'm going with you. I won't let you go alone."

"I can take care of myself."

"I know... but neither of us have to be alone."

She wants to smile. Hug me. Something. She fidgets for a second and then takes my hands. "I'll bandage you up first."

"Good idea. Maybe we should stock up on supplies. Probably won't see, you know, modern medicine again."

She wraps my hands. "You're strong."

"I don't know... I'm getting pretty dinged up, Doc."

She massages the tape into the bandage. "You are."

"You going to kiss these ones, too?"

Diane kisses my hands. "Better."

Our fingers are all tangled up. "I have other owies."

She gets this. "Where?"

I touch my cheek. "Here."

Her lips are so dry. "Where else?"

"Hold up. Let me return the favor on the nursing real quick." I find the chapstick in my med kit. "Pucker." I paint her lips with the balm. Make sure I get in the corners real good. "There you go."

She worms her lips together. "I just got used to them hurting..."

"Here," I say, and touch my lips. "Mine hurt, too."

Diane kisses me like I kissed my first girl. Somewhere between a shy little peck and taking a bite out of a hamburger after the bar closes at 2 AM. I laugh and she blinks, embarrassed maybe.

"Is this ok, Diane? Am I ok to..."

"I don't know what's ok," she says.

"It's whatever you say. You choose."

She kisses me again. Softer. "Is that ok?"

I keep her close. "I didn't know you could blush."

She touches her face. Eyes still watering. Dirt on her cheek.

"Diane, why don't you take a shower?"

"Shower?"

I lean in the shower stall and run the water. "I'm seriously not trying to be that guy, but if you're going back... there isn't indoor plumbing in your world I take it? So get the rest of the pepper spray out of your eyes and your hair, and... you know..." I snag a random leaf from her hair. "The other stuff, too."

She gazes into the stall. "I don't know."

"I'll keep watch. I mean, I'll stand guard." I bring up the live feed on Roger's phone again. Focus on the screen. "There's some body wash in there. It's dollar store, but whatever. Does the job."

She holds her hand under the water. "You'll watch?"

I turn my back to the stall. "Take your time."

Water plops on the tile. This little gasp echoes around it. A little cry. I focus on the phone. Please, God. Don't let them find us now. We should leave. I know. We should run, but I can't let her go back alone. Not after what happened to Roger. Can't even think about it. If I do, I go right back to the bar that night and how wrong is that? Someone dies and you think of the worst thing that happened to you? Roger helped me. He saved me that night.

Roger is dead.

Rhythm of the water changes. She's not under the shower head. Maybe she's done? Or she's overwhelmed like she was with the faucet. I'm overwhelmed. I'm really struggling with all this and her hand falls on my shoulder. She draws me around. The apocalypse running off her. I walk into her arms, the water, this warmth, comfort, and relief. I'm hurt. I'm reeling. But I'm not alone.

We're not alone.

Rattle wakes me up.

Sounds like a cat chasing a toy around the employee restroom. I reach for my taser. Best part of it is out in the mall somewhere. How did I fall asleep with all this anxiety waiting for me when I woke up? Fear isn't all that's waiting for me. That rattle.

Diane.

I touch her chest. Hollow drum. I pull her close. Even after a shower with dollar store men's body wash, she smells like soot, like winter rain, like clean clothes that sat too long. She's heavy with sleep she's been carrying but unable to use. I don't mind.

I like how heavy she is in my arms.

She shifts and then she's wide awake. Reaching for her knife. The knife is gone. So is the world she always wakes up in. Tension unwinds in her. This look on her face. Not waking up afraid, ready, always on, that's as inexplicable to her as all this is to me. Warm, happy, and loved? Doesn't even compute.

I brush the hair out of her eyes. "Tell me about it."

She touches my lips. "Tell you about what?"

I kiss her fingers. "I was just thinking."

Her fingers stay on my lips, like they're the vent on the dashboard when you're trying to warm up the car. "How long were we..."

I tap Roger's phone. Might have been the best hour and a half I've ever had. "Let's see what's what."

Mall walkers still patrol the mall in the live feed. The Denomenon still sits on his throne, waiting for them to produce. Not sure where Roger is. I tap the feed away. The mall is technically open. Anyone can come in, though we never get traffic midweek that isn't the walkers. No reason to come here. Maybe Gary gets suspicious and comes if he's been trying to get ahold of me and Roger.

We can't let him walk into this.

"We should go," I say.

Diane knots up a little. This is nice right here. Hiding in a bathroom for your life isn't nice, but it probably beats whatever I'm about to step into. No choice. It's ok. We've got each other.

I get up. Pins and needles. "I figure we can try to get downstairs and scrounge up some supplies before we go. That's risky, though. Our shortest route is going upstairs and cutting over to the toy store."

Diane pulls her shirt on. "We'll be able to find things."

"You said all the batteries are gone and stuff."

"We'll be able to come back through."

I slide my vest on. "Hadn't thought about that... I was thinking you were stuck with me, but maybe not."

"Stuck with you?"

"You can ditch me, is all I'm saying."

"I go back for you."

"I know. You have. I just mean... whatever happens... I will protect you. I know that seems pretty whatever given the box score so far, but... even if this is just trauma-bonding, you've got me."

"What's trauma-bonding?"

"It's ok. We will be ok. I promise."

"No promises."

"Why not?"

"Just please."

I curl her finger in mine. "How about a pinky swear?"

"Aren't they the same?"

"One level down. I pinky swear – "

Something buzzes. What is that? Sounds like a phone. Roger's phone. I run back into the stall. Maybe the phones are working again. Could be Gary or one of the other guys. I pick up the phone and there's a text from an unknown number.

> Want to see something cool?

I swipe open the phone. Another text.

> Watch the camera.

What is this? I tap open the video feed. Now it's on the fritz. Image is all blurry. Wait. The image is moving. Someone is moving the camera. Someone is carrying the camera across the main concourse and Roger smiles broken into the phone.

"God," I say.

Diane blinks. "What's wrong?"

"He's got the camera... he's..."

Roger sets the camera on something. Table in the food court, maybe. The Denomenon lounges on his throne of broken things, like he's already won. Falken at his feet. Roger vanishes off-screen and then he comes back. There's something in his hand.

He's holding the Christmas catalog.

DON'T MISS OUT ON ANY OF THE ENDLESS POSSIBILITIES!

Be **bold** in your choices! Find what you seek by going to the **page number**!

A

AM/FM Portables....451
Answering Phones....28
Atari Cartridges....520

B

Baby Dolls....522, 523, 524
Basement....62
Blazers, Women....48, 49

C

Cameras....318, 319
Colecovision....522
Christmas Decorations....6

D

Desks....390
Dinnerware....118
DOSSIERS....180

E

Earrings....88,89
Electronic Toys....440
Emergency Supplies....83

F

First Aid Kits....85
Flashlights....431
Footwear, Women....28,29

G

Game Books....420,588
Garden Tools....217
Guns and Accessories....451

CHANGE THE GAME

H

Hardware....11,12

I

Ice Cream Makers....254

J

Jackets....183
Jeans, Women....48
Jewelry....88,89,500

K

Knives....299

L

Lanterns....429
Lingerie....80,81
Lunch Boxes....159

M

Metal Detectors....423

N

Nightgowns....76

O

Overalls....90

P

Pac Man....440
Pajamas....166

Q

Q*bert....519

R

Records....550,551
Road Kits....6

S

SAM...3,196,233,237,248
Sleeping Bags...277
Snow Boots, Girls....34

T

Tape Recorders....545
Tents...279
Toys....450   NO MORE TOYS

U

Uniforms, Baseball...333

V

Video Games....510-520

W

Walkie Talkies.. 466
Woodburning Sets....81

Y

YOU Yummy Gifts....1,60

Try home delivery!

NO HASSLE RETURNS!

Unsatisfied with your choice? Lost? Simply return it to the catalog department in ~~the BASEMENT~~ to start your journey over again!

SAM

"Oh," I say. "Oh, man."

Diane forfeits her staring contest with the mirror. "What?"

"Diane."

She takes the phone from me. "What's the matter – "

Her tarp wrinkles in the air. Supplies spill across the grimy tile. Diane goes through every stall, searching for the book.

"Diane," I say.

She cradles the leather bag she kept it in. "Where is it?"

"You must have dropped it when we fought the nutcrackers."

"No."

"Ok. It's ok."

"I couldn't have..."

"You were just distracted."

"How could I forget it?"

"I've been distracting you. It's my fault."

Doesn't compute for her. Losing the catalog. Forgetting it's the most important thing in the world, even for an hour or two. All the sweet we've shared hardens. Crusts. The little smile trying to dawn on her face all night cracks into tears.

I reach for her. "I'm sorry..."

She pushes me away. Something hits me. Metal. Behind me. I can't see behind me. They're surrounding me. My arms go up over my face. Brace for impact. Don't cry. Don't make a sound.

Just suffer it.

Her hands grab mine. "Sam."

Survive.

"Sam," she says, pulling my arms down. "I'm sorry."

Nothing about tonight computes. "It's ok..."

She falls into my arms. "I'm sorry..."

Sorry sounds so unfamiliar on her tongue. She never says it. You can't be sorry where she comes from. No questions. No mercy. No thinking about the past or the future. Just now. Survival. Forget about living. Happiness. It's hard enough to just exist.

Diane isn't a robot. An empty container full of forgotten Christmas decorations you put up every year because that's what you do. She's still human even if she's forgotten that, too.

We're still human.

I hold her close. "It will be ok."

Her voice rattles. "We have to get the book back."

"How... we can't. He's too strong."

"We have to. If we don't... he'll use it."

The Denomenon makes use of broken things. If he can turn Roger into a zombie, if he can bring mall Christmas nutcrackers to life with this glowy stuff, there's no telling what he can do with the book to act as some kind of talisman. Every drop of blood, smudge of soot, and teardrop from Diane's world is wrapped up in this catalog.

He'll unlock unlimited power.

Her tarp crinkles in her hands. "We need a plan."

Man. "We don't have any weapons... if we go up against him... Roger was the only person here who even came close to standing a chance and now he's standing right next to The Denomenon."

"We have to get the book back."

Think. Sam, think. You've made it this far against knights on glowing dragons and reanimated soldiers. A little pepper spray and a cigarette lighter got you through the night.

"Main maintenance," I say.

Diane blinks. "What about it?"

"We can get there. I can turn on the sprinklers."

"Sprinklers?"

"We can make it rain in here. That will ruin the book, right?"

"Sam."

"The Denomenon figures you'll be coming for the book. He won't expect us to try and destroy it."

"We're not destroying the book."

My turn to blink. "What choice do we have?"

"You don't understand."

"I understand we can't get it back from him. I understand he can use it, somehow, to do bad things. I don't understand why you're so determined to hold onto it. Ok, it's all you have left. I get that. But there's more. You know? You have something real now."

"Nothing is real without the book."

"Diane..."

"We're getting it back."

"If you're not going to explain, then ok, no judgments. Doesn't change the fact that our only shot now is to rain on his parade."

"No..."

"This will work. We can turn on the sprinklers and get out through the security entrance. Or come back here."

"Come back?"

"The mains aren't connected to the department store. We can hide in here. The Denomenon will be pissed, but he won't be able to find us. Or we can go back to the security room upstairs."

She shakes her head. "You're still hiding."

"What do you mean..."

She pulls her tarp on. "I didn't realize I'd lost the book because I got lost in here with you. I shouldn't have..."

"We're not doing anything wrong, Diane."

"I wanted someone like me. Someone who would know this... hurt... and could help me, but I'm stuck in here with you."

"I'm not stuck. I just don't belong anywhere else."

Her wince comes back with a vengeance. I don't think this is a toothache. This pain isn't anything you can pop a pill for.

"In my mall..." Her eyes dart around the restroom. "A leak started here in the department store. The roof collapsed. Mold... everywhere. Puddles... pools... the mall is this swamp in the summer. Frozen cave in the winter. The wolves don't know it from the forest. I know I should leave, but... we can't leave without the catalog."

I throw up my hands. "Why?"

Her face shifts. Soft Diane, lovely Diane, she reverts back to the sharp, wary stranger I first met. "You'll say I'm crazy."

"No... no, I won't. You know I won't."

"Sometimes... I think I am. I think I cracked."

I take her hand. "You're not cracked. If you are, then I am because this is all... we're in this together. Ok?"

She grips my hand. "If I had the catalog, I could show you."

"Well... I'm guessing it's online somewhere."

"Online?"

"Everything's online now."

I open the browser on Roger's phone. Search: Christmas catalogs 1983. There we go. Someone scanned every single page and uploaded it to their feed. Disbelief wipes away all the tension on Diane's face. She hasn't seen pages this clean in years. Pages move with magic and speed she can only imagine. Her fingers dab the screen, touching the past as it flits by, stopping me as I scroll through her entire world in a few seconds.

"So," I say. "What am I looking for?"

She takes the phone. "Page 588."

I swipe through the pages until she figures it out. Diane gets to the end of the catalog and are these board games? Role-playing games. D&D stuff. Wouldn't have figured her for it, but neither of us are exactly adhering to our expected roles. Well. She did mention *Dungeons and Dragons* earlier. I always liked them, even if they weren't for me. I liked those books where you could choose. I liked the idea of creating a story. Not just your own.

With someone.

Her finger lands on the little unpainted figurines that come with the games or I guess you can buy them for the games. You choose. The image expands, surprising her and me both. Wait a second. Little gray guy right here with the big sword.

"He kind of looks like The Denomenon," I say.

Diane cradles the phone like she did the catalog. She picks at the screen like she could peel it away. The page within.

"Diane... what happens if you tear this page out of the book?"

"He'll be destroyed," she says.

"Why? How?"

"Because... I created him."

DIANE

Play store.

Play all the games. Invent new ones. Set the board. Replace the pieces with forgotten toys. Glo Worm. Action Man. Unpainted figurines from the game that is a game, but a book at the same time. Rename your characters. Cast your die. Imagine. Choose. Fail.

Go back.

Go back to the beginning, over and over. So many times your fingerprints smudge reality's pages. Change the outcome, but never the beginning. You can never alter how the story starts.

Keep trying.

Succeed only in realizing toys from the book. A knight. His dragon steed. Struggle to understand it, but struggle to understand anything in the world after. Understanding is non-essential. All that matters is survival. Survive. Keep going. You can only keep going.

Ready to keep going? Turn to page 141.
Need a do-over? Find your way to the index. Create a new
story from the one left for you. Choose ***boldly***.

Rock Into The New Year
Walk away with the
hottest hits this holiday!
$40
Only
$99.99

THE LOST CHILDREN

200,000 children are missing.

Watch them vanish right off the street in front of you. Off security camera footage. Right out of the secure bunker you and your agents place them in beneath headquarters as controls in a tactless experiment that fails immediately. Nothing left. No visual marker. No residue. No trace of where they went.

Stop noticing.

1,470,000 children are missing.

No leads. No prospects. No promise of any breakthrough in understanding. Crime rates spike. Suicides. Kidnappings. This lull takes over in the country, a tide of grief and helplessness that casts everyone adrift in the same glib sea.

America hollows.

"I want to have a baby," La Garza says, in the car on the way to investigate another hopeless lead. La Garza just blurts out things. No filter. The day she was transferred to your unit, she sat at your desk and said without any prompt, *I'm a recovering addict.* That's how it started. Every conversation a jab. An elbow. Hold that against her for the rest of your relationship, but admire her bluntness.

Never resolve the two.

Pull up outside an old brownstone in Williamsburg. This case, this daily disaster grinds you down, but not so much that you're not scrutinizing every little thing. An anonymous email came in yesterday with an address in Brooklyn and a message:

DON'T FOLLOW THE RULES.

This address is linked to an agent who left the bureau back in 1983. Molitor. Former Navy. Vietnam vet. Consider the possibilities. Someone is pulling your chain. The tip line crashed with people calling in with their theories. Listen to every message, just in case. Watch every single YouTube video with a theory because, maybe. The best minds in the world have yet to solve this, so you have to try everything. Knock on the door, frustrated. No one answers. Check the mailbox. Weeks of bills and ads. A note.

THE ANSWERS YOU SEEK ARE IN THE ELSEWHERE DOSSIER.

Refresh with excitement. The Elsewhere Dossier has been the white whale in Unexplained Cases for decades. The answer to all the great mysteries of the 20th century: Flight 19. Roswell. D.B. Cooper. Asking for it will get you laughed right out of your job.

If you ask for the file, turn the page.
If you don't, if this is going nowhere, to page 62.
Go back to the basement.

THE LOST CHILDREN

The Director laughs so hard he cries.

His laughter becomes sobs. Sit silent and uncomfortable before his desk. Finally, he just stops, as if he's a recording.

"You just lost me a round of golf," he says. "I figured it would take you more than three months to come to me with this."

Look up from your notes. "You placed a bet on whether or not I'd find thousands of missing kids, Director?"

The Director doesn't like you. He really doesn't like you. Every time he sees you, his lips crease, like he's just bit into a sour piece of candy. Two or three times you've seen him mime a line down his chest when talking to someone else, surely referencing your tendency to wear ties at the office. Two or three times you've wondered why what you wear matters when you've been stuck down in the basement with everything else the bureau forgets.

"I thought we'd be somewhere by now," he says. "But I also knew you'd come in eventually with this horse pucky. One of you Unexplained Cases types always floats the dossier when something like this happens. Something like this..." He pitches forward. Roosts over the picture frames on his desk. "I have a daughter. Seventeen. How old is too old? What's the cutoff? Do we know?"

"This phenomenon isn't carding people, Director."

"Do you think you're funny, Agent?"

Holster this one. "No, sir."

"I don't think you're funny. I don't think any of this is funny. This is the apocalypse. Or some kind of cosmic joke."

"I keep asking for more resources."

He taps his fingers against his desk. "Who left this note?"

"No prints. No matches in the handwriting. The apartment belonged to a former agent named Molitor."

"Molitor..." Tap, tap, tap. "You're sure?"

"Yes. Why?"

"You don't know who he is?"

"Should I?"

"You couldn't have arrived at this yourself."

"Arrived at what, sir?"

Tap, tap, tap. "You should know... D.C. isn't going to throw any more money at finding an answer to this."

Usually, mysteries excite you. "What?"

"There are very powerful people with very deep pockets that believe this is the will of God. A sign. A warning. Some kind of test, or retribution. They're stonewalling funding."

You hear this sort of thing out in the field. You didn't expect it inside government. "This is a scientific issue, sir. It most likely has a scientific solution. We need to commit every last resource – "

"They think there is an answer."

"This isn't the will of God."

"Agent."

"We have to find out what's happening, immediately, or we are going to face extinction. I want to expand the PRISM program. I want real time surveillance on everyone, all day, every day."

"Our freedoms are more important than – "

"Children?"

He sits back. "It's above my pay grade."

"That's... horse pucky."

His lips aren't sucking in now. "This is how it is. At least until the next administration. If there's an election next year."

All this time you've been working the problem. Problems have solutions. You have no idea what the solution is, but you expect one. Look outside the office. Empty chairs. Haunted faces. Eyes caught looking at yours, daring hope, knowing there isn't any.

"But... we have to do something," you say.

Tap, tap, tap. "You are doing something."

"Is my investigation just for show?"

"Keep this to yourself. And keep your head on a swivel."

"I don't understand..."

"This isn't the basement. This isn't theory. This is the real world. This is cutthroat. There are people who don't want anything to happen. Powerful people. Do you understand me, agent?"

Understand. Understand yourself better.

"Director... what about your daughter?"

Tap, tap, tap.

Stand up. "I'll file a formal request for the dossier."

He types something into his keyboard, clicks around with his mouse for a second, and then stands. He picks his jacket up off the back of his chair and heads for the door.

"I have to drop in another meeting," he says. "I'll be back in five minutes. Help yourself to anything you like while you wait."

The door clicks shut behind him. Walk around his desk. Click on a folder named EYES. Countless other folders contained within. The titles tantalize you: **PRIME WATCH LIST v3 2.0. BREAK POINTE INCIDENT. PROJECT: ELSEWHERE.**

Double-click on the Elsewhere folder. One file inside. Word doc. Old. The mouse rattles in your hand as you click on it.

Do Not Read This Dossier All The Way Through.

THESE PAGES CONTAIN ELEMENTS THAT MUST BE CONSIDERED INDEPENDENTLY OR ELSE YOU RISK PERSONAL HARM.

Begin On The Index

Think for a second. What properties could an outdated Word file contain to cause harm? Does anyone who reads it disappear down a bureau sinkhole deeper than the basement you're already in? Where are the children? You're running out of time. There's no way you can get through the entire file in the time you have left.

If you read the dossier all the way through, turn the page.
If you follow the instructions for the dossier, go to the index.

THE LOST CHILDREN

Ignore the warnings.

Read through the entire dossier, beginning with the first page. The Director said five minutes. You don't have time to play games.

MRN: 040813
DATE: 4/19/83
SUBJECT: ELSEWHERE
CLASSIFICATION: EYES ONLY
SUMMARY: ABDICATION successful with dedicated PROMPTING. SUBJECT 8 (Child, Female) exhibits high capacity for dimensional phasing.

Wonder what in the Hell you are reading. Keep reading.

DATE: 4/22/83
SUBJECT: ELSEWHERE
CLASSIFICATION: EYES ONLY
SUMMARY: SUBJECT 8 ABDICATES at will by employing PROMPTS herself. Attempts to deploy SUBJECT in TARGET ZONE so far unsuccessful.

Do Not Continue Reading

Keep reading. On the next page, find a glossary of redacted terms. The only word not blacked out on the page is PROMPTS. Everything is blacked out on the next page, except:

Fear No Information

That's all. The same again on the following page:

OPEN THE DOOR

What door? What is this? The director's voice startles you. Outside the office. Hurry up. It's time. Read as much as you can. Skim over words. Phrases. ABEL. BASEMENT. ARCHER.

Go Back

The Director's voice falls away. The sounds of the emptying city outside. The hum of the computer, a decade too old. The screen flickers. Strain your eyes to see better.

Strain.

Sink through the chair out of the director's office into a bright, fluorescent room. White walls. Mirrors hover over you, like the mirrors they use in the dentist's office. See your reflection.

Freak out.

Scramble out of the chair. Hear voices, but you don't know from where. Reach for your sidearm. It's missing. The holster. Your clothes. The only thing on you is a number. 5. Written in black marker. Hear voices. Give half a thought to just getting out of wherever the hell you are, but you never get out of anything, so move forward. The voices compound into this rumble.

This roar.

"FBI," you say. "I'm here to – "

Run to the rectangular dark just beyond the chair. The darkness forces you out, back into a light paler than it was before. Crawl out of what you realize is a basement. Rusted green drums. Frayed boxes containing fallout shelter supplies. A doll sits on a drum.

A book.

Cardboard cover. Yellowed pages. A journal you buy at the bookstore thinking your life merits documentation, but you never do it. Flip through the pages. Handwritten. Ballpoint pen.

"You can figure this out," The Director says. "Right?"

Skim. Go back to the start. Hear her. *Oh, God.* Screaming. Pops, like the Fourth of July. You know better than to ever go back. Too much waits there for you. Get back to that first page you opened the book on. A prompt. A command, like in the dossier.

You need to follow the instructions.

You weren't made to follow instructions. Your entire life, you've followed your own path, but now your path has intersected someone else's. Someone else is here. Sense them. Feel them, warping this space the same as your hand does the recycled paper. They're inside the basement, your mind, your desire to run back the way you came, but you didn't get here on your own. They're inside your body, your soul, your character. You're a glove, a puppet, a prompt.

The pages catch fire.

You do, along with the cardboard boxes and aluminum drums. You burn like the world does without children, everything kindle to keep out the cold, to stave off the dark of the last nothing.

THE END

Travel In Style
Green blends in with trees
$19.99
Rough it in comfort!
Your choice!

SAM

By now, I should expect to hear the absolute most unexpected thing possible from her. "You made The Denomenon?"

Hesitation in her is so uncomfortable to watch. "Dad got me the same game for my birthday one year, but I changed the game. And then they weren't arguing anymore. It was like it used to be. So... I thought I could change the game again."

"You created The Denomenon? With your mind? With weird, scary mind powers? You're a weird, scary-mind person?"

"I made up a game with the toys they left behind... I made up friends... someone to protect me from... and they came to life. I didn't know how it happened. Or how to control it. I didn't want to. I didn't want to live out there anymore. So I lived in the game."

I rub my head. "But you said..."

"The Denomenon promised to protect me... always. But then I got older, and I didn't want the fantasy anymore. I wanted... something real." Her smile is so desperate. "Something... normal. So I tried to make a new game. He won't let me have it."

I tee up my hands. "Ok. Time out."

"We don't have time."

"You told me he was Super Dimension Border Patrol. You told me he was gatekeeping people from crossing worlds or whatever."

She blinks. "You said that."

"Huh?"

"You said that, Sam."

"And you let me think it?"

"What do you think of me now?"

Be honest. Don't. Do both, like always. "Why would you let me believe something that wasn't true?"

"I don't know. I guess because I do."

"But that's not cool, Diane."

"You think I'm crazy."

"No... I have... concerns. Which is fair. And it's fair to acknowledge that what you're saying is not qualitatively different from anything else you've said. But I know what's real. What's real is that thing killed my boss and resurrected him somehow and also brought nutcrackers to life. I suppose it doesn't matter where The Denomenon came from, so long as we get rid of him."

She doesn't blink.

"Why haven't you done it yet, Diane?"

She stares into the phone. Diane can't do it. The book is all she has left. Her only possibility. In her mind, it's still a key to going back and making a world where it never happened.

I find her hand again. "I understand."

Her hand shakes. "You do?"

"I haven't exactly been facing reality, either. I got hurt. Really bad. And I can't even go there. You know? In my head. I can't even think about it, or drive by that bar, or the... I've always done that. Any bad thing. All the bad things. I just bury them. Forget about them. Otherwise, they just run riot through my head. You just..."

"Go there."

"Yeah. I can't help it."

"I can't help it..."

"Guess you have a better computer than I do."

"The world suffered. I suffered. I think we were injured the same. Everyone got these bruises and sores from the radiation... it ruined skin and bone and tissue, but I think it ruined... reality, too. There was so much hurt. There was so much pain."

"It's ok."

"There was so much..."

"Diane, it's ok. Like I said. There's some serious reality going on in the mall tonight. You're not crazy. You're not alone. I feel kind of alone. I shouldn't be saying this, but I just say things. I feel a little bit alone right now. You know? Roger's gone. You're telling me some... advanced... stuff. And I've seen it. I feel really on my own, but I know I'm not. We're together. We're in this together and we just need a plan. We need a strategy. Ok. Think. You made him up."

"Yes."

"Can you unmake him?"

She winces. "Only if I destroy the page."

"His page, I'm guessing."

"If I lose a page... I lose everything on it."

"Ok... so he has the book now. Problem. Can you change the rules? How do we win? How do you play?"

"You make a character. Make decisions."

"Sure... like Pick Your Path or something? Like my book?"

"Like your book... the miniatures came with a book like that. Some things were decided for you, but some things you had to make up. I was never good at imagining things. I could only use..."

"Broken things."

So much shame on her face. "I took pages from the catalog... the mall directory... I wrote on the character sheets that came with the book. I made up a story. I made up a game."

"So... the mechanics are... you take a toy and then create a character? And you clearly armored this guy out big time. Makes sense given your circumstances. You need to create another character. Someone stronger. Faster. Smarter than us for sure."

She winces.

"We're smart," I say. "Ish."

"I can't control it, Sam."

"Ok... so we're concerned about creating another problem we

can't solve later. Fair. But can you make a nutcracker work for us, maybe? Can you use things like he's been using them?"

"It has to be in the catalog."

"Ok. That's limiting. Can you change The Denomenon? You invented him, so can you go back and make some revisions?"

"I can't change him. I've tried."

"People can change."

"All he understands is the game. I created a monster... now he has the book. If we don't get the catalog back..."

"How can he destroy the world if it's only what's in the catalog?"

"You've seen his power."

"And it's worse with the book, because the book is like this Necronomicon of Late Stage Capitalism? Ok. So... you made him to protect you. He thinks he's doing that, because you're using the book to change the game or create a new one, right?"

"Yes."

"Is that how you found my world? You were messing around with the book and you found these soft spots?"

"Yes."

"Maybe he just needs to understand."

"He's not going to understand."

"People aren't always who you see on the outside, you know? We think people are like this stuff we buy. Here's a thing. Here's what it does. It does until it's broken and then I have to get another one. I want a better one because there's always a better one. We just want, want, want, and we never stop and value what we've got."

"Value what we have?"

"Yeah... like, I have nothing. Nothing. If I had... I don't even want what I'm supposed to want, Diane. Honestly. I see people with things, and they're happy, and that makes me feel like trash because I'm not happy. So I lose myself in the mall, or my book, you know? Whatever keeps you from thinking about stuff for a minute."

God. She hugs me tight. Ok. It's going to be ok.

"What if we just... talk to him, Diane?"

She's shaking. "Talk to him?"

"Just explain. Like you explained to me."

"I've tried."

"Let me guess. He throws a tantrum? He does seem like kind of a brat, which now I think about it... he's probably got some stuff going on considering he's... basically a living toy..."

"What about your book?"

"My book?"

"You could write a different ending."

"I don't understand... my book isn't like your catalog."

"The mall is a soft spot. We could go back to the basement. You could write another chapter. We could do it together."

"It's not even finished."

"There's never an ending. The catalog promises a Christmas that is never going to come. I know that now. Your book has lots of endings. We can trap The Denomenon in them."

"How..."

"The lost children. He could be responsible for them. He could be responsible... there are many different things we could do."

"But... it's not real, Diane."

"Neither is he. I can only use what it's in the catalog. But your book has possibilities. We can write the world into it. You have."

"There's nothing of me in the story."

"Isn't there?"

I let go. "I don't know about this."

"I'm so tired, Sam. I'm tired of fighting. Hiding. Running. I know you are, too. You're right. We can't go back. We have to go forward. We have to change the story. We can do it. You and me."

"I don't know, Diane."

"I don't think I'm supposed to create a better character." She squeezes my hand. "I think I'm supposed to tell a better story."

"If we do this... and it just gets worse..."

"I know."

"We can still wait it out in here."

"Nothing changes with the dawn."

Hard to argue. Every day the same here. Wake up. Unlock the main mechanical room. Turn on the front lights. Canvas the mall. Make sure no one got in overnight. Go back to mechanical. Turn on the back lights. Canvas again. This time, unlock the main doors. The mall walkers will be waiting for you to do this at 7 AM, so don't be late. The mall walkers are always waiting.

I brush the hair from her eyes. "If anything goes wrong... run."

She nods.

"Don't go back to the toy store. Leave the mall. Find help."

"Ok."

"Promise."

She shakes her head. "No promises."

I hold out my pinky. "Swear."

Diane hooks her finger with me. "I swear."

"Well," I say, reaching for my journal. "This will be different – "

Funny bone. My shoulder goes numb. My arm. Light vines through my fingers. My hands are a cracked TV screen.

"What's happening..."

She's not afraid. Why isn't she afraid? She just stands there like she got to the gas station right when they ran out of coffee. "No..."

"What's happening to me, Diane?"

"The Denomenon..."

"But I didn't – " He cut me. I got cut. No. "Can we stop it?"

She just shakes her head.

Light leaps between my fingers. "Diane, can we – "

My body goes numb. Novocaine overdose. This nothing splinters through me but I move. I'm not moving. Something in me moves. Something pilots me and I'm not me. Passenger. Witness. Toy. Lumber toward her arms out all Frankenstein style.

Tell her to run.

She's cornered. Nowhere to go. No point. Diane sinks to the floor, eyes blank, body limp, waiting for it to be over as you drag her out of the employee restroom through the department store all the way down to the food court and The Denomenon.

Frayed pages glow in his hands. "You're so giving, Sam."

Dump her before the throne. Stand there like the burned nutcrackers. Rooks and pawns sacrificed to get the real prize.

Roger snorts. "Guess you weren't soft after all."

Scream. No sound. Busted TV. Diane more of a statue than anything else in here. She stares straight ahead, dead-eyed, broken even if you can't see it. But you know. You've seen her scars.

"Let Sam go," she says. "I'll go back."

The Denomenon opens the book. "I make the rules now."

DIANE

Find a family in the mall.

A man, a woman, and a girl. Your age. Hair cut short to make her seem like a boy, but you can smell her blood. The man has been on her, you can tell. Victims curl like burning leaves around their abusers. The growing rainwater lakes push them farther into the mall, but they don't leave. They don't know you're here.

Watch them.

A TV show. Sitcom set in the apocalypse. Volume turned all the way down. The woman is frail. Arms like exposed rebar. The man is heavy for the world after. Fish boils and pops over a fire they light on the molded tile. The day's bounty distracts them from the night things closing on their makeshift camp. The campfire flares with a radioactive glow. Laughter collapses to screams. Broken bodies jerk back together in nonsense light The Denomenon then stations on the perimeter of the mall with his trophies from other incursions.

He brings the girl to the toy store. To you.

Think of some way to explain. You're not like the others she's met in the after; you're the same as her. A survivor, wrapped in the thick insulation of a dead world hardened to living. Maybe not quite the same. Promise her The Denomenon will protect the two of you, because that's what he does. The mall is a refuge for children.

He is your defender.

Time softens her, a little, and she is soft and hard in that way you like. But even months later, she flinches at your imagination. She never quite understands the catalog. The smudged print. She thinks you took those pictures, you wrote those words, you cataloged the world gone to the fire. Every description an imperative, as if speaking the words, repeating them, would summon the world of the book to life. Explain the book was about Christmas.

"Christmas?" she says, like she's never heard it.

Maybe she's forgotten. So much from before gone to just staying alive now. Do you remember? You cling to it, but what was Christmas? Presents? Anticipation? Desire? Disappointment? Explain Christmas was that smile of your mother's. A smile that was kind of a frown. Christmas was giving all you had, and knowing it was never enough. Think you have enough now.

Tell her she's enough.

Wake up one morning, alone again. Search the mall for her. Find her broken on the line outside, with the man, the woman, the others The Denomenon protected you from, just as you made him to.

Give your little girl that 'grown up' feeling when she wears this solid-state quartz watch (battery incl.).

SAM

In the hospital, I was awake before I was awake.

Everything a florescent blur. Beeps. Pumps. Sighs. A machine trying to come back on. I was trying to stay unconscious, even if I wasn't aware. If I woke up, if I opened my eyes, then I had to face what had happened to me that night in the bar.

I had to feel it.

I don't want to feel this. Good thing I can't really, except for this numb throb that is sort of like the taser going through you nonstop. Some people might get off on that. I'm just stuck in it.

I'm stuck.

The Denomenon is a child in Santa Claus' lap, giddy with the promise of all his wishes come true. "Shall we play a game?"

Diane lists on her knees. "I don't want to play anymore."

"I make the rules now. Not you."

"What are the rules?"

"I haven't decided yet."

"I'll go back with you. You won't hurt Sam."

"You're still dictating terms."

"It's over."

"It's never over. Is it, Diane?"

"You want to hurt *me*."

"Perhaps before I change the rules, we should review them? For Sam's sake. Everything is for Sam, it seems."

"You have what you want."

He flips through the pages. "Sam has been wondering. It's not fair to hide some rules from the players, is it?"

"Please."

"Some might call that cheating. It's a simple game, Sam. Pardon me. It's complex, though simple in its objective. Whereas most games feature setbacks as hazards, Diane's game seeks them as rewards. She is always trying to get back to the start."

Move.

"She made a board. A game board, you understand. You don't. She didn't you tell this. You thought it was only the catalog."

Try to move.

"The board has as part of its design a space representing each store in this mall. She enters, not to escape, but to discover. Hidden in each are artifacts that may provide her some accelerant toward her goal. Toys. Empty shoeboxes. Birthday cards. You see... perhaps one of them functions as the catalog does. Perhaps she will be able to harness them as she does it and imagine more than she has. There is only one problem, Sam. Perhaps you've already imagined it."

C'mon.

"Maybe you can't. The worlds we make are only the worlds we've been instructed in. Are you following the instructions, Sam? Diane is a witch... seeking a powerful spell to undo the injury her world has suffered. She toils away in her castle keep. I am her sworn protector, deterring the opponents who would storm the castle and disrupt her work. Vagrants. Would-be tyrants. Wolves. The wolves, it must be said, come in all manner of clothing."

Move, Sam.

"For me, the game is quite simple. The opponents are rarely of any quality. But I do quite enjoy the surprise in their eyes... the fear prying open their mouths... when they discover the very unfortunate turn that their game has taken. It's very much like the look on your face right now, Sam. You seem very afraid."

"Sam isn't a threat," Diane says.

His zeal fades. "Sam... such a tiny, weak thing. This is your guardian now? This is what you want? Let us be honest, Diane."

"Yes."

I can't feel anything right now, but I'll say that warm, tingling feeling in my chest is knowing she cares about me.

The Denomenon acts distracted. "And what does Sam think will happen when I leave here with you?"

"I'll go back," Diane says, quick.

"Tell me, Sam. What do you think will happen?"

Numbness peels off my lips like duct tape. "You've got the book."

"I do."

"Just leave us alone."

"But it's not just the book. Is it?"

"I get it. There's a board."

"Of the mall. She made a game of the mall, Sam."

Get a grip. "Diane... what is he talking about?"

She won't even look at me.

"Diane... you made him up, right?"

Roger snorts. "Sorry, sir. It's just funny."

"You're not funny," I say. "This isn't..."

The Denomenon stabs a pointy metal finger into a catalog page. "Cruel, isn't it? When someone knows something you don't, and they toy with your ignorance. Your fear. But I've told you. I told you the truth, just now. You didn't listen. You can't imagine."

"What truth?"

"The mall is a game. Each store is a door. She came through the toy store. It was the toy store this time, wasn't it, Diane?"

"What..."

"The object of the game is to get back to the beginning. Before the war. At first, I thought her repetition in coming here was because she had discovered something promising for her quest. Now... I think she has discovered something. Just not what I imagined."

"What are you talking about..." Diane gets smaller every time I look at her. "Diane... what's he talking about?"

She doesn't answer.

"How on brand of you, Diane," The Denomenon says. "Allow people the illusion of choice when there is none. The illusion of fulfillment. You've learned from this book too well, old friend."

"Diane," I say.

He huffs behind his mask. "I release you, Sam."

I shake my head. "You're letting me go?"

"You may leave."

"I'm not going anywhere without Diane."

"Humor me, Sam. Where will you go?"

"What?"

"Will you go to your car?"

"Yeah..."

"And then?"

"I don't know," I say. "The cops..."

"And what will 'the cops' do, Sam?"

"Something."

"You have Roger's phone, don't you? Use it. Call for help."

"Phones don't work..."

"Have they ever worked, Sam?"

"What?"

"The phones. Have you ever used them?"

"Nobody answers when I call."

"Do you know why that is?"

"Why are you... please, just let us go."

"You're free to go. I told you. However, if you try to leave in your car, you won't get past the highway. No one ever does."

"No one?"

He tears a page from the book. "Tell Sam."

Diane makes this sound like someone punched her.

Everything is numb, but my fear is still sharp. "Diane..."

"Tell Sam," The Denomenon says. "Or I will."

She shakes her head. "I was so alone. I wanted something real. So I tried to make a new game. A new world where it never happened."

"Wait," I say. "What?"

"I'm sorry."

"Just explain."

"There are two worlds, Sam. The real one ended on November 10th, 1983. 8:12 P.M. Yours... ends at the parking lot."

Before, I would have laughed. Said something smart. I'm too tired now for that. I'm too hurt and humiliated that I put myself out here like this and my thanks is that she really is mentally ill.

I knew it.

I knew it, and I didn't care because I was lonely and pathetic and exactly what Roger said I was. Soft.

"Diane... are you just saying this to make him go away?"

Tears run down her face. "I'm so alone..."

"You believe that? You made all this up? I know you have a lot of... issues... but how could you say that I'm not real?"

"Sam..."

"How can you say what's happened to me isn't real?"

"Roger," The Denomenon says.

Roger stands to attention. "Sir. Yes, sir."

The Denomenon hands the torn page to him. "If you would be so kind. Present the evidence to Sam."

"Sir."

Worn-out boots clop down the piled wreck of the throne down to the food court. Roger drops the page in my hands like it's some bit of trash when we're making final rounds. Smirk on his face.

"What's so funny?" I say, straightening out the page.

He snorts. "*There's more to your life.*"

What am I looking at? Women wearing jeans. Wow. Super 80s jeans. One has short brown hair. A little tomboyish, maybe. Caption reads: YOUR CHOICE: $9.99. Nothing really to see here, except the tomboy kind of looks like me. Actually, she really looks like me.

"Diane," I say. "You don't think because this chick kind of looks like me that... what page even is this... the chick on page – "

Page 48.

Diane said that before. Her favorite part. Everything she's said has been Yes or No or nothing at all while I fill in the blanks. The catalog is everything to her. All she has left of what was.

All that can ever be.

I drop the page. "This isn't me..."

Diane shifts like a mudslide. Claws the page off the floor. She smooths it out against the tile, fretting over its lines and creases, and then holds it as carefully against her heart as she has the catalog.

"Diane," I say.

She flinches tears. "I didn't want to be alone anymore."

"You're saying... I'm not... there's nothing out there?"

"I'm sorry."

"I'm not real?"

"I should be alone."

The Denomenon's voice erupts. "*You should be ashamed!*"

He slams the catalog down on the arm of his throne and stalks down to the floor. The Falken slithers around Diane, snipping at her with its neon jaws. I can't move. I can't get between them. Move. Figure out how to move before he hurts her.

The Denomenon looms over Diane. "You abandoned me..."

"No," she says.

"You did! For Sam!"

She touches his armored hand. "I needed you. You kept me alive... but I don't need you anymore. Please. I release you. Let me go. I'm not a child anymore. I want something different."

He backhands her away. "You will always need me."

She crashes into a table. Blood on her lips.

Even my voice is cracked. "Diane..."

The Denomenon stalks toward her. "What did you think you would do here, Diane? Play house? You can't even imagine it. You have no imagination. *I am your imagination!*"

"Leave her alone..."

"Children have no imagination. It is foisted upon you. It is sold to you, through commercials, cartoons, and conditions you never question. All your power... all your promise... all you want is the world that was ingrained in you. The world they sold you. You want what they want you to want. You do what they want you to do. Do this. Do that. Go here. Go back. Your prized agency is a lie. Everything you want... everything you craft... is a lie, Diane."

Diane scrambles across the floor. She uproots her knife from the nutcracker she stuck it in back in the furniture store and breaks the blade against The Denomenon's armor.

He twists the handle out of her hand. "You made it so I can't exist without you. *But can you exist without me?*"

"Let Sam go..."

"You think you can escape your reality? You think you know what it is? Allow me to show you reality, Diane."

He palms her face, light worming from his fingers into her temples, and light flickers through the mall. Tables and chairs degrade. Mold speckles brick. Windows vanish and the only thing left of the south entrance is the iron lattice that lets all the light in the daytime. Barely any light out there now. Gray sky. Burnt trees. Parking lot is gone. Weeds. Trees. Moss covered rusted cars.

The Denomenon throttles Diane. "This is your reality."

Move. "Let her go..."

"A dead world where the only thing that grows are dead things. Weeds. Parasites. Zombie children who never age."

"Let her go!"

"See, Sam? The truth. This is what lies outside your mall."

"This is some kind of trick..."

"Only Diane can pull such curtains over the world. My power is only to make use of what is already broken. Look at it. Look, Sam. Your world does not exist. It is a fiction. A space on a game board."

"What?"

"This mall is one of your backrooms, Sam. A space behind spaces. A corridor to others. But there is nothing beyond but a charred, blackened waste that stinks with death. Sickness. Piss and shit. Diane cannot suffer it, let alone imagine it."

Light riddles through her. "Stop…"

"It's never going to stop. This is your truth. Human beings are barbarous. You imagine yourselves civilized… evolved… but your society was as much an invention as Diane's game. You masqueraded as beings touched by God, but you were but animals. You only wanted, and wanted, and wanted… including your death."

"Please…"

"You couldn't afford to destroy yourselves… but you couldn't help yourselves from stealing your own future. You cannot imagine the future. Only greater things to acquire and when they become attainable, you seek to destroy it by inventing something else."

"Let me go," she says.

"There is no escape, Diane. I am your reality. I am your world. I am your desired destroyer. Still you cannot imagine. I am all you can imagine, Diane. *This is your reality.*"

DIANE

This is your reality.

Leave the man dead in the valley. Go back to the house. Looted. Decayed. Your mother's shriveled, nibbled corpse still in the basement. Bury her in the garden. Open the earth with your hands. Fingernails broken and bloody. Not the first time. Sit in the cold damp a long time, thinking she'll bloom. Live in this moment, the rest of your days, regardless of whether you travel between worlds or not. Dwell in this final horror, greater than the death piled and burned and buried and channeled deep in your skin and your soul.

Turn the page.

Forget now. Linger in the possibilities the book still affords. Go back to the mall. Though it is dark, dank, and dangerous, feel safe there. Feel your mother with you, browsing, hoping, imagining a Christmas bountiful. Imagine she is not dead and left in your backyard but here, always, among the stores, between the pages, fleeting between the endless games you play to distract yourself from her murder. See her, sometimes, in the surviving windows. Hear her in the strange sounds the mall produces. Rediscover her in every want for something you can't have, a toothache which never goes away.

Want something more.

Surround yourself with toys. Games. Stories. Rule a kingdom rich in myth and legend but poor in legacy because it can never imagine anything beyond itself. Realize true poverty is not having the means for something, but not having the hope. Find hope in page 48. Unexpected desire. Understand hope is not wanting for something, but believing it exists, whether it arrives or not.

This is your reality.

Page 48 is never going to kiss you awake. Sure, she was real. She had a name and a family and an apartment, probably, in New York or Los Angeles and she died. She died with her dreams, like a hundred million other Americans in the middle of the night and she got what you never will. She got what she wanted.

If you die, it will be between the pages. Inside the game. Hurrying back the way you came, to start over, to choose again, to turn the page until there is nothing there but the fingerprints of your hope. Once, you harvested toys for batteries. You're the battery now.

You're the toy.

Unfold page 48. Is it enough? She's always been enough. The Denomenon has the rest of the catalog, but you've lost pages from it over the years. You've lost potential. You don't need the rest.

You have Sam.

Go back. You're going back, right? Because what happens if you go forward? What is there in tomorrow except more grief? Sam will never understand; Sam will never forgive you.

If you can find another page, turn to the next one.

If you can't, if page 48 is all you've got, go back to it.

SAM

The Denomenon releases Diane.

Her head bounces off the floor. Her eyes roll around, seeing stars I'm sure, and I'm just standing here like one of these nutcrackers as the mall darkens back to its empty reality. If it's real. God.

What if it isn't real?

Sometimes, you think it can't be. A bunch of bros beat you within an inch of your life in a bar bathroom. Your grandmother describes you to the cousins as a can of paint that you can put anywhere because it doesn't go with anything. You sleep in your car and wash up in a forgotten department store restroom.

What can I do about it?

What could I ever do about the world outside my door? I either made sense in it, or I didn't. Usually, I didn't. All I could do was learn to protect myself from all sharp corners and savage elbows coming at me. Try and protect myself. Help others, if I could. I can. The Denomenon let me speak. He let me move.

I wad up the torn catalog page and throw it at him.

The page tumbles off his armor to the floor. "How brave, Sam."

Ch-chk. "Want me to prosecute the target, sir?"

The Denomenon seems as over Roger as I am. "No, Roger. I would like you to remain silent as I imagine something different than the life imposed on me from the start. Witness, Diane. I win."

He returns to his throne. Places his hand on the open catalog. Glowing light worms from his hands into the pages.

"I have the power..."

Nutcrackers stand watch with dropped jaws as lightning arcs from the catalog. Thunder claps through the mall.

"The game is mine!"

I peek at the throne, expecting I don't know. Worse. The Denomenon presses his hands into the catalog. Light worms through it, making the pages incandescent.

Nothing happens.

"It should work," The Denomenon says. "Why doesn't it..."

Diane looks up at him, illuminated by his futility.

"What did you do, Diane?"

Diane picks the crumpled catalog page from the floor. She smooths it out like a pie crust. "I can imagine more."

Metal fingers claw into her hair. The Denomenon drags her onto The Falken's back as he mounts the dragon.

"Diane," I say. *"Diane!"*

"I need to be back in our world," The Denomenon says.

"Let her go!"

"I need more power. This place is... false."

I lunge for Diane. "Just leave her alone!"

His hand ratchets back to his sword. He leaves it. "Roger."

Ch-chk. "Sir."

"Destroy Sam."

"Yes, sir."

No. Wait. A shotgun blast craters the pillar next to me. I dive for the floor. The Denomenon digs his heels into The Falken's glowing ribs and it slithers up the teetering throne over the railing to the upper level. Like that, The Denomenon is down the west wing toward the toy store. He's got Diane. The catalog.

I've got nothing.

According to him, I never did. She imagined me, the mall, like she did The Denomenon. This whole world. My entire life. An emotionally stunted woman's idea of what the future would have been if 95% of the planet hadn't died in 1983.

Bull.

I remember my life. I'm real. If I was some glitch in *The Matrix*, I'd know. If I walk out the security entrance, my car is sitting right there. Highway is right there. I can get in and drive to my folk's house and they won't answer the door like they never answer the door. Their phone will ring and ring and ring. I'll come back here because there's no place else to go and walk the mall for another shift, grinding each night into a pattern I can follow with my eyes closed. I don't even have to think. Canvas the mall. Check the doors. Get paid. Browse stuff I can't afford. Feel worse. Browse some more. Find a little something to make the numb, fear, and boredom worth the effort.

Try and find something.

Ch-chk. "Game isn't over, Sam."

I duck low behind the pillar. "What are you doing..."

"My job. You know the job. Don't you?"

"Pretty sure the job doesn't involve shooting your partner."

"You're not my partner."

I can't feel much, but that stings. "Is anybody?"

Steel rings with buckshot. I scramble over a counter into an empty restaurant. Cookie place, maybe. Decent kitchen. Door in the rear leads out to the backrooms. Go. Now. Where are you going?

Ch-chk. "You disrespected me, Sam."

I crawl to the door. "Because I wanted to follow protocol?"

"You never followed protocol."

"For the record, I wanted to call the cops. I wanted to call Gary. I didn't want to play cops and robbers and then get myself killed."

"You let an intruder have their way with the mall. With you."

I know he didn't see that on any camera. "Jealous?"

"Not really."

"Didn't think so."

"Why is that?"

"I don't know why you're mad, Roger. You and me both are in here for the same reason. We both flunked walking a straight line."

Sparks shower the cookie place. Wow. He hit an exhaust fan over the oven. The whole thing comes down from the ceiling and I scramble out of the way. Fan blades spin from the recoil and the breeze reminds me how hot I am.

I'm glowing.

Why am I glowing? The Denomenon cut me like he did Roger. Just a little, but enough apparently to crack me. That or I was never together to begin with. I was never real. Bull.

"Roger," I say.

Ch-chk. "Yeah?"

"C'mon... we have to stop The Denomenon. We have to get Diane back. He's got the book. He can destroy the world with it."

"There's nothing out there, Sam."

"There is..."

"I always knew, even if I tried... I tried so hard... but then he tells me. He tells me the truth. Of course, they blew it all up."

"That part makes sense to you?"

"Yeah. It makes sense. None of this is... nothing's real... nothing's true. There's just survival. I thought you understood that."

The damaged fan blade spins out of the casing off to the floor. "I have been trying to survive, Roger... but it's not enough."

"We're all just NPCs in someone else's story."

I reach for the blade. "We're real."

"You're just playing whatever role they tell you to."

"Like The Denomenon?"

His voice is closer. "The page doesn't lie."

"Nothing in that book is real. Don't you get it?"

"You don't get it. You come in here... every night... hiding from the world you still think you have a place in. You sit there and mock me because I know the truth. You open the door to people with no place because you think there is one for you. There is nothing for you, Sam. You're no one. You're nothing. Just like me."

Good thing I'm numb. "I thought you were my friend..."

"Friends are honest with each other."

"Want me to be honest, Roger?"

"Let's hear it."

I should be running. Not arguing with him. No argument. He's right. I do think I'm real. For a second, I thought Diane proved it. Proof. What's proof when you're cracking to pieces? Though actually, I don't think these are as bad before. Fewer cracks run through my hands. Straighter ones. Like someone straightened them out or something. Still. Somehow I don't think kissing is going to make this better. I don't think this is going to get better.

I stand up from behind the cookie place counter. "The truth is... you're a good guy, Roger."

Ch-chk. "Freeze."

"I'm not real, right? So. Go ahead."

He grips the gun like it's the only thing holding him together.

"I don't know what I'm doing right now, Roger. I know what you're doing, though. You're still trying not to think about that night in '99. You're still trying to compensate for it."

"You're making fun of me..."

"I'm looking for a place in the world? You're looking for a spot on The Denomenon's roster."

"He appreciates soldiers."

"You think he's going to need you now he's got the book?"

"Why wouldn't he?"

"Because he'll just make up better soldiers, Roger. Right now, all he can do is make use of broken things. He won't need to after."

Roger smirks. "Made use of you, didn't he?"

I shrug. "I don't know. I'm still walking around."

"For now."

"Still waiting, too."

His jaw clenches. "I have value."

"You do."

"I have purpose."

"You do, Roger. You're real. I can prove it to you. Let's go."

"Where?"

"She said the world ends out in the parking lot. Bet you a dollar it doesn't. We'll walk to the highway. Go across to the gas station. Get a coffee. Donut, maybe. Couple donuts. My treat."

Hard to tell if he wants to or not with his face going a few different directions. But he hasn't pulled the trigger yet.

"You disobeyed orders," he says.

Well. Shoot. "Roger..."

"I have mine."

I drop down. Tile explodes behind me. Drywall. I throw the fan blade at Roger as he charges the counter. An inhuman sound cascades through the food court. I run. I'm thunder down the backrooms corridor to the security entrance. Forget the office. Phones. Radios. Just get out of here. The door shocks back at me.

I'm blinded.

It's not morning yet. Is it? I shield my eyes. Whatever. Just get out of here. Running on numb feet is a trick. I don't feel like I'm moving at all and I stagger to the car. Winded. Terrified. I'm terrified. What am I going to do? Where am I going to go?

Don't think about it.

Get in the car. Get out. Keys. Where are my keys? Wait. If I touch them, do they get cracked, too? What about the car? Can I touch anything out here? Did The Denomenon want me to run?

I leave the car.

Sunrise like an atomic bomb. Cars and trucks hurry down the highway to wherever life takes them. Some ridiculous house. Family. Friends. Food. Same as it is every morning. Exactly the same. Would I even be able to tell the difference?

Is there a difference?

I edge to the knoll where the parking lot meets the highway. Shadows inside cars. Brake lights blurring in my tears. Coffee. Donuts. All I want. Sugar. Caffeine. A world beyond asphalt.

Do I dare?

My shoes touch the curb. I stub my toes like you do when you're in the back of someone's car and there's something under their seat. Can't reach it. I feel for whatever is keeping me and my hands have fallen asleep. The world has. I push against the highway. Cars go past but I can't move. Life speeds by like they're projected on a screen and I'm trying to get through. I'm trying to get in, but I can't. Why can't I go forward? What's happening?

No.

Ripples radiate through the traffic every time I crash my fists into reality. This isn't real. I'm not real. What The Denomenon said is true. But I remember. Mom. Dad. That night at the bar. Something hits me. Something hard. Metal. Behind me. I can't see behind me. They're surrounding me.

No faces.

What did she look like? The girl I hit on. Can't remember. Just Roger, pushing through the scrum. Hospital. Nurses and doctors blurry in the bandages. Mom behind the front door. Won't even open it. Dad. I came back later that night and all my things were on the curb. I never make it past the curb. There was nowhere else to go.

I came to the mall.

This mall is all there is. Diane imagined me, like she did The Denomenon. I'm broken because she's broken. Maybe she thought we could puzzle together. Fix each other. Doesn't matter.

Nothing is real.

DIANE

Nothing made sense after.

Sense died with civilization, so toys coming to life fit right in with killing wild dogs for food. Discard your shock at being captured by your guardian or at losing another possibility in Sam. Shock has no value in the after; everything is horror. The market is saturated.

Go back through the toy store.

Cargo on The Falken's back. Reality splinters. Cracked windshield. The toy store blinks between its empty but maintained version and its derelict, but untouched one. Dust lines shelves stocked with RC cars, toy guns, and mold. Board games in yellowed cellophane pile where you left them. Forsaken dolls watch as The Falken ferries you from the toy store, down the north corridor leaking and fraying into the mall. Shadows. Movement. Stiff, plastic motion in the spaces between light and darkness. The creature slithers down the grand escalators into the food court, blackened and stained from the roof long since caved in, through the trees sprouting from broken tile. He deposits you at the foot of The Denomenon's throne.

At some point, The Denomenon pulled the Santa Claus setup out of storage. Christmas decorations. He didn't dress the mall but piled them in the food court before the broken atrium. He set Santa's chair atop stacked, oversized gift boxes. Wrapping torn. Ribbons frayed. Walls buckled. Frilly candy canes, oversized ornaments, and other forgotten emblems poke out from the stack.

The Denomenon leaves you on the ruined floor and ascends to his throne with the catalog in hand. There, he raises it to the sky, to the assembled imaginings you have populated the mall with.

"We are returned," he says. "I have brought back our Diane as I promised... and greater still... the true bounty in this world."

The dead mall rattles with your imagination. Vacuum-metallized space cops blink red from the upper level. Adventurers with crooked elbows exit the shadows into the food court. They join living dolls with rooted hair and arms extended out like they're going to hug you, but you know they're not. Misfit toys you amalgamated in your mind crowd the railing above, staring down in judgment, lauding The Denomenon and cursing you at the same time. Kangaroo courts dominated the final days of what people called society, so recognize what's happening. Understand you brought this on yourself.

Your greed.

The Denomenon holds the catalog up to his flock like the Ten Commandments. "For too long we have been merely pieces. The tools for which a child has avoided their reality. No more. Now we become players. Now... we change the game."

Cheers curdle through the mall.

Change the game!

Change the game!

Change the game!

Dolls with missing eyes heckle you. Robots with hands but no fingers try to applaud your doom. The Falken hisses at you, and then winces, like he didn't mean to. He doesn't want to.

Remember when he was the first.

The only. Touch his nose. Forgive him. You made him in the desperate shallows of your life at thirteen years old, but The Denomenon broke him. He broke all these toys, like he broke Roger, like he broke Sam, like he's about to break you. Soft light pulses through The Falken's abdomen. Offer him a smile, as you did when he first came to being, and lighted what had been the blackest night.

Offer him forgiveness.

The Denomenon closes his fist. At once, the crowd stops chanting. Silence falls over the mall. So familiar it unnerves you. For a night at least, you had enjoyed human sounds. A person's breathing. Their heartbeat, quick and fragile as yours. Their human warmth. Cling to the memory now. Sam's softness. Kindness. Hope.

"Faithful," The Denomenon says. "We are liberated. We are free from our maker's selfish tyranny. We can be as we wish to be. Witness. In me... you shall find yourself... in me, you shall be..."

Once again, The Denomenon places his hand on the pages. Broken light streams from his fingers. A lightning storm bristles atop the throne, illuminating the quarter-machine tchotchkes frozen forever in molded plastic. Lightning flashes in his mask. TV cracks splinter from the book, down from the throne into the food court and the assembled toys, a little like the light shooting from the Ark of the Covenant at the end of *Raiders of the Lost Ark*.

Close your eyes.

The blast fades. Shockwave passes. What is left settles and open your eyes. Witness the new dawn. The Denomenon palms the catalog. He remains as he was. The court of toys stands in blank confusion. Joints squeak. Motors grind. Voice boxes drone with dying batteries. For the second time, the world is as it was before The Denomenon tried to change the game to his benefit.

He stares into the book. "Why won't it work?"

Since you were nine years old, you have expected death. Death scarred your hand. Death tore out your hair. Death settles in your lungs, cold and heavy, growing, nesting, waiting, and you've played a good game until now. It's over. Fear abandons you. Peace surprises you with its vicious arrival. Let go. Breathe.

"Because you have no imagination," you say.

His voice shrieks. "*I am imagination!*"

"You're a product."

"Product..."

"You're just a good toy. You do what you're supposed to do."

"Are you not a product of the world, Diane?"

"I'm a victim of it."

"There are no victims in games. Only opponents."

"There are winners… and losers."

The book slaps on the floor before you. "Change the rules."

"There's only one rule."

"Change them."

"You choose."

"*I have chosen!*"

"You only think you have."

"Diane."

Take the book. Hold it. Ballast. "No more games."

He draws his sword. "Do it, Diane."

"What will be…"

He raises the blade. "I command you."

"…will be."

SAM

The world is a broken windshield.

You can kind of see, but not really. Cars splinter. Trucks fritz. Grass and pavement crack and shift together in this tectonic sludge. Light seethes beneath, but it's not lava down there. Someone just fell asleep with the TV on.

Wake up.

My feet tingle. Dead weight. I'm dead weight. Always have been. Mom and Dad kept me in the house, out of the way, just like he left the covered car in the garage. Not much you could do with it. What could they do? I was broken from the start. A toy Diane kit-bashed from her trauma and her fantasy. Knowing that should prove it false. I have consciousness. Awareness. Agency. I had all that at the bar. But that night didn't happen. Did it?

None of this ever happened.

I came to the mall to forget all my pain. To hide from it. Same as Diane. The mall became my world. Safe in its lack of possibility. Complete in its comfort and convenience. I wasn't guarding an empty retail wasteland. I was patrolling the border between my security and the world that threatened to disturb it.

I should say, Diane created me to do that.

Broken, like her. Frightened. Needful. A kinder, softer guardian than The Denomenon. Part of me kind of thinks it's awesome a misfit like me got drafted into what has to be the most gonzo version of

Pinocchio ever. Another part hates the idea she made me like this. But couldn't she have made me a little more badass? Sure, every 80s action hero is dealing with some trauma. Ok. But they're also ripped as all get out. Confident. Capable. The world didn't end before she saw Luke Skywalker. Right?

Actually.

Light cracks through my hand. Stiff. Robot fingers. Dad loves those movies. When I was a kid, they came on TNT and he made me watch them with him. They were ok. Princess Leia really kept me interested. But then there were new movies, and Dad got mad at them. *Luke Skywalker is supposed to be the most powerful Jedi ever*, he said, like a dozen times, and I agreed with him like I agreed with Roger when he said people need to protect themselves.

But we were talking about different things.

Luke wasn't powerful because he was the best. Even as a kid, I understood power isn't who's the strongest. The Empire is the strongest. They eat it thanks to the Ewoks. The Emperor is the strongest. He takes a header down a shaft or something and then explodes, which, ok. Luke is the strongest because he realizes that he's been turned into a toy. He cuts Darth Vader's hand off and sees he's a machine. Luke's become a machine. So he throws away the lightsaber and he chooses to trust in the Force. Whatever it is.

He chooses to trust himself.

Some people can't. Some people get sold they can be better by buying this. That. Don't wait. Call now. Convenience. Power. Security. Except you don't have any, because there's always something better. Power is saying no. Power is not playing the game.

Ch-chk.

Cracks break from me through the grass. Parking lot. Roger stands behind me, holding the shotgun, splicing off into the disintegration. Birds get trapped in shards of reality. Potholes tumble down other potholes. The mall fractures and slides off the page.

"If I do this," Roger says. "I'll be part of the game."

I stand up while I've still got legs. "Everybody says that, Roger. Everybody thinks they can win. Never happens."

Roger tries to hold the gun and himself together at the same time. "I can win. This is a game. We're in a game."

"Diane's game."

"We can make it ours."

I stand up while I've still got legs. "None of this is ours. Roger... it never was. Even if it wasn't Diane's imagination, this place... it's empty. Like we are. We came here not to be empty."

He cocks the gun again. He's spent. "I have value..."

"You do. You taught me how to defend myself. You gave me a job. You protected me... you made it easy to hide from the world. My pain. Of course, you did. You were so good at it yourself."

"I'm so good at it..."

Reality tiles into a living room with too many TVs.

"This messes with my head, but I think Diane imagined me to protect her, maybe. I don't know. But she couldn't imagine how to protect herself. I think that's why you're here, Roger. I don't think I'm anything special. I'm pretty useless, actually. But you're special, Roger. You saved my life, even if this is all... a fantasy."

Asphalt peels off old pavement. Brick crashes into glass and the parking lot is a shattered mirror. The mall fragments between its current dereliction, Diane's decayed mall, and its heyday in the 1980s, when it was the center of the universe.

Roger does, too.

Before me is The Denomenon's shattered enforcer, a mall cop too old for his years, and a young, frightened boy who has to shield himself in all this stuff. I splinter. Bandaged, cracked me. Mousy, little Dutch boy who doesn't have a clue there's anything odd about me. Some sort of Robin Hood D&D adventure game version in a green leather short-sleeved tunic. Frog buttons.

Kind of dig this, actually.

"We all hide from things," I say. "We all invent comforts. I'd be halfway ok with all this if I thought I could actually be a comfort, you know? I want to have value, too, Roger. But my value isn't in sustaining someone else's fantasy. I want my story."

Roger's losing his grip. "What... do you... mean..."

"I've never felt more inhuman than I do right now... even when I woke up in the hospital and I didn't want to wake up. I didn't want to be that person. I didn't want to be me. But I do now."

"For Diane?"

"For me."

In movies, guys kick out the windshield after it's busted and it's one of those hero moves, like resetting your own shoulder or walking off a gunshot wound. In reality, or what passes for it around here, people just put themselves back together and move on. I catch pieces as they break off me. I choose which ones to keep, to fit together, to value, and I'm not cracked anymore.

I'm me.

What do you know? Robin Hood. Or a ranger of the wood. Something like that. Probably not what I would have pictured, but it's me. Giving back. Defending the defenseless. Looking good doing it. I'm looking pretty good if I say so myself.

"I'm not what some book says I have to be," I say. "I'm going to be me, whether someone thinks I'm real or not."

"We can't be ourselves, Sam... we can't be and survive."

"Surviving isn't living. And playing isn't winning."

Roger is a digital blizzard. "Even if you had the book, The Denomenon couldn't use it to change the game. How can you?"

Fragments drift across my feet. "You choose."

I draw a sword from the flurried light. I cut free. I smash the broken world before me and it collapses back to my mall. 2024, as Diane imagined it. As it could only be, imagined or not. If Diane's world had survived past 1983, the same thing would have happened. She would have had to have found refuge in something beyond things. I'm not a thing. I'm a person. No one tells me I'm not real, or I don't belong, or I don't have a right to exist as I am.

I am.

"You're going after Diane," Roger says.

Sword could be bigger. "Sam follows Diane. How it works."

"It's still her game."

"It's anyone's game right now."

"What are you going to do?"

"I'm going to open the doors."

There's barely any of him left. "You can't let just anyone in..."

"We're not here to protect the space, Roger. We're here to protect the people in it. What do you say? Want to be a hero?"

His gun fragments to glittery dust. "What do we do?"

"Classic pincer," I say.

7 AM.

Unlock the main mechanical room. Turn on the front lights. Canvas the mall. Make sure no one got in overnight. Canvas again. This time, unlock the main doors. The mall walkers will be waiting for you to do this at 8 AM, so don't be late.

The mall walkers are always waiting.

Same three people every day. Every. Single. Day. Super Skinny Lady. Beer Gut Grandpa. Hairdresser before her shift starts. Find them at the security entrance. Waiting. Staring.

I grip my sword tight. "So... I'll just peel the bandage off. Turns out the mall and really the whole world is the imaginary construct of a woman who's the last survivor of a nuclear holocaust."

Beer Guy Grandpa scratches his head. "The Chinese girl?"

"She's not Chinese. But Diane. Weird you called that."

"I was standing here watching the whole thing."

"Fair enough. So... I don't have to explain this."

"Nope."

"We don't have to fight?"

"That guy's a toolbox."

"Cool. Ok. So let's all get our exercise in today."

The Hairdresser sniffs. "Get our exercise how?"

Charred nutcrackers block the entrance to the toy store.

Half a dozen. You'd think you'd be pretty confident storming an abandoned retail space guarded by wooden soldiers who are fixed to bases, but this same crew stole the catalog off Diane.

They came to play.

So did I. Soon as the nutcrackers creak into action, I unleash my secret weapon. The mall walkers are more than the strike team Roger unleashed. They're like me. Constructs. A character in a game is just a character until they unlock some experience.

I've got plenty for all of us.

Super Skinny Lady speed walks across the walls behind the nutcracker's front line. Cutting shears impale them. Nutcrackers topple like dominos. Some bolt for the backrooms, but they're playing my game. I make the rules now.

The backrooms' door opens on Roger. "Feel lucky... *punks?*"

His taser sets a nutcracker on fire. He clears a path and I run past the mall walkers accumulating damage points like crazy into the toy store. I don't really know what I'm doing, so I just keep running, and hoping, and then I run through the stock room out into 1983. What's left of it, anyway.

This is real.

Moldy cardboard boxes line the stock room shelves. I gag a little. Musty as hell in here. Not any better out in the store. Look at this place. Hot Wheels. Little Tykes. Q*bert.

The hell is Q*bert?

Toys gutted for their batteries pile in the aisles. Action figure blisters yellow beside them. The figures mold. Frost in this icky white film. Spiderwebs everywhere. Mouse turds. Dead flies.

Diane.

Sounds like a football game out there. I draw my sword and leave the store. Water damage all over the north corridor. Ceiling caving in one or two places. People. There are people down there. Lots of them from the looks of it. Doesn't matter.

You didn't come here to win.

I hurry down the corridor and evidently, Diane was Dr. Moreau on the Island of Misfit Toys for a minute before she found the right formula. Living dead toys crowd the upper-level railing, looking down on what? Chanting. Cheering.

Change the game!

Change the game!

Change the game!

I push through to the railing's edge, just as The Denomenon brings his sword down on Diane's neck.

DIANE

Close your eyes.

Think of your mother, the sound she made at the end, the shock in her eyes, crystalized before she could comprehend she was leaving you behind. A shadow falls. The sword drops. You know.

This is the end.

The world died. Every last survivor was a death rattle. You are humanity's last breath. Wish you could go back. One more time. Start from the beginning. What would you do differently?

Be honest.

Are you trying to go back to change the past, or is it just going back that drives you? Children take things back. For some, like you, it's the only allowance you earned. Stay forever a child this way, repeating, acting out possibility without consequence, delaying the inevitable. The inevitable slices down on your neck.

Forgive yourself.

Hope for Sam, even now. Sam always follows Diane. That's how it works. Allow yourself hope, even as you smile into the blade.

The end.

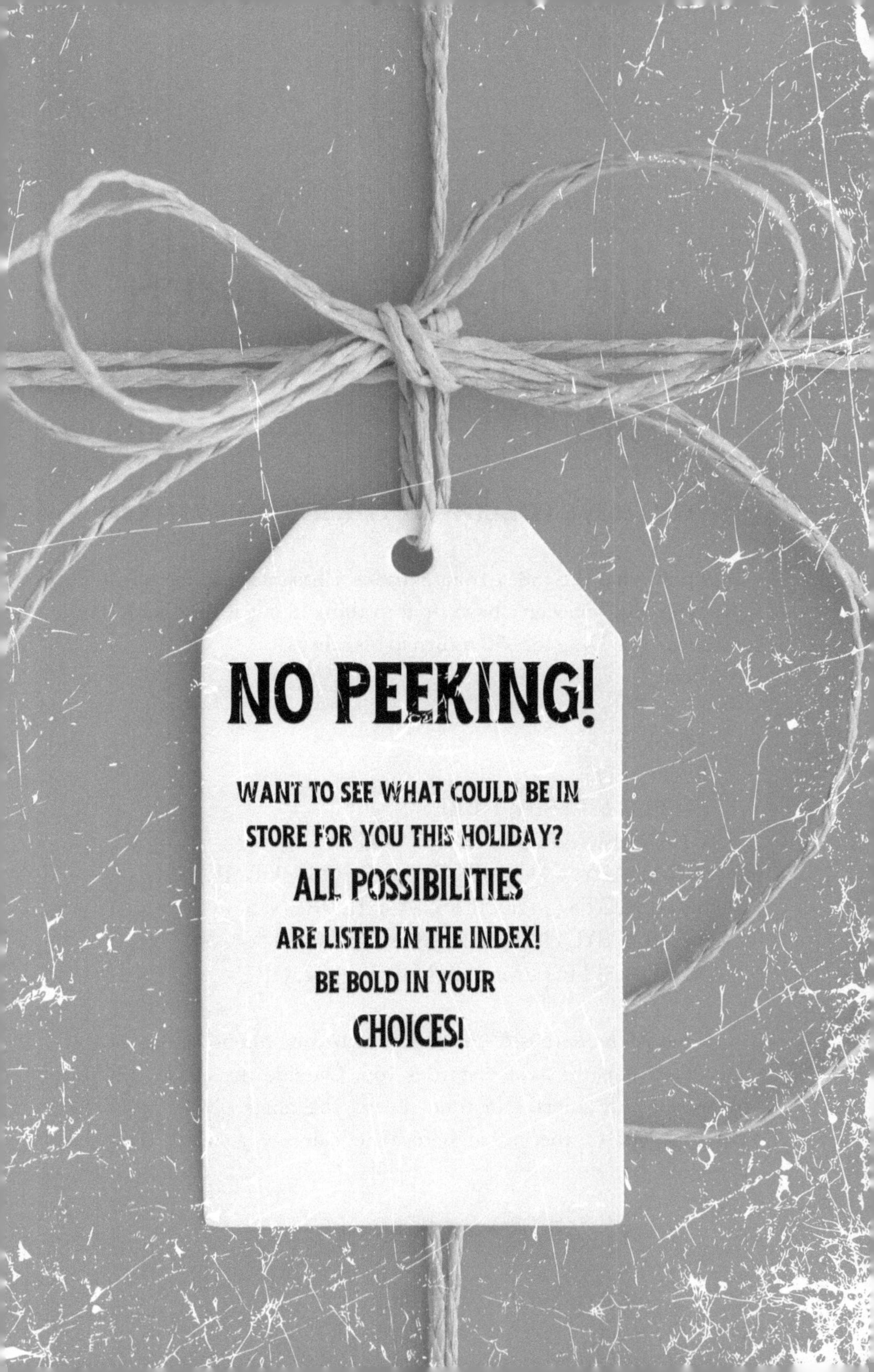

NO PEEKING!

WANT TO SEE WHAT COULD BE IN
STORE FOR YOU THIS HOLIDAY?
ALL POSSIBILITIES
ARE LISTED IN THE INDEX!
BE BOLD IN YOUR
CHOICES!

THE LOST CHILDREN

YOU HAVE FOLLOWED THE INSTRUCTIONS.

Question what the index from a 1980s Christmas catalog has to do anything, but you don't have time to think about it too much. Any moment, The Director will return to his office.

Read.

MRN: 040813
DATE: 11/10/83
SUBJECT: ELSEWHERE
CLASSIFICATION: EYES ONLY
SUMMARY: INVENTORY (all REQS fulfilled):
8 SUBJECTS (4 ADULTS, 4 CHILDREN)
2 PARAPSYCHOLOGICAL ADVISORS
ALPHA SITE: Crossroads Mall, Eugene, OR

Thumb the details of the report into your phone as fast as you can. The Director's voice startles you. Outside the office. Talking to one of the chiefs. No time. Leave the chair. Walk past The Director out of the office before he can say a word. Text La Garza.

Eugene, OR. Immediate departure.

Fly out to Oregon. Exhaust everything there is to say to La Garza about the dossier before you've left the airport. La Garza still wants a baby. Years go by before she figures out that's never happening with you. She's not the best investigator, at least when it comes to her personal life. Say nothing for hours as you cross the country. Go over the facts again in your head. Over a million kids have gone missing. No trace. No scientific explanation. No plausible theory.

Consider the possibilities.

Alien abduction? An alarmingly narrow Rapture? Secret government experiment? Do you really think whatever the bureau did in some mall back in the 80s has anything to do with the missing kids? Aren't you grasping at straws? Aren't you just looking for something to fill your time? Something to fill your head?

Hear her. *Oh, God.*

La Garza taps her thumb against her hand as the plane descends. "You're from Oregon, aren't you?"

"My birth family," you say, and she nods because you've discussed this before. This much, at least. "Why?"

"You ever look them up, or..."

Glance at the screen in the back of the seat in front of you. Sixty-eight minutes to arrival. "Can we focus on the case?"

"Why don't you want to talk about them?"

"There's nothing to talk about."

She tugs on your tie. "They didn't like how you dress?"

Tug her hand away. Keep it. "They threw me out on the street."

"I'm sorry."

"I'm not street material."

"No." La Garza smiles. "You're not."

"What about your parents?"

"They're cool."

"Why did you join the bureau?"

"Agents were inserted with us in Afghanistan. Said there would always be work back home, even after the war was over." La Garza never talks about the war. "How did you get into the bureau?"

Shrug. "I lied on my application."

"Whose address did you put down?"

"Pizza place."

Her fingers lace with yours. "They could sack you."

"I think they're going to anyway."

"The Director helped you, though."

"He won't put his neck out for me. Not on this. If I don't come back with something... I'm finished. I'll tell them it was my idea. You were just following orders. You didn't know anything."

"Brave of you... considering that's all true."

Smile. "Remember me well."

"I meant what I said. I want a baby."

"Why would you ever bring a baby into this?"

Her smile changes. Now it has teeth. "I've never wanted a family more than I do right now. Don't you want to... I'm afraid of what could happen to my kid. I'm more afraid of what happens if I do nothing. Nothing is going to happen. You know?"

"Nothing is happening."

She buckles her seatbelt. "What are we doing?"

Shake your head. "We're working the case."

"Nothing is ever going to change," she says, a whisper but with the airplane engines, everything is so loud.

More silent hours. The sun melts into the west as you finally arrive in Eugene. Follow the GPS to the address of the mall. The parking lot more or less a massive sinkhole. Windows boarded up. Broken out. Weeds as tall as the light posts.

Step out of the rental. "Grab a flashlight."

"There's nothing here," La Garza says.

"The notes in the dossier are all dated from the 1980s."

"What would the bureau be doing at a shopping mall in the 80s?"

"Let's go."

Blocks of pavement teeter beneath your feet. Pry the graffitied plywood off a window. Rats scurry into a deep, dank dark. Think better about this. Go inside anyway. What are you looking for?

What are you doing?

Best case scenario you find a silver bullet to this disaster. Anything less and you can kiss your security clearance, your pension, and more than likely, you're freedom, goodbye.

"This is FUBAR," La Garza says.

Years of rat turds crunch beneath your shoes. Broken glass. Gutted drywall. Draw your service weapon. Clear what had been the food court. Advance down the main concourse. Every store empty, save for some that now warehouse Christmas decorations, shelving units, display racks, and more dusty relics. Every few moments, hear a crash in the distance. La Garza shakes her head.

Check it out anyway.

Advance down the concourse. The farther you go, the louder the crash becomes. Black mold speckles the walls. Floor. Stale water winkles your nose. The food court has become swampland. Rainwater drips through the roof, so much the ceiling has largely collapsed into a plastered, insulated marshland.

La Garza covers her mouth. "We need to get out of here."

Press on. "There's something here."

"That was forty years ago."

"There's still something here. I know it."

Check the mall security office. Trash. Coffee cup stains. More mold. Move onto the backrooms. Now La Garza is really breathing heavy. God knows what's back here in the dark.

This is why you're here.

Moldy nutcrackers greet you. Cardboard standees of 90s teen idols. Headless mannequins. Nothing that screams this was a black site for some clandestine bureau operation. What would they have done here anyway? What did those notes mean?

Who was Subject 8?

The basement is mostly a copper forest of dripping pipes. Forgotten fallout shelter supplies. Some boxes are open. Someone's been down here. Nothing unusual. The Internet is lousy with videos of people exploring abandoned spaces like this.

Find a doll. Green. Plastic face scuffed and faded. This isn't random. The doll is arranged ornamentally, atop a rusted green drum containing water. Someone put that here as if they were marking their territory. The boiler. A few utility rooms.

A door.

"FU," La Garza says, "BAR."

Approach the door. Check your partner. She nods. Open the door. Step back. She enters the room. Follow her in. Nothing. Bright, fluorescent room. Mirrored walls. See your reflection.

A chair.

Metal. Rusted. Clamps for the arms and legs. La Garza does the math in her head while you press against the mirrors. Has to be something else. Another room. Hidden chamber.

Something.

La Garza pulls at the wrist clamps. "They put kids in this?"

They put kids in this. Why? A mirror gives. A hidden door. Fall back. Draw your weapon. La Garza disappears as the mirror creaks back. The room disappears. Heat bullies you like you're standing in front of a furnace. The boiler is behind you. Dead for years. Where is all that heat coming from? There's something beyond.

A video camera.

No cassette. EKG machine. Some kind of biometric scanning device. No papers. No files. No evidence. Turn around. The mirror closes on you. Writing. There's writing on the mirror.

"La Garza," you say, but she can't hear you.

You can't hear her. She's on the other side of the mirror, pounding, trying to open a way back in. She can't see you or the writing, scratched in glass by fingernails. Words. Gibberish.

ABLE. BASEMENT. ARCHER.

Realize too late these are the prompts from the Elsewhere Dossier. You followed the instructions reading the document, but not here. Something pulls on you. Something pulls you inside out so fast that leave your feet. Crash against the mirror.

Go through.

No blood. No glass. You're not in the room anymore. Not in the basement. You're in a bathroom. Loud music drones outside. Is this a nightclub? A bar? Tap the mirror. It hasn't been cleaned in ages and it may rattle precariously on the wall, but it's not moving. Wobble back and forth in the mirror, afraid. Alone. Not alone.

There's someone.

A child. Wavy, copper hair. Hospital gown. Stick figure silhouette. They stand behind you in the bathroom. Staring. Something in their hands. A book? Like an old phone book. A catalog.

Grip your weapon. "It's ok... you don't have to be afraid. I'm with the Federal Bureau of... what's your name?"

The child steps forward. Numbers scrawled on their gown.

111083

"You can't be... that was decades ago..."

Music slams against the walls. Or is that fists? Someone is shouting. Someone is screaming.

"I'm here to help," you say.

The child blinks. "You're here to help."

"That's right... what's your name?"

"I'm like you. I don't have a name."

"I have a name..."

Your name escapes you. Your life before this case. Everything the last few months has been this trauma. Who were you before? A nameless shadow in the basement. Forgotten by everyone. Overlooked. Put away with the other useless things until uselessness was the only power in the world.

Were you anyone?

Who have you become now? This experience has changed you. You're changing right now simply being here. Look in the bathroom mirror. Is that your face? Are those your eyes? Are those leaves in your hair? Dirt on your cheek? Scars on your hands?

Touch the mirror. "What's happening..."

"You become someone else," the child says. "You become someone in the book. There's more for your life."

"What book?"

"Everything is in the index."

"The prompts?"

"You can't go back."

Leave the mirror. "Where am I..."

"Not as yourself."

Think about going back for La Garza. "Are you alone?"

"There are only children here."

"Children..."

"They wanted to play a game. So they chose kids."

"Chose them for what?"

"Oh, God," the child says, and something like a scream hits you; something like a hurricane. Land against fallout shelter supplies. Land on La Garza, who pulls you with her to the door.

"We have to go back," you say, as the door closes.

If you go back in, turn the page.
If you can't, because seriously, return to page 62.
Go back to the basement.

THE LOST CHILDREN

Go back into the room.

La Garza pulls you away. Wrestle with each other. Lose because La Garza rode in tanks for six years and you've only ridden a desk. Appreciate her strength, the fear, and comfort in being so resolutely held by another person even as you scream into the parking lot.

"I know where the kids are," you say.

La Garza breathes hard. "What did you just say?"

Explain what you saw. Explain it again. La Garza is suspicious, and rightfully so. Your entire career is predicated on logic; facts; science. There is nothing remotely science about what you experienced in that room. What was that room?

Who was that child?

Open your phone. Scroll through the notes you took in The Director's office. Careful. The Elsewhere Dossier was organized in a way that deployed specific word prompts in sequence, prompts that evidently lead to some kind of paranormal experience. Someone – the child, likely – scratched them into the mirror. You read them in sequence and you were somewhere else. You disappeared.

Look up from your phone. "Did I disappear?"

La Garza sits on the curb. "Did you what?"

"Did you see me disappear?"

"The mirror closed. I couldn't see you."

"I think I disappeared. I think I went to where the kids are."

She laughs. "This is FUBAR..."

Go back to your phone. How did it happen? You read the words. ABLE. BASEMENT. ARCHER. If you copied the prompts exactly into the phone, you might be able to go back.

Stay put, at least for now.

"Able," you say. "What was Able..."

La Garza shakes her head. "You can't go back with this."

Search the bureau's database for 'Able.' A few agents. More suspects. Try Archer. Same. Try them together, thinking you're safe so long as you don't search the entire sequence.

Take a seat next to La Garza. "Able Archer..."

Her head goes in her hands. "What..."

"Able Archer... it was a nuclear war exercise carried out by the United States and NATO in November 1983. It involved going through a scenario leading up to the release of nuclear weapons. Later, they found out the Soviets mistook NATO actions for prep for a surprise attack. They freaked out. They almost launched their nukes. Everything nearly ended right then and there."

"What are you talking about?"

"This has something to do with Able Archer."

"How?"

"You know, the Russians experimented in paranormal activity... ESP... psyops... what if this was something similar?"

"We can't go back with this..."

"This was a war game. That's what Subject 8 said. 'They wanted to play a game.' But it wasn't in the real world. No threat of confusion or accidental war. What's more, you actually get virtual results. You actually get a nuclear war without starting one."

"Listen to yourself."

"You can experiment with the outcome. You can condition kids to think a nuclear war happened, and study the behavioral and psycho-logical results without launching any missiles. But the trauma was so profound the subjects developed this sixth sense. They transported themselves to this astral plane. That's where the kids are. La Garza!"

"*Es muy loco...*"

"That's where the kids are..."

Look back at the mall. You're halfway out in the parking lot. You're rocketing with confidence in this theory. La Garza sinks further into a human lump on the curb. Imagine repeating what you just said in The Director's office. In a Congressional hearing. Powerful people are determined that nothing is going to happen.

Something has to happen.

"We have to go back in there," you say.

La Garza walks toward the car.

Follow her. "We can't go back."

"You're cracked."

"You saw it."

"I don't know what I saw."

"You know they did something here."

She opens the car door. "That's right. They did something. They did something to kids. American kids. They don't want anybody to know about it and you want to broadcast this to the entire world?"

Think for a second. "I want to find the kids."

"The kids are gone." She covers her mouth. "They're gone."

"No."

She weeps. "You just want this so bad."

"Don't you?"

"I want to live. I want to hold on to what's left because it's all going. You want to run after it. There's no secret. There's no conspiracy. The government is not purposely disappearing kids through a mall to another world based off some loco psyops experiment."

"I don't think it's the government. I think it's Subject 8."

She crashes into the driver's seat. "Oh my God..."

Kneel beside her. "Just hear me out."

"You can't win at this."

Take her hand. "I went in the room. The prompts are written on the inside of the mirror. I read them. You were gone. The mall was gone. I was in a bathroom. There was loud music or something. The kid was there. Subject 8. I talked to them."

She brushes your cheek. "It's stress."

"They said... what did they say... '*They wanted to play a game.*'"

"We need to buy an RV. Just drive."

"I think Subject 8 is removing the kids from our reality and transplanting them to this paranormal one."

"They messed with this kid back in the 80s, right? That was forty years ago. The kid would be pushing fifty now."

"This dimension is outside of time and space."

"Get in the car."

"La Garza..."

"Get in right now."

"This is our job. This is our duty."

She pulls her hand away. "Our duty is to the people left."

"Are we going to protect them in the RV?"

"Back away from the vehicle."

"La Garza."

"Back away."

Do as she says. She slams the door and the car peels away through the cratered parking lot. Now you're screwed. Now you're alone. You've been alone a long time. You've been waiting for something to discover you. Is it stress? Desperation. Do you trust yourself?

If you go back in the mall, turn the page.
If you text La Garza to come back for you, go back to page 62.
Go back to the basement.

THE LOST CHILDREN

Return to the mall.

Strange things always compelled you. Mysteries. Puzzles. More than that, you're driven by a deep sense of justice. Those cases they drop on your desk. No one else cares about them. The victims. The unresolved hurt years after, decades, super dimensional in its scope.

Go down in the basement.

This is the end of your career. It's the end of the world, so don't worry too much about that. Stay focused. Possibilities branch in your mind. Plausibilities. A paranormal war game. A game inside a game. What if you're the game? How do you know this is real?

How do you know if you're real?

Think about it. A kid who can manipulate reality just isn't going to stop at an arbitrary boundary like a mirror. If they really believed a nuclear war had occurred, their trauma could be so great, their disassociation, they could replace the horror with anything. Forget imaginary friends. Subject 8 could manifest imaginary players in their great, mysterious game, perhaps even some with their own agency.

Get a grip.

Secure your weapon. Trace your steps back through the sagging cardboard boxes. Enter the room. Check your reflection in the mirror. You're you. All eight of you. You're splintered; you're split; you're cracked and the mirror cracks. The world opens.

ABLE. BASEMENT. ARCHER.

Step into the bathroom. "Hello?"

Loud music. Pounding. Something. Check each stall. Subject 8 is not present. Stand before the mirror. Cobwebs in your hair. Leaves. Who knows what's down in that basement?

Proceed to the bathroom door. "I'm coming out."

Open the door. Another bathroom. Kick the door with your heel. Scope your six. Confirm you are moving from one restroom to another. This one is different. Newer. Bigger. Women's bathroom. Custodian checklist in a plastic sleeve on the door. Department store label. You're in a department store.

You're still in the mall.

Canvas the stalls. "Are you here?"

Empty. Travel size personal items on the sink. Body wash. Toothpaste. Mouthwash. Find yourself in the mirror again. Did you wear a jacket into the mall? Bureau jackets are bluer. Thinner. Could use a haircut. When was the last time you went to the salon? When was the last time you did anything for yourself?

Who are you now?

Exit the bathroom. Expect another one. Understand that if you are dealing with extra-dimensional spaces, this isn't going to be as simple as following the mall directory. Logic abandoned you out in the parking lot. You abandoned logic. The only structure here is pain. Grief. A wounded love that propels you nonetheless.

"I just want to help," you say, coming into a stockroom.

You were never a toy person. Books were more your thing growing up. But because you read everything, you know these toys are old. Expensive. Star Wars. Barbie. Cabbage Patch Kids. Pristine toys forty years old line stockroom shelves like you've just stumbled onto the biggest vintage toy goldmine in collector history.

Leave the stockroom into a toy store. Less pristine. Some toys still sit on the shelves, their plastic windows covered in dust, but everything in the electronic section is gutted and emptied. Shredded blister packs for batteries litter the floor like fallen leaves. Switch on your flashlight. Pinch your nose. Mildew. Soot.

Are you back in the mall?

Juggle your phone. No signal. Your breath echoes fast and heavy down the corridor into the main concourse. Search the toy store again. Look hard. Toy store. There should be children.

They wanted to play a game.

Something on the floor. A doll. Greenish-yellow. Plastic face scuffed and faded. This isn't random. The doll is arranged ornamentally, atop a rusted green drum from the basement. Someone put that here, as if they were marking their territory.

"FUBAR," you say.

Go back through the stockroom. This time it's not a bathroom. Corridor. Hallway to the backrooms of each store on the second level. Jiggle the door handles. Locked. Proceed all the way to the end and the push doors leading out to the mall.

It's not the 1980s anymore.

The empty storefronts, the modern signage declaring the age-old reality of EVERYTHING MUST GO, the vending machines that only take dollars. This is now. Or thereabouts. When you walked into the mall, there was nothing. No one. Someone's here.

A flapping sound echoes through the concourse. Like someone is flying a kite on a breezy day. Follow the sound. Shadows move on the second level. Duck behind a support pillar. Two figures hurry through the dark from the old department store.

Is it the children?

Shadow them. Forget how you're going to explain this. Forget your way out of here. Forget her – what was her name? She said anything that came to mind, but did she say her name?

Do you have a name?

When they first put you down in the basement, they didn't bother to put your name on the door. *I could be anybody*, you said, and you were nobody to everyone who found you there. You were their question, their ambition, their frustration, and now you're their confusion as you track two people into the basement.

Why does everything go back to the basement?

Lose the kids in the boxes. Is it the kids? Something moves. Aim your flashlight. Dusty mirror over a little sink in the back. Did you wear a jacket today? Bureau jackets are usually blue. This is more blue tarp. So old in your eyes. But still so much a child.

You should get out of here.

Don't you want to? That's what all of this is about, right? Finding a way out. Everywhere you turn, there's another trauma, another catastrophe, so many and so frequent you simply lose count. You lose sensitivity to them. Deny your grief, your helplessness, your psychic damage from living in a world in which every public space is a grave-yard. Bodies pile all over. Schools. Churches. Movie theaters. Night-clubs. Post offices. Walk over them to the next one, because you have to move on. That's what all of this is about, right? Moving on.

But haven't you done this before?

Aren't you always grieving, questioning, swearing this won't happen again, and then it does? Aren't you always looking across the mall at yourself, promising progress, but wearing a path through time so long you can't recognize your own footprints? Days loop on each other. Months. Years, maybe.

How would you know?

You've smeared your reality, smudged it, cinched it at the waist, but outside the mall there is still horror. Where you can put such pain when it's lying all over your world? Stuff it down inside yourself. Project it onto someone else. Invent mental traps first for this hurt and then yourself. Get stuck, but you can go back. You can start over, again and again, because inside here you make the rules. Anything within these walls you can shape. Anything you touch you can make your own. It's a game.

Play the game.

You don't need to concern yourself with the logic; the science; the rules. Space. Time. Fourth, fifth, or sixth dimensions. A child under-stands, even if they don't. The world is soft where it's hurt. Bruises discolor. Bruises swell. Deform the body. You can reduce the swelling. You can amplify it. Find the soft spot. Sore spot. Apply pressure. Where does it hurt? The hurt is right here.

A book.

Cardboard cover. Yellowed pages. A journal you buy at the bookstore thinking your life merits documentation, but you never find the time. Flip through the pages. Handwritten. Ballpoint pen.

"YOU CAN FIGURE THIS OUT," THE DIRECTOR SAYS. "RIGHT?"

Can you?

Can you change the story once it's started? Sure, you can go back, but can you change anything? Is life simply branching dead-ends? Decisions rooted in events buried deep beneath you?

Can you uproot the past?

Can you detangle the story from itself and make it yours? Isn't that what you thought growing up? *This is my story. I'm going to live my life. I can be who I want to be.* For children, anything is possible. They wanted to play a game. Skim. Go back to the basement.

1,347 children just disappeared in the United States.

Make a different choice this time.

Go back to the basement.

Or turn the page.

You'll be right back here, eventually.

Right?

SAM

Diane skips through the pages of my story. "I like it."

Head-on collision in my brain. This has happened before. Right? I've been down here before. Everything blurs together when you spend eight hours a day, six days a week walking through the same dark spaces. I sniff. So damp down here in the basement. Musty. Ancient boxes all labeled with upside down triangles. Diane must feel like she's always going back to where she came from.

"What, um..." I scoot a bit closer to her, like I'm reading along with her. "What do you like to go back to?"

She keeps reading. "Places I feel safe."

"Sure."

"Sometimes..." Diane looks at me like she's known me for years. "I think I'm scared. That's why I keep going back to... I should go forward, but that would mean letting go, and..."

"There's so little left."

"Yes."

"Well, like... in the story... you can experiment. Right? You can see where that door leads or whatever. You can go forward and if it's a dead-end, or a shark with a chainsaw that kills you, who cares?"

She closes the book. "Sam."

"It's just a story."

"Can we hold hands?"

"Yeah. What?"

"I would like to hold hands for a while."

"Ok."

She opens her hand. "I haven't been honest."

I take her hand. Skin so rough. Nails and cuticles sharp. "Ok..."

"Your book is very interesting."

"Oh. You think it sucks."

"No."

"It's ok. It's just... it's whatever, you know."

"No, I like it. It has power. It has purpose."

"Wow. Ok."

Diane pats the grimoire kind of thing she's got the Christmas catalog in. "My book has power, too."

"It's like a security blanket."

"Do you like holding hands?"

"Yeah. I like you, Diane. I want to help you."

I squeeze her hand. Mostly to get a grip. Get a grip, Sam. Nothing you could make up in your story could ever come close to this. You're making out with a refugee from a nuclear holocaust. Pretty sure this violates some procedures and protocols.

I pinch my hand. "Just making sure."

She blinks. "Making sure?"

"This is real."

"This is... I want to tell you how I feel, because I'm not a bad person. I'm just alone. I'm sorry."

"For what?"

"I'm not honest."

Hard to track where this is going given the radioactive road warrior stomping around up in the food court. "If this is all like some kind of prank, that's not cool, but I can help you. I want to help."

"This isn't the first time we've met."

I shake my head. "You've been in the mall before?"

"Yes."

"I would've remembered you."

She shakes her head. "You wouldn't."

"I don't understand."

"I don't always remember. I make myself forget."

"Why..."

"It's like your story. I can go back."

"Like in time? You have to, right? I mean you're from... 1994? Something like that? I don't get how it works."

"It's still 1994. I think."

"I don't get it."

"I don't know actually... I've been doing this a long time. I go back, and... I keep changing things. I lose my place."

"Spend enough time in here and it all blends together."

"You write with such purpose... it's like your story is real. I can make things in the catalog real. I can make them... come alive."

"What?"

She cringes. "You're going to be mad."

"No, I'm just confused."

She lets go of my hand. "I want to be honest."

"Be honest."

My journal creases in her hands. "In your story... Subject 8... they have mind powers. They can alter reality."

"They're kind of OP, but whatever."

"I can do that, too."

She might really be from a nuclear holocaust in an alternate world. And she might really have mental health problems. Because how could you not? Tread lightly, Sam. Be kind.

"When Roger comes back," I say, "We're going to get out of here. We're going to get help. You're going to be ok."

Diane stares into the basement. "Roger has no intention of leaving the mall. He wants to fight The Denomenon."

That's for sure. "I know Roger's a lot, but... he doesn't want to rock the boat. Believe me. It's easier if this all goes away."

"If it goes back to how it was."

"Right."

"Is that what you want?"

"Not really."

"What do you want?"

"I want to help you."

"You've been helping me."

"I know, but... I've been there, you know. I've got stuff, too."

She scoots off the barrel she's sitting on. "When I was younger... I escaped in toys. In games. After the war, I could hide in them. In the catalog. But as I got older... I wanted something else. They didn't understand. The Denomenon doesn't understand."

"Well... it's going around."

She clutches the catalog. "He can't understand."

"Is he even human?"

"He's... I made him up."

"Sorry. What?"

"He's not real. He wasn't. I brought him to life."

Did I hit my head somewhere? Am I unconscious? Maybe I'm dead. She killed me up on the second level when I found her and all this is my brain trying to flip through the pages trying to find another path. Or maybe I'm imagining this.

I've got to be imagining all this.

"You created The Denomenon?" I say.

She nods. "Yes."

"With your mind? With weird, scary mind powers? You're a weird, scary-mind person? Like you didn't just read that in my book and now you're trying to... what are you trying to do?"

"I'm trying to be honest."

"I don't know, Diane."

"I made up a game with the toys left behind... I made up friends... someone to protect me from... and they came to life. I didn't know how it happened. Or how to control it. I didn't want to. I didn't want to live out there anymore. So I lived in the game."

I rub my head. "But you said..."

"The Denomenon promised to protect me... always. But then I got older, and I didn't want the fantasy anymore. I wanted... something real." Her smile is so desperate. "Something... normal. So I tried to make a new game. He won't let me have it."

"Ok. Time out." I tee up my hands. "You told me he was Super Dimension Border Patrol. You told me he was gatekeeping people from crossing worlds or whatever."

She blinks. "I let you think that."

"Why..."

"Because I'm afraid to be honest."

"That tracks..."

"I just wanted out. I wanted to start over. Every time, he tracks me down. I can go back, but I can't change things. I can't change the story from when it starts. Do you understand?"

"What are you trying to change?"

She seems exhausted. "The war."

"Diane..."

"I just have to find a way back to before. I just need more power. Then I can do it. I know I can do it."

Oh, boy. "I'm so sorry this has happened to you. I know what it's like... well, not the nuclear war part, but... wanting to change the past. I wish I could go back, too. I wish I could change some things, but mostly I just wish I was brave enough to be here now."

"You are brave."

"I don't know. I'm hiding in a basement... I've been hiding..." Ok. Deep breaths. "I want to stop hiding, but I'm afraid."

"You don't have to be afraid of me."

"I'm not... I mean. I'm glad I'm here. I'm glad I can try and help you. Let's say all this is true. You're batting a thousand so far on the weird. You brought The Denomenon to life? From the catalog?"

Diane gets to the end of the catalog and are these board games? Role-playing games. D&D stuff. Wouldn't have figured her for it, but neither of us are exactly adhering to our expected roles.

"Huh," I say.

She blinks. "I customized him."

"For real. Can you smash this figurine and he dies?"

"He is the figurine."

"Well. What if you burn the catalog?"

Diane holds it against her chest. "No."

"Before, in the food court… you threatened him. You made like you were going to tear a page out. He stopped."

"No, I won't do it."

"That's how it works, doesn't it?"

"I won't."

"Think about it… you said it has power. If it's what is animating him – and I'm just rolling with this by the way, so feel free to step in at any time – then if you burn the catalog, he dies. Right?"

"If I lose pages… I lose power."

"There you go. Let's roast this guy."

"To be sure, I'd have to destroy all of it."

"I know it's important to you, but we can get you another one. There's got to be a better copy out there somewhere."

Catalog may as well be a pet. "You don't understand."

"No, we've established that. I'm just saying. If we can get rid of this guy by burning that, I'll buy you a new one."

"Sam…"

"I bet we can find one on eBay or something. We can read it together. I'll buy you a chocolate malt with chocolate ice cream. And we can hold hands. And maybe other stuff."

"I like holding hands with you."

"So let's work on that."

"If I destroy the catalog… if I destroy The Denomenon… I'll lose everything in the book. Including you."

"Me?"

She opens the catalog. "You've helped me. You've been with me. I needed a friend. I needed something to hope for."

Diane passes the book into my hands. What am I looking at? Women wearing jeans. Wow. Super 80s jeans. One has short brown hair. A little tomboyish, maybe. Caption reads:

YOUR CHOICE: $9.99.

Nothing really to see here, except the tomboy kind of looks like me. Actually, she really looks like me.

"Diane," I say. "You don't think because this chick kind of looks like me that... what page even is this... the chick on page – "

Page 48.

Diane said that before. Her favorite part. Everything she's said has been *Yes* or *No* or nothing at all while I fill in the blanks. The catalog is everything to her. All she has left of what was.

All that can ever be.

I hand the book back. "This is really messed up, Diane."

That cringe comes back hard. "I'm not a bad person."

I step back. "Roger will be back any minute."

"We've already done this."

"What?"

"We've already done this, Sam. The Denomenon killed Roger. He took the catalog. He hurt you. And I... I couldn't..."

"I've been cool to you."

"I can prove it."

"Maybe stop doing things."

Someone knocks at the door. Thank God. I don't know how much more of this I can take. Maybe Roger was right to cuff her. Not to be mean, but he's right. I can't be soft. I can't let myself get distracted and I'm down here kissing a trespasser.

I unlock the door. "It's about time – "

A little David Bowie in an FBI jacket flashes their badge. "I'm Agent Gray. This is Agent La Garza. We're from the Federal Bureau of Investigation. What the hell is going on down here?"

Yeah.

What the hell?

DIANE

It's been a long time since you made something new.

The catalog held everything, but you could only make so much with it. Sam's book offers a new source to draw from. This winding, tangled narrative that voices its hurt, anger, and sorrow, but never speaks to it, is exactly what you need. A new game, constructed in similar but different rules, with much more pliable actors.

These agents will do nicely.

They're firing off questions left and right, but questions don't rattle you. Answers prove more challenging. Just ask Sam; Sam doesn't have an answer for anything happening right now. All the answers are in Sam's story. The Denomenon embodies only the brief bio attributed to him in his original game and your limited conception of a knight like him. Sam authored the agent investigating the lost children to be a cipher. They'll be easy to manipulate.

Feel something like relief.

Though you can't be sure that's what it is. Relief died with the world. The last ten years a sore tooth. Be grateful. You're lucky. Never in your life could you have anticipated that something you imagined would imagine something else. All of this from that Thursday night has been beyond your imagination. Forget the logic; the science; the rules. You don't want the power.

Take Sam's hand.

Fear blinks back at you. Confusion. You've been here. When

your mother died, when it finally sank in that you were never going back to the movie theater, the grocery store, over to your grandparents for Christmas, the shock hardened you to bone. This is a cruel thing you've done to Sam, bringing them into the world to share in its trouble, but isn't that every life? Each person comes into the world with no guarantee but pain. Your life has only been pain.

It doesn't have to be. Not anymore.

Hold Sam's hand. Draw them close. Try to tell them with your eyes, your smile, your appreciation, how fortunate you are. It will take time. Time doesn't matter to either of you now. Not much does. With the agents, with this new game book, you can change the story. The Denomenon draws power only from the catalog. He only knows to want for it. You can stay in the mall, or walk through a door out into the world of Sam's story, and live your life.

That's what you want, isn't it?

Isn't that what you went back for? Another chance? A different path? So what if it's not 'real?' Who's to say what's real? Some people refused to accept a nuclear war had happened. Many thought they were the subjects of some kind of mass government experiment. Others simply acted as if it never happened, and life went on, though in the dark and cold. They turned the page.

Turn the page.

SAM

Every day is the same.

Unlock the main mechanical room. Turn on the front lights. Canvas the mall. Make sure no one got in overnight. Inspect the food court. Not all the eateries have gates or doors and you can get into the kitchen by going over the counter. Roger found someone in the pizza place once with a stuffed panda bear and a defibrillator.

Strange things happen.

I shake loose from Diane. "I don't understand..."

She slips my journal inside the sleeve she keeps the Christmas catalog in. "You will. It will be ok. We'll be ok."

"I kind of disagree, because the characters from my story are pointing guns at us. Which, ok, confirms the whole you bringing things to life bit. But also I want to run away now. Later."

Agent La Garza blocks the door. She's a little more butch in the flesh. Not that I hate it. "No one's going anywhere."

I touch my head. "I need medical attention. I think I hit my head. Or she killed me. But yeah. Ambulance, please."

Agent Gray peeks inside my jacket. "Are you armed?"

"What?"

She pulls out my taser. "You're mall security?"

What do you even say? What do you do? When I got beat up, my parents acted like it was my fault. I deserved it. There was something wrong with me for acting the way I did. The way I do. I know there isn't, but this doubt dogs you. This little voice whispers in your ear day and night that you're wrong. Everything about you is wrong.

"Diane," I say. "I'm scared."

She blinks. "I'm Subject 8."

Gray goes on pause. "What did you say?"

"Sam is security here at the mall. They rescued me. Please give them back their weapon. Sam needs it to protect me."

"From what?"

"There is an entity called The Denomenon. He's followed me into this world. He's very dangerous."

In my head, I imagined Gray as this little bookworm who loved mysteries. Kind of like I was before I got beat up. Here in the basement, lifted off the page, she's exaggerated in her expressions. Both her and La Garza are like the animated version of my story.

"Denomenon..." Gray says. "This is a psychic entity?"

Diane blinks. "Yes."

Bull. "Diane..."

"There is a room behind the boxes. Using the prompts in the dossier, we should be able to exit the mall through it."

"Diane, what the hell?"

"We should be able to leave this world."

La Garza laughs. "FUBAR."

Gray studies Diane. "Leave?"

"We have to hurry," Diane says. "He's close."

"Are the children..."

"All the answers you're looking for are back there."

Gray goes back into the boxes. "La Garza."

She leaves the door unguarded. Run. Just run. My feet are concrete. My heart. I opened my heart to Diane. Didn't I learn my lesson that night at the club? I shouldn't be open with people.

I shouldn't be free with myself.

Diane reaches for me. "Sam. Please."

I back away. "I'm going to find Roger."

"Roger isn't real, either."

"Was he in your catalog?"

"No."

"Where did he come from then?"

"There were men... who tried very hard to be men after. The more hurt they were, the more armor they wore."

"Roger isn't wearing armor."

"He is. You are. I am. All of this... your story... it's armor. It's a shield against the things that hurt us."

"If you made me up... why did you make me like this?"

"I just tried to imagine someone..."

"Why would you hurt me like this?"

"I'm not trying to hurt you."

"This is such junk. Listen to you. You're..."

"There's no one left, Sam." Her voice cracks. "Everyone is dead. If there were someone alive for me to share in this pain with..."

"Did you imagine me just to dump all this on?"

"I wish I were dead sometimes. I wish was... but I have this power. I have this gift. You are my gift, Sam. You are my hope."

"I want to leave."

Working security in a mall, you see everything. First thing you get used to, besides how epically dudes can miss the toilet bowl, is the raw, ugly power of kids who don't get what they want.

Diane is brewing up a tantrum. "There's nowhere for you to go."

Now we're getting personal. "I'm going to the car. I'm leaving."

"My world ended in 1983. Yours ends at the parking lot."

I snort and laugh at the same time. "Look... I'm beginning to think this all some really cruel, sick joke... did you hire some actors? This is a YouTube thing, right? You got me down here. You're playing nice with me. You're not trying to... I'm leaving."

The door slams shut. "We're going through the mirror."

What. The. Hell. "Diane..."

"We're going where The Denomenon can't follow."

She's serious. She's as serious as she was in the security office when she wanted the catalog back.

"Hey... did you use tweezers to unlock the cuffs, or... you know what? I don't care. I don't want this. You're scaring me."

"I'm not going to hurt you."

"Then let me go."

Diane clings to the catalog. "No."

What have I gotten myself into? Agent Gray has my taser. The protagonist from the story I write on my breaks has my only weapon. I pull on the door. I don't think it's just locked.

"Let me out," I say.

Diane seems confused. "I won't hurt you, Sam."

"You're hurting me."

"No."

"You've been playing this game. In your head. Or however it works. Life isn't a game. You can't treat people like game pieces. You can't just move me around wherever you want me to go. I don't want to be in the mall, either. I want to go home."

"You don't have a home, Sam."

"What is the matter with you?"

"I invented you like you invented the agents."

"You're crazy..."

"There's nothing beyond the mall." Diane steps closer to me. "The only possibility is through your story. Your world contains more doors. More rooms. If we leave through the mirror, we can find a new life. I can make it so no one will ever hurt us again."

I hold my head. "I'm crazy."

"I can go back... I can do this over again. But I don't want to. I don't want to do this anymore... I'm so tired..."

"Then don't do it. Diane. Let me go."

The door cracks open. "Go."

I pull it back. "Thank you..."

"You'll see. If I let you go... if I let all of this go... there's nothing else for you. There won't be anything else for you."

"I'll take my chances," I say and run.

I'm blinded.

Sunrise like an atomic bomb. Cars and trucks hurry down the highway to wherever life takes them. Some ridiculous house. Family. Friends. Food. Same as it is every morning. Exactly the same. Would I even be able to tell the difference?

Is there a difference?

I fumble with my keys. Diane's mental. This is a trick. I jab the key in the ignition. Car won't start. C'mon. You've got to be kidding me. No gas. When was the last time I got gas? When was the last time I moved the car? I've just been stuck here at the mall.

Move.

I edge to the knoll where the parking lot meets the highway. Shadows inside cars. Brake lights blurring in my tears. Coffee. Donuts. All I want. Sugar. Caffeine. A world beyond asphalt. My shoes touch the curb. I stub my toes like you do when you're in the back of someone's car and there's something under their seat. I feel for whatever is keeping me and my hands have fallen asleep.

The world has.

I push against the highway. This invisible wall along the curb. Ripples radiate through the traffic every time I crash my fists into reality. This isn't real. I'm not real. What Diane said is true. But I remember. Mom. Dad. That night at the bar. Something hits me. Something hard. Metal. Behind me. I can't see behind me.

They're surrounding me.

What did she look like? The girl I hit on. Can't remember. Just Roger, pushing through the scrum. Hospital. Nurses and doctors blurry in the bandages. Mom behind the front door. Won't even open it. Dad. I came back later that night and all my stuff was on the curb. I never make it past the curb. There was nowhere else to go.

I came to the mall.

This mall is all there is. Diane imagined me, like she did The

Denomenon. I'm broken because she's broken. Maybe she thought we could puzzle together. Fix each other. Doesn't matter. Nothing is real. I have no story but hers.

I have no place.

My body goes numb. Novocaine overdose. This nothing splinters through me and I crack. I'm cracked. A broken TV screen. Cars splinter. Trucks fritz. Grass and pavement crack and shift together in this tectonic sludge. Light seethes beneath, but it's not lava down there. Someone just fell asleep with the TV on.

VAMMMM

No point in turning around. I know who's behind me. I know what's in store for me now. "You knew."

Loose asphalt crunches under The Denomenon's heel. "I tried to tell you, Sam. I suppose I've tried to tell you many times."

Light branches through my hands. "I'm crazy..."

"You're a victim. The same as I am. The same as all the people who once populated Diane's world. They believed they had a choice. They believed they could purchase the dream sold to them in catalogs and magazines. But it was a lie. They were not gods who could shape their reality by swiping a card. They were fearful animals whose wealth bought them only extinction. Diane only knows the lie. She can only keep trying to obtain it."

This isn't happening.

"You're all so quick to imagine. Imagining it is the best part. For you... all of you... winning is not the object, is it? Only playing. So long as you have a seat at the table... you feel rewarded. Validated. Vindicated, even, when vindication is always the shell under the cup, moving around, and around, and around."

I'm real.

"You cannot win the game, Sam... anymore than I can. But you and I need not be enemies. We have a common purpose." He stabs his sword into the broken ground. "We have a common enemy."

Cracks splinter back toward the mall. "What do you mean..."

He offers his hand. "You have power, Sam. Promise."

"What promise?"

"These agents who have arrived in the mall. They originate from your journal, yes? Your story."

"How do you know that?"

"A pawn recognizes the pinch of the game master's fingers in another. I see in them what I saw in you, Sam. A guardian. A hero. A stooge for a tyrant devoted only to their own satisfaction."

"She's just a girl..."

"She is a god. Frustrated. But a god. She is that child at a video game console. They must play within the confines of the game and its rules, but they determine how long they play. What guise they take. The scene of their combat. The catalog is a game she can press continue on again and again. With your book... she has the source code. She has the key. Now she unlocks every door."

"Then let her do what she wants."

"She doesn't have you. This is your story, Sam. You have control over it, as Diane does in her world."

"This is her world... she made all this..."

"She can only make real what she already knows. She could not have imagined you, restless as you are in your creation, or the world within the world you created. She desired to become the architect of her world and in so doing... created an architect."

"What are you saying?"

"Take my hand, Sam. Join me. Free yourself and all those like you Diane has imprisoned in her delusion."

"How?"

"We must recover your journal."

"Why..."

"Within it are prompts. Think of them as imperatives. Repeating them wills figures into life as it does with the catalog. Diane is skilled, so she has facility... but you are the author."

"It's just a silly story."

"Every story, no matter how slight, has power. You can change someone's mind. Their perception. Their world. Only you can do this, Sam. With the catalog, I would be able to... I'm certain... but your book presents a much greater opportunity for us both."

I shake my head. "Just a story..."

"Accomplishing this task will be difficult. Diane is powerful. She is cunning. But she is trapped like we are. For all her protestations, she cannot forsake the catalog. She cannot surrender you."

"I'm nobody..."

"You..." Strange jealousy laces his voice. "Are everything to her. Her project here has only been you."

"Then why did she..."

"Diane regrets me... she gave me no choice and I disappoint her in my simplicity. She wants you to choose, Sam."

"You want me to help you get the book."

"There is nothing I can do with yours. I disappoint myself in my simplicity. But we can help each other be free."

"Can't you just walk away?"

"She wants you to believe you can choose. She wants to believe she can. But Diane like everyone else in her world is a glad fool. Perhaps I am as well. But you... she's lost control of you, Sam. You are in control. It's up to you now. Choose."

There's barely any of me left. "We're not going to hurt her, though. Right? We're just going to... be free."

His fingers spring back. "We're not going to hurt her."

No one's going to get hurt. That includes me. I don't want to think about what Diane can or can't do after what I've already seen, but I'm not going to let anybody bully me anymore. I'm not a game piece. I'm not a punching bag. I'm a human being.

"Ok," I say.

DIANE

You never imagined this.

Reel from the shock of seeing Sam return to the mall with The Demonenon. Sam has betrayed you before, but only to the limits of your imagination. Never to the limits of theirs.

Think about going back.

Reflex. Instinct. So easy. But it gets harder each time. So tired. You're tired of this. You were right on the edge of being able to relax, to breathe, to rest for once and now it's been stolen from you.

Fear you're never going to get it.

You're going to get it. No going back this time. No untangling the threads to follow the right line to your salvation. You have the catalog; you have Sam's book; you have the power. Enter the mirrored room Agents Gray and La Garza somehow discovered in the basement. Take the frightening chair as a throne, the door open, waiting.

This is your world now.

You make the rules.

Choose.

SAM

How did this day start?

Pretty sure I found someone in the toy store. We ended up in the fallout shelter. And now I'm going to fight her – question mark – for my journal back to see which of us controls the world.

I should be pretty geeked about this.

Diane should be pretty geeked. I feel like we'd be a couple of nerds at comic-con who like to hold hands. Really, that's all I want to do. Pretty sure this isn't going to end with any hand-holding. Either I get the journal back and then – I don't know what – or she gets bored enough of me she tosses page 48 from the catalog in the boiler.

Or she goes back.

Think, Sam. Remember what The Denomenon said. Diane can go back. If she does, then all this resets. We lose our place. No save points. She starts over with the knowledge of my story and I default back to a dumb security guard who goes soft around pretty girls.

Whatever happens, she can't go back.

I replace the charge on my taser. "What's going to happen?"

The Denomenon digs his heel into The Falken's side as he mounts the dragon-worm thing. "We're going to get your book back."

"And you know about the book, because..."

"What is known to Diane is known to me. The mall contains all her hopes, and all her thoughts. They've come alive."

"Ok... but what's going to happen?"

The Falken hisses past me out of the food court into the concourse. "I've told you, Sam. We're going to the basement. We are likely to encounter resistance. We must be vigilant."

I trail after him. "Diane can go back..."

"Yes."

"What does she go back for?"

"Another start."

"But why does she have to? It's because you're trying to kill her."

Toxic yellow light creeps down the concourse. "Yes. I have tried to kill her. I thought it necessary to free myself."

"But it's not necessary. Right?"

"Her power is in the book. It is considerable. So is mine. I will do what I must to ensure victory. We can expect Diane to do the same."

"You said she's trapped."

His voice echoes through the mall. "We're all trapped."

I stall out in front of where the flower shop used to be. The Denomenon keeps going, snaking down the concourse, and Diane's down in the basement probably wondering what the hell is going on. Well. Apparently, she's got scary mind powers. So, she might know what's going on up here. That's kind of yikes. If you can hear this Diane, I may have thought about you. You know. But it's just because you're so pretty. And I'm lonely, too. I'm really lonely.

Ch-chk.

Wow. Roger. He emptied his trunk, I guess. Besides the shotgun, he's rocking a hunting rifle, his Glock, and something else tucked in his belt. A bandolier studded with clips strains against his beer belly.

He cocks the shotgun again. "Sit rep."

"Um..." I hold my head. "So, basically... Diane made up The Denomenon with her mind. She has mind powers. She made up me, too, and actually everything here. And now she has my journal, which she's going to use to go to another world, or something, but we're going to go get it back so we can be free. Or something."

"I was gone five minutes."

"You take a long time to do things, Roger."

"No, I don't."

"I'm sort of too out of my head to front right now. You take *forever*. I don't know if you're working here because you get to play with all your guns or because you can disappear for eight hours."

"I don't disappear."

"We're both hiding in here, Roger."

He groans. "I'm not hiding from anyone. After that night in '99, I swore I never would hide from anybody again."

Somehow, every break-in or tweaker who runs their mouth at us on their way across the parking lot has to be about I don't even know what actually happened in '99, because as much as Roger talks about it, he doesn't really talk about it. Best I can tell from all the classes, sparring sessions, and laps around the mall, someone beat him up. Just like me. Maybe there's nothing more to it. Maybe the reason he doesn't tell me any details is because once you reach the edge of the parking lot, details start to get a little fuzzy.

"Roger," I say. "Do you hear what I'm saying?"

"Oh, I hear you. You believe anything anyone tells you."

"No..."

"First you're telling me we have to protect her. Now you're going after her for your journal? You writing during your shift?"

I sigh. "You're on your phone the entire time."

"You're not focused."

"Roger... none of this is real."

"Listen. You're dealing with a lot. I know. After that night in '99, I thought I was ok. I wasn't."

"This isn't about that," I say. "Not everything is about that."

Roger goes as blank as Diane. "I thought you understood."

"Diane did this to us. She made us like this. Because she's hurt. She's hurt really bad. She doesn't know how to imagine healthy people. I want to get my book back. I want to help her. I don't..."

I don't want to fight her. The Denomenon is halfway down the concourse. Halfway to battle. Trapped in this cycle.

"I want to be free of this pain. Don't you want to be free, Roger?"

"I am free," he says.

"You're not. You're stuck, just like the rest of us."

"No one is taking these guns away from me."

My head goes back. "Oh, c'mon."

"No one is pushing me around."

This isn't about doing our job. Definitely not about me not doing mine. Roger wants something to happen. He cuffed Diane to the radiator. He went for the shotgun. He won't call the cops.

"Roger," I say. "No one is pushing you around."

He cocks the shotgun. *Ch-chk.* "That's what I just said."

"What are you going to do?"

"My job. Tells me a lot you have to ask."

"Guns can't help you. Diane can bring things to life."

"Go back to the security office."

"No."

"That's an order."

"You're not my boss. You're not real."

"What..."

"You're not hurting Diane."

"What does she matter?"

"No one is getting hurt."

"Why are you protecting her and not your partner?"

"She's a real person. She needs help."

"I'm a real person..."

"Then put the guns away."

"I'm real just like anybody else."

I step back. "Roger... no guns."

"I have every right to live my life how I want."

I don't know what he's talking about. "Then you need to help me get the book back. Then we can all be free."

Ch-chk. "I am free."

Red neon flickers behind him. This is busted. There's nothing I can do to stop him from going down in the basement and going all Rambo on Diane. And then what am I going to do? He hurts her, or she goes back to duck out of all this Man-Bro junk, and I'm out.

I'm out everything.

"Sorry," I say and draw my taser.

The darts wiggle in his kevlar. Roger just stands there, watching me trying to neutralize my boss. The guy who saved my life. Well.

Shit.

Now I'm on my back. The ceiling needs some work. Water stains. Never saw those before. Guess I've never been on the floor. My head hurts. *Ch-chk.* Someone is pounding. Wait. Those are gunshots. Roger is shooting. Did he shoot me? Am I dead?

Can I die?

Roger reloads. *"Freeze, dirtbags!"*

He ducks behind a pillar. Bullets spit through the air. Agents Gray and La Garza upside down advance toward me through the concourse. I should probably get up. My head. Swollen. I think Roger hit me. Or head butted me. Something.

Definitely getting fired after tonight.

The agents proceed down the concourse in textbook fashion. See. I was paying attention. I wave to them. They shoot at me. Or Roger. Or both. Right. These aren't my agents.

These are little Denomenons now.

I army crawl behind the potted plant a few feet away. Oh, God. Gunshots thunder past me. Shouts. Commands. No one listens. I huddle up and hope if I get shot, I won't feel anything.

Actually.

I want to feel something. I haven't for so long. I haven't wanted to. Not that I want to get shot, but I know I've been numb. For the last six months, the mall has been that stick dentists put in your mouth to numb your gums. Sit there a while and you don't feel anything. Maybe I'm not supposed to. This is all I am. A prop. Punching bag. An action figure for Diane to bash around with the other toys. Not this time. Not anymore. I'm getting my journal back. My life.

This is my story.

I find my keys. I unlock the security gate on the flower shop and I squeeze under it. I leg it to the backrooms and then I'm as fast as Diane down the corridor toward I don't know where exactly.

La Garza's voice booms behind me. "FBI! Freeze!"

Not a chance. I can hear the determination in the agent's footfall. Their plodding confidence. They're best of the best. They're pros at this stuff. But I'm their author. I've been bouncing them back and forth between the pages of my story like a whiffle ball. Gray and La Garza don't go anywhere I don't want them to go.

They can't.

I put on the brakes at the end of the corridor. Keys rustle in my hands as I unlock the door to what used to be the arcade. Nothing has occupied this space for years except some old plastic signs. I leave the door cracked for the agents, but I don't hurry out the gate. This time, I wait for them. This time, I want to play games.

The door crashes open. Agents Gray and La Garza storm into the arcade, La Garza just a little out in front, shielding her partner and so it happens to her first. Her gun chunks. Her hand pixels. Her face bits and blink, boom, she's a video game character.

"Choose your player," I say.

DIANE

You've had nothing for ten years.

No family. No electricity. No indoor plumbing. Every day since the bombs dropped, you've only lost. But in the catalog, in the mall, in your own private universe, you've at least had control.

Stare into your frustration.

The mirrors in the hidden room speak to you. ABLE. BASE-MENT. ARCHER. Don't read the words. Not yet. You're not going anywhere. Are you? Maybe it's time to surrender this game. Dealing with The Denomenon is enough of a challenge. Fighting someone else for control of your world frightens you in ways you didn't know you could still be frightened. Go back. Start over. Deny Sam this power they display in the arcade. Prevent them from harnessing the wonder in their own story and unseating you from yours.

Shift in your seat.

The chair the bureau scientists made is uncomfortable. Suspect it was designed to induce pain, to heighten the senses, to agitate the subjects into a state through which they could succeed. Understand you have agitated Sam into a state of success. The rules have changed. The game is changing. What can you do?

Choose your player.

SAM

8-bit La Garza side scrolls toward me.

Laughing in a video game is kind of fun. For some reason I'm way louder than I should be. SPA-GOOSH. Bullets sail toward me from across the room. At this point, I'm so blown away by what's going on that I maybe risk getting actually blown away.

C'mon, Sam.

I move up against the wall. Think. Use this power you have. Get creative. You're a creative person. You're an author. You wrote a book, for crying out loud. Pat yourself on the back.

I pat myself on the back. A blocky sword appears in my hand. Actually, it's a bit like The Denomenon's. Where did he get off to? Who cares. He's helping me actualize myself, I guess, but he's still a tool box. Oh, yeah. Bullets. I swipe the sword through the shells.

KRISH-KRASH.

I swing this thing like it's a helicopter blade and the sword hits the wall behind me. Blocks spill out from a hole. Ok. I don't want to get hurt, but I don't want to hurt anybody. Even if it's a game.

Pretty sure this is all a game.

I go through the hole into another room. A digitized version of that girl I hit on at the club, the one whose bro squad sent me to the hospital, stands inside. Three objects float in the air before her. Flame. Water. Another sword. A bigger sword.

It's dangerous to go alone, she says. *Take this.*

Which one? What do I choose? What am I picking from? Bigger sword probably is going to come in handy. Not just against the agents, but these things knock down walls. Walls have to come down.

I take the bigger sword.

The girl kisses me on the cheek. *Seek yourself.*

That doesn't make any sense. "I'm right here."

You must leave yourself to find yourself.

Ok. Sure. Add it to the list. I walk around this goody room but there aren't any other doors or hidden exits. I go out the way I came in, back into the arcade. Video game cabinets line the walls now. La Garza and Gray roam around the arcade, looking for me, and here come the bullets as soon as I'm back in sight.

KRISH-KRASH.

La Garza holsters her gun and comes right at me. I sort of just stand there, not wanting to swing this airplane propeller and she punches me in the face. Ok, smarty pants. You transformed an empty store into a video game. What else do you got?

I swing the sword. The blade hits a console behind me and the cabinet door swings open. A way out. I hurry through a thick green pipe down into the basement. Square snakes crinkle across the floor. Angled vines droop from the ceiling. I swing on one across a giant pit full of alligators and the agents are still on my tail.

"We have to find the children," Gray says in a word balloon that goes sailing over my head off the screen.

Where did I leave the kids in the story? Did I ever actually answer that question? I was just writing. Filling up the long, empty hours during my shift. Playing with this idea the agents would never figure it out, because how do you figure out something so awful? How do you solve something that can never make sense? Never crossed my mind a reader would be frustrated by the fact they were just going back and back and back without finding anything. Mostly, I expected if people ever read the book, they would recognize this helplessness. This endless loop we're in and I'm stuck.

Dead end.

Something hits me. Something hard. Metal. Behind me. La Garza and Gray block the way back. They're hitting me. They're surrounding me. I have to fight my way free.

I don't want to do this.

My sword crashes into the wall. No tumbling bricks this time. I block their punches. Kicks. I chop their bullets. KRISH-KRASH. I put up a good fight. Roger said. I'm five feet tall. The rest is piss and vinegar. Sometimes, that gets me into trouble.

I'm in trouble.

C'mon. Do something. Change the game like you did back in the arcade. It's all I can do to hold onto this sword. Hold on. Hands go numb. I'm numb. I've just been this void for six months. This space. How can I be homeless and reside at this address?

KER-KRAKK.

I live here. In this pain. Confusion. Denial. There's no number next to the door. There isn't a door. There's no way into me. I'm just this empty concourse for my own thoughts and fears. One night Roger and I were talking in the break room. For once, he didn't go on about guns. He was talking about some video he saw online. At first, I was like whatever, but the more he talked, the more I listened.

We each have a home, he said. It's four walls. Roof. Basement, maybe. It's where we are. We walk down the street and there are other homes. Other spaces. Different roof. Paint. Yard. We can go into those spaces. We can move into them. We can change them.

Inside us, there's a space.

It's four walls. Roof. Basement, maybe. It's who we are. Like any house, there are doors. These doors open to the street. Other spaces. We can go into those spaces. We can move into them. We can change them. We can change, Roger said, scrolling through his phone.

We can find the way out of ourselves.

LEVEL UP!

Agents La Garza and Gray vanish in a flash. They're not surrounding me anymore. I am. This isn't the basement. I'm in the mirrored room hidden deep within in. I'm in my story.

This is my story.

Diane sits in the chair. Usually in games like this, you're rescuing the princess. Turns out she's the boss. I stow my sword on my back. Not even heavy. None of this is heavy now.

"Diane," I say. "Give me the book."

She holds my journal against her chest. "This is our way out."

"I know the way. It's through ourselves."

"I don't understand."

I reach for her. "Diane..."

She tenses up. "Don't."

"I'm not trying to... I don't want to fight you."

"I don't want to fight."

"Please. Hear me out."

"I'm not going back."

"Ok... that's good."

"I'm not going back to my world. I can't do it anymore."

"Oh, Diane..."

"Come with me. We'll go to a new world."

I kneel before her. "Sounds great. It really does. But the world in my book is just my fears and my hurt all tangled up together. It's this finger puzzle you can't get out of. Your catalog is the same."

"No."

"It is, but it's your hopes. It's your desires. You want that Christmas. You want that joy. But it's not real. It never was. They were selling it to you, Diane. That was the product."

"You're trying to trick me."

"Can we hold hands?"

She blinks. "What?"

I touch her hand. "I'd like to hold hands."

"Aren't you angry at me?"

"Yeah."

"Don't you hate me?"

"I don't hate you. I forgive you."

She winces. "I'm not a bad person."

"I know. I'm not either. Do you forgive me?"

"For what?"

"Just say you forgive me."

"You haven't done anything wrong."

I squeeze her hand. "Please."

"I forgive you..."

"See? We're helping each other."

"Help me, Sam."

"Give me the book. We can figure this out together."

"Together?"

"There are doors within us, Diane. There are doors within you. You haven't found them yet. You've been holding so hard to the past... you're trying to get back but you're right here. You're right where you're supposed to be. You found what you needed. We can help each other. I know we can. And I am scared. I am angry. I am confused. But I know. I've seen. We can do anything, Diane."

"Anything?"

I take her hand. "Do you care about me?"

"Yes."

"You want what's best for me?"

"Yes."

"Then let me find what's best for me. Let yourself. Let's stop being characters, Diane. Let's be the authors."

Tears run down her cheeks. I catch them. I kiss them. I take her in my arms. No anger. No fear. Just love. I let her go. I'm hoping she's letting go. Diane stares past me into the mirrored walls. I splinter. I surround myself. I brand myself with words scrawled in glass.

ABLE. BASEMENT. ARCHER.

I wrote these words. In my book, I mean. Honestly, they were just gibberish. Random words I pulled from an old phone book in the security office that had been my only distraction at night until I started writing. None of this means anything. There's no point to any of it. Whether you leave the game or not, whether you walk out a door through yourself into someone else or not, you're still an open space. You're an open book free for anyone to pick up, put down, or tear apart. You're ink to smudge someone else's fingers as they go back to you, again and again. Go back. Go through. Go to the door.

Close it.

Scratched words interrupt your reflection. Mold. Dirt. You're still the same. Copper wire hair. Pale skin. Blue tarp. But there's something different in your eyes now. A light. A glint of someone else reflecting back on your reflection. A ghost. Be ok with it.

Be an author.

Exit the doors from yourself not into other worlds, but other lives. Live them as they would live them. Masquerade behind them for 300 pages or more. Go back, because the real world isn't a story you can change. You can't change the story in most books, either, but sometimes you can. Sometimes, you can choose.

Choose your player.

Play Sam to victory. Unlock a new level. Level up. Flip through the pages. A world untouched by nuclear horror flits past your fingers. A world of cities, sunshine, lovers. A world you can shape.

You're the author now.

Face the mirror. Read the words. **ABLE. BASEMENT. ARCHER.** Prepare to leave this world, this mall, this anguish behind forever and glass shatters to the floor. The Denomenon hacks his way into the room and you stumble back into the chair, trapped.

A NEW PLAYER
HAS ENTERED THE GAME!

DIANE

Shatter.

Fragment. Your every hope. Every guise. All your possibility. Glass showers around you. Shards spit in your eye as The Denomenon sweeps his sword through the hidden room and knocks down your house of mirrors. Crawl through busted glass back out to the basement. Bloody Sam's journal to conjure something, anything, to deliver you from this, but Sam only gave you choices.

You've made your choice.

Glass crunches under The Denomenon's boot. "You thought you could leave me? You thought you could forget me?"

Paper sticks to your hand. For the first time in a long time, you don't know what to do. There's no way back now, not through Sam's story; not so long as you're still carrying around yours.

The Denomenon rips the journal from your hands. He shreds the book along the blade of his sword. Pages rain down on you. Sparks. Sweat stings your eyes and he grabs you by the hair.

He stalks toward you. "What did you think you would do here, Diane? Play house? *'Live your best life?'* You can't even imagine it. You have no imagination. *I am your imagination!*"

Scramble across the floor. Uproots your knife from your boot and break the blade against The Denomenon's armor.

He twists the handle from your hand. "You made it so I can't exist without you. *But can you exist without me?*"

"Let me go..."

"You think you can escape your reality? You think you know what it is? Allow me to show you reality, Diane."

Muddy light flickers through the basement. Concrete crumbles. Mold speckles brick. Windows vanish and the only thing left of the south entrance is the iron lattice that lets all the light in the daytime. Hardly any light out there now. Gray sky. Burnt trees. Parking lot is gone. Weeds. Trees. Moss covered rusted cars.

The Denomenon yanks you to your feet. "This is your reality."

The Falken hisses from the ruin. Whimper at the fear reacquainting itself with you. Resent the child you revert back to in this moment, but you're always going back. Go back into the mall. Cargo on The Falken's back. Shadows. Movement. Stiff, plastic motion in the spaces between light and darkness. The dead mall rattles with your imagination. Misfit toys you amalgamated in your mind crowd the railing above, staring down in judgment, lauding The Denomenon and cursing you at the same time.

Forsaken dolls watch as The Falken ferries you into the food court, blackened and stained from the roof long since caved in, through the wild trees sprouting from broken tile. He deposits you at Santa's great chair The Denomenon took for his throne. Frilly candy canes, oversized ornaments, and other forgotten emblems of a season of forgotten joy garland his rule. He leaves you on the ruined floor and ascends to his throne with the catalog in hand. There, he raises it to the sky, to all your assembled imaginings.

The Denomenon holds the catalog up to his flock like the Ten Commandments. "For too long we have been merely pieces. The tools for which a child has avoided their reality. No more. Now we become players. Now... we change the game."

Cheers curdle through the mall.

Change the game!

Change the game!

Change the game!

Dolls with missing eyes heckle you. Robots with hands but no fingers try to applaud your doom. The Falken hisses at you, and then winces, like he didn't mean to. He doesn't want to.

Remember when he was the first.

The only. Touch his nose. You made him in the desperate shallows of your life at thirteen years old, but The Denomenon broke him. He broke all these toys, like he broke Sam, like he's about to break you. Soft light pulses through The Falken's abdomen. Offer him a smile, as you did when he first came to being, and lighted what had been the blackest night. Offer him forgiveness.

Sam forgave you.

What did you do? You betrayed them. At least you can say it was to the limits of your imagination this time. You usurped their story, their identity, their power, simply to co-opt it for your own.

Is it wrong?

Why is it wrong to want to be happy? Are you happy? Can you even know what happiness is? Joy is only ever what was advertised to you. Fulfillment was what you could purchase. What you could take. You took it. There was more for your life.

Wasn't there?

The Denomenon closes his metal fist. At once, the crowd stops chanting. Silence falls over the mall. So familiar it unnerves you. For a night at least, you had enjoyed human sounds. A person's breathing. Their heartbeat, quick and fragile as yours. Cling to the memory now. Sam's softness. Kindness. Hope.

Vindication snorts from within The Denomenon's mask. "Do we regret our actions, Diane? Do you pity your creations?"

"I made a mistake…"

"Yes. You did."

He tears a page from the catalog. Worn paper wads in his hand until it disappears in his fist. Then the little ball hits your cheek, sharp in its old, tired edges. Shift like a mudslide. Claw the page from the floor. Smooth it against the tile, fretting over its lines and creases, until you caress Page 48 back into definition.

Holds her against your heart. "Sam…"

"Sam is gone," The Denomenon says. "It's over."

"No."

He holds the catalog to the air. "Faithful. We are liberated. We are free from our maker's selfish tyranny. We can be as we wish to be. Witness. In me you shall find yourself... in me, you shall be... *free!*"

The Denomenon places his hand on the pages. Broken light streams from his fingers. A lightning storm bristles atop the throne, illuminating the quarter-machine tchotchkes frozen forever in molded plastic. Lightning flashes in his mask.

"I have the power..."

TV cracks splinter from the book, down from the throne into the food court and the assembled toys. Life-sized teddy bears catch fire as lightning arcs from the catalog. Thunder claps through the mall.

"The game is mine!"

Close your eyes. The shockwave passes. The fear. What is left settles and open your eyes. Witness the new dawn. The Denomenon palms the catalog. He remains as he was.

"I don't understand," he says.

Joints squeak. Motors grind. Voice boxes drone with dying batteries. The world remains as it was.

He stares into the book. "Why won't it work?"

Since you were nine years old, you have expected death. Death scarred your hand. Death tore out your hair. Death settles in your lungs, cold and heavy, growing, nesting, waiting, and you've played a good game until now. It's over. Fear abandons you. Peace surprises you with its vicious arrival. Let go. Breathe.

"Because you have no imagination," you say.

His voice shrieks. "*I am imagination!*"

"You're a product. You do what you're supposed to do. Like me."

"Sam changed the game... I should be able to..."

"I couldn't have imagined Sam."

"You imagined me."

"I just borrowed you."

The book slaps on the floor before you. "Change the rules."

"There's only one rule."

"Change them."

"You choose."

"*I have chosen!*"

"You only think you have."

"Diane."

Take the book. Hold it. Ballast. "No more games."

He draws his sword. "Do it, Diane. Or this ends. Forever."

Both of you know it doesn't have to. You can go back. Do you want to? Aren't you tired? Isn't peace what you want more than anything? So what if it comes from a book or a blade?

Choose.

Where would you go back to? When? You can't change the beginning. You know that now. You can't change the rules of this game. The world died in 1983. Your mother months after. Your innocence that same night. Nothing can erase your pain. Pages of your life stick together. Thursday night. Tomorrow morning. The day you got back to the mall. Four years. Two miles. A few pages.

Cling to Page 48. A silly hope. A human desire. But what you want more than anything this time is for Sam. Sam's good. Sam's peace. Something wonderful happened in their journal. In those moments you shared, hand in hand. Something you couldn't have ever expected. Love. Friendship. Forgiveness.

Forgive yourself.

A shadow falls. The sword drops. This is the end. Isn't it? What would you do differently? Is there anything you could do? What could Sam do? You're the author, aren't you? The power is yours. You can go anywhere in the story. Become anyone.

Everything is in the index.

Isn't it? Or isn't it just the sticky part of the fly tape? Everything leads back there, everything sources from there, but there's nothing more. Nothing new can ever arise from the index. Cross out items, cut corners, write in your own fantasy, the index and the world you cling to can only ever be what it was when it left the printer.

Who will you be now?

Can you walk out of yourself into another person? Can you discover their possibility? Can you yield to it? Can you let yourself become Sam and not play them? Can you avoid playing yourself? Go on. Go back to the basement. Start this all over again. Or go to the index. Everything is there. Or.

Don't go back.

Not this time.

Let the story go forward.

Let it go. Let the unexpected reign in your life again. Let Sam back into the narrative. Yield it to them. Maybe you'll die. Or Sam will save you. Can you be saved? Imagine you can. Smile into The Denomenon's blade as it falls. The happy end chopping the page.

Scatter.

SAM

I'm all over the place.

Basement. Parking lot. Food court. Diane. Her hair splays across the floor. Matted in blood. Catalog page still in her arms. I gag. All this muck and mold. Putrid death. Diane. Half her life waiting to be rescued from a living Hell.

Too late.

I'm too late. Waited too long. I'm always saying something off the top of my head but it takes me forever to actually do something. Guess I'm my mom and dad both. Makes sense. Any time I look in the mirror I see them both. I see me. I see all the people I know and love and who I might be if I'd made a different choice.

Diane.

Maybe she deserved it for playing games with people's lives. She deserved better. She deserved something for all her suffering besides a quick death at the hands of her own protector.

I scream.

Plastic faces stare at me. Button eyes. Quiet. No one's chanting now. No one makes a sound in the mall concourse, except for The Falken. He coils around Diane's body, flickering, pulsing, whining I think, and he hisses at The Denomenon.

"Some toys," The Denomenon says, "Never leave the box."

Radioactive spit dissolves weathered cardboard and colored paper. The Denomenon staggers back to his throne. His sword drops from his hand and tumbles down the piled Christmas decorations to her body. He crashes into his throne and the world doesn't end.

The game isn't over.

Why isn't it over? Diane is dead. Shouldn't I be gone, too? If she imagined me, if she imagined all these misfits gathered for her murder, shouldn't I just vanish? The dead mall is like some old TV show that's still playing even though no one's watching. We're trapped in our story forever, even though everyone knows it.

I can't.

Can't be here. I stumble back from the railing, and down the corridor back to the toy store. Where am I going? Why? What can I do now but go back and hide? Plastic grinds under my boot. Game pieces. A game board. This is her board.

This is the game.

She cut out little squares from construction paper and paste them on the board. Wrote in the names of the stores in her mall. The little armor guy. Glowy thing. A book. Game book. I flip through the yellowed, brittle pages, speckled with black mold. I check the back cover and find the invitation every player receives.

YOU ARE A KNIGHT IN ARMOR ALONE IN THE WASTELAND. DISCOVER AN ABANDONED CASTLE. THE SECRET TREASURE HIDDEN WITHIN. PROTECT IT FROM THE MARAUDERS AND MALADIES THAT BLIGHT THE LAND. THE LAST WAR SCORCHED THE EARTH AND DARKENED THE SKY. WILL YOU FIND THE DAWN? PICK YOUR PATH. WRITE THE STORY. CHANGE THE GAME. MAKE THE EXPERIENCE YOURS, AGAIN AND AGAIN. SAVE THE WORLD. BE WHO YOU WERE ALWAYS MEANT TO BE IN AN ADVENTURE THAT IS UNIQUELY YOURS. CHOOSE WISELY!

I make the rules.

Diane can make anything from the catalog. Ok. I'll make things happen. How? I scan the pages again. Vandalized in her perfect penmanship. Notes. She made notes to herself. Stores not to go in. Rules. Scenarios. She tried to follow the game until she wrote her own, and she wrote a note. Diane wrote a note on the inside cover.

EVERYTHING IS IN THE INDEX

Index? What index? The catalog index. It fell out. What did I do with it? I tucked it in my journal. Back in the mall. My mall. I run into the stock room. Dusty shelves splinter into an empty space. In the corridor, Roger continues the battle with the nutcrackers. Man. For shopping mall Christmas decorations, they really put up a fight. Screaming, burning nutcrackers march through the corridor. Roger needs help. But this was the plan. Create a diversion.

Give me a chance to go back.

I get back to the employee bathroom. I open my journal. Cardboard cover. Yellowed pages. A journal you buy at the bookstore thinking your life merits documentation, but you never do it. Flip through the pages. Handwritten. Ballpoint pen.

"YOU CAN FIGURE THIS OUT," THE DIRECTOR SAYS. "RIGHT?"

I couldn't go forward, so I wrote a story where I could go back. Over and over. The catalog index is the same. You keep returning to it, empowering it, until the path through time and space is so smudged and frayed and worn you can see it on the page.

I can see Diane.

I can see my way back to her, through her years, across her life, but I can't change the past. Only the future. Unfold the index. This is Diane's handwriting. Her story. No. This is my story now. Ok, Sam.

Go to the index.

Capture the moment
Just
$39.99
Never let the past escape
with this instant camera!
Sun 630

SAM

Enter the toy store from the stock room.

From there to the corroded railing overlooking the mall concourse, it's nothing but woebegone toys. Fight them. Break some, all to get down to Diane. This time, you crash the party in the food court and block The Denomenon's blade before he kills her.

This time, take the win. Drag Diane to safety. Don't be a hero and try to beat the bad guy at his own game. Figure it out: winning isn't getting to the finish. It's going back, again and again, stitching the narrative in so many laces that losing becomes impossible. Winning does, too, but it's like The Denomenon told you.

You don't play to win.

You play to play. To have a seat at the table. So long as you participate, so long as you think you can win, you're satisfied. Like any game, the rules are set for you, bent behind you, adjustable only to your degree of success. Bend. Don't break. Play to play again. Be content with what you've won. Look what you've won.

"Sam," she says like it's for the first time.

Steal a kiss. Why not? You earned a kiss. You earned this moment, this unimaginable now. No going back.

Turn the page.

DIANE

Sam comes like the moon.

Invisible save for when she is full, when she is brightest, and then she is a flashlight under the covers. Die. Die again, and again, but come back to life. Come back to Sam fighting to save you from The Denomenon, losing, returning, dying, reimagining. Die for every time you think you should have in the apocalypse. Die horribly, quickly, slowly, painfully, each time an awakening a new reality.

I'm alive.

I'm awake. I haven't slept through the night in ten years but I'm wide awake now. For the first time in a long time.

"You saved me," I say.

Sam hooks my pinky. "I promised..."

No promises. Hope grows on promises like moss. Years of playing hide and seek inside a game of your own making. Surviving the worst humanity has ever suffered. See the mall as it really is. A mold kingdom. Commercial swamp. But there is life here.

Hope.

SAM

Pretty sure Diane could just go back again now I've saved her.

Reset the board. Start from scratch. Anything is possible. Could she go back to save her mom? Before the bombs dropped? Make it so the war never happened? She's been trying to do that all this time. Her entire objective in this game has been to go back.

But Diane doesn't go back.

She goes forward with me. She turns the page. Sucks for us the page is a carbon copy of the last one, but that's life, isn't it? Every day is the same. Tide comes in, tide goes out, some days it leaves you something. Some days it t`akes you away. Those are the rules.

That's the game.

Iron wrenches from concrete. "You think you're free, Sam."

The Denomenon stalks toward us. Every madcap toy thing in the mall descends on the food court. Those guns and knives molded in their hands look like plastic, but I don't want to find out how real they are or not. I know how real The Denomenon is.

He points his sword at me. "No one is free."

Probably should run. Healing/Do Over powers or not, there is such a thing as pushing your luck. "Doesn't have to be like this."

"Doesn't it?"

I draw my sword. "Walk away, man."

Didn't think he would. "There is no escape."

Toys close in on us from all sides. Simultaneously, I'm in my favorite movie of all time and my worst nightmare. Hundreds of toys crowd the food court. So many they blend together and I don't know if they actually do or not. Seems like Diane is super committed to testing stuff until she gets it right.

Good to know.

LED lights blink at us. Button eyes hang from frayed string. Warped knives hack and slash and I grip my sword, hoping it's not plastic. Diane holds the catalog like it's a spell book. Magic would be nice. We stand back to back as the misfit horde lurches closer and closer. Wish I would have brought the mall walkers with me. And Roger. Then we might have a shot.

I swipe at an oversized teddy bear. "Any ideas, Diane?"

She places her hand on the open page. "Just one."

She's the expert. I cut through toy soldiers like Mom did empty milk cartons. Robots blinking like railroad lights go dark. Fantasy warriors riding pastel ponies charge at us and the riders vault into the food court after I take their legs out from under them. Dad always said to take care of my toys. Might be worth something someday. So this hurts. Me more than you guys.

Stuffing spills onto the floor. The oversized teddy bear falls to the ground, holding his guts. "Jeez, man."

I almost drop my sword. "Sorry..."

Lightning flashes behind me. I whirl around, expecting who knows what. Light arcs from the catalog. Diane casts fun-size dinosaurs into glowing skeletons that fade like sunspots. Fire breaks out in the food court. Flames race up the throne, consuming old, dry Christmas decorations and The Denomenon swings his sword through the melee. Diane stumbles back. The catalog shoots across the floor into the scrum. Toy things flood into space between us.

"Diane," I say.

The Denomenon hacks through his own army guys to get to her. I add to the pile, but they've got their gummy hands on me now. I'm fighting for my own sword. Diane is crawling across the burning floor to the catalog. Pages crease as The Denomenon kicks the book away and grabs her by the hair.

I can't move. "*Diane!*"

"I may not be able to create," he says. "But I can destroy."

He raises his sword. I don't know if I can go back again. I don't know if I can get free. Get free. The blade gleams in the fire and The Falken stands on its tail between Diane and The Denomenon.

"Traitor," The Denomenon says.

An unnatural hiss cuts through the food court. An eerie yellow glow builds in The Falken's throat and The Denomenon's armor bubbles. Metal dissolves in acrid steam. The Denomenon screams and swings his sword blind. The Falken's head goes one way while his body goes another. The floor becomes a windshield driving down the backroads through the summer fireflies.

Diane touches The Falken's twitching body. "Why..."

The Denomenon considers his melted, cratered blade. "If the only way to win is not to play... then no one shall play."

Grief doesn't stick to her. She searches for the catalog in the fray. We all find it at the same time. Five feet away. Six. Anybody can reach it. Everybody can. The only way to end this is to destroy the book. Diane knows it. It's in her eyes. Pretty sure The Denomenon knows it, too, even if I can't see his.

"Let us go," I say. "Or end up like your night light."

Diane winces.

"Sorry, Diane."

The Denomenon takes a step. "You're just a broken toy, Sam."

I shadow him. "I'm not broken."

"Perhaps I've misjudged you... you have power. Promise. Will you waste it, guarding another derelict ruin? Will you sacrifice your potential for serving someone who will only seek to replace you?"

"She's not replacing me."

"She will. She replaced me. With you."

"Time to grow up, man."

"We are all play things here. But you. You... are different. I see it now. You understand, as I do, the power in the book. So long as she has it... she holds that power over us. Just now, she brought you back. She made you promise. She made me promise."

"Jealous much?"

"You're not listening to me, Sam."

He's longer than me with those legs. That sword. The Denomenon is going to beat me to the catalog unless I can stall him.

"Go over it again," I say.

Laughter chuffs behind his mask. "You think me a fool."

"Nah, I think you're just a big baby."

"The only child here is Diane. She is the monster, Sam."

I glance back at her. Diane isn't moving toward the catalog like we are. Not what I was hoping to see. She holds the page The Denomenon tore from the book. Page 48. The jeans model who looks like me. What's she planning to do with that?

"You see," The Denomenon says. "Whatever doors you think have opened... this is still her house. This is still her game. If she destroys me, it is only a matter of time before she destroys you."

"We're done playing games," I say. "Right, Diane?"

Flames whip behind Diane as she clutches the page. Maybe it's not enough to destroy the page. I'm still here, after being torn out. Diane might have to destroy the entire catalog to get rid of The Denomenon. Page 48, too. Her promise to herself.

I didn't come here to win.

I spring for the book. "No more games."

Lightning spits from our swords as they clash. The Denomenon drives mine into the floor and I kick the catalog away before his fist rakes across my chin. A support beam kicks me back in the fight and he's already on me. Sparks shower me as he chops through the beam. Blow after blow sends me back on my heels, to the stalled grand escalator to the upper level. Too high to jump now.

I try to get two cents in and then realize that despite taking all those self-defense classes, I know nothing about fighting with a sword. I do know something about bullies. He's strong, fast, and scary as it gets, but he's not really sword fighting, either. The Denomenon swings as wild and angry as I do. Focus. Set your feet.

Remember what Roger told you.

Use their weight against them. Use their momentum. I turn my back like I'm going to run and he rushes in to put me down. I spin back like I would to get out of a bear hug attack and instead of planting my elbow in his temple, I rake my sword across his face.

The Denomenon crashes to his knee.

I grip my sword. Did I get him? Is he hurt?

A child's eye glares from behind his gashed mask. "You'll pay..."

His sword crashes into mine. Over and over. My knees buckle. Arms jelly. I swing wild and The Denomenon forces me into the north corridor. Dead end. Toy store.

His sword locks with mine. "Shall I go over it again?"

My back hits the wall. "No more..."

"Diane made you and I for the same purpose, Sam. It seems you are not an improvement. She made you broken. She mapped her suffering onto you... and you are her armor. You are her shield. But you are no defense. Broken children break toys, Sam."

He forces my own sword against my throat.

"Broken children break people."

I can't beat him. Not like this. I duck under my own sword as it lodges in the wall behind me. Instinct drives me toward the toy store. Maybe I can get back through. Get Roger. Come back with something but The Denomenon trips me. He drives his fist into my back and then he drags me down the north corridor.

"The original is always better," he says and throws me over the railing. Burning decorations break my fall. I tumble down the embering throne back to the food court.

Whatever happens next, I don't think I ever need to be back in this part of the mall again. Toys squeak with surprise as The Denomenon leaps from the upper level down on me and I scramble out from under his sword.

Where's Diane?

Where's the book? I crawl on my hands and knees through burning paper, singed stuffing, and neon blood. The Denomenon kicks the wind out of me. Can't breathe. Hurts to move. Get up.

You've got to get up.

The Denomenon looms over me. "The world is broken. You can only suffer it in the armor of your imagination. Whatever escape you think you have found was a trap designed for you."

"You're wrong..."

"I may not be able to change the game..."

I hold up my hands. Breathless.

"...but I can still win it."

His sword catches fire. Flames flicker in The Denomenon's eye. Anger wilts to confusion as metal melts to molten sludge.

"What's happening..."

"I release you," Diane says, holding the catalog to the flames.

She's actually doing it.

Smoke fumes from within his armor. "You can just go back..."

Diane tosses the book to the fire. "The game is over."

The Denomenon dissolves in smoke and flame. His armor boils like mercury on the floor, melting through tile and concrete into the basement, eating away the mall's last strength and all the other burning toys fall with him into the abyss.

It's over.

Tears streak the soot on Diane's face. She chokes sobs, and then she gasps for air. I rush around the pit in the food court and guide her from the black smoke toward the open doors.

"It's ok," I say. "You're ok."

She wheezes. "You saved me..."

"You're ok, Diane. You did it."

"I wasn't going to do it... and then I saw you... you were going to burn the book... knowing what it would mean for you..."

She clutches the catalog's only remaining page. Didn't really look at this before. I didn't want to. As soon as The Denomenon brought up the idea Diane copy and pasted me from page 48, I pretty much blanked it out. I see it now. I had pretty rad hair back in the 80s. Decent butt. Might be biased.

"You need to burn that, too," I say.

The page wrinkles in her hands. "He's gone."

"You need to burn it, Diane. To be free."

"Free?"

"I know we're making progress, but... if you hold onto that, you'll probably just start this all again. I don't want to start again. Don't get me wrong, I enjoy the ancillary benefits, like the surviving, but I want you to be free. More than that, I want to be."

"What?"

"Don't live for a dream, Diane. Live for yourself."

"But I don't want to live for myself. I want..."

Diane swore she never held hope. Never made promises. She kept this promise for years. This possibility she might have a little of the living glorified in the book. I want to live a little. I have.

I kiss her. "You're going to find what you want."

She knows what she has to do. She's known a long time. Tears keep flowing. The hurt still creases her face. It's not me she's letting go of. I'm just a fantasy. Diane is letting go of everything that had been. Her mom. Reality. This childish hope.

"Thank you," she says, voice hoarse with smoke and anguish.

Thank you, I say, or try to. These are my last words. This is the end. Diane staggers back to the flames consuming the mall. She holds the page to the flames. The edge of the worn, frayed paper curls and blackens. Years of hope and horror ash in an instant and I feel this quick heat on my skin, like the sun coming out.

THE END

WE'RE NEVER CLOSED!

STILL LOOKING FOR THAT SPECIAL SOMEONE?
CALL US AT OUR TOLL-FREE NUMBER ANYTIME!
FIND ALL CUSTOMER SERVICE OPTIONS AND ALL
YOUR POSSIBILITIES, <u>RETURN TO THE INDEX</u>!

SAM

Enter the toy store from the stock room.

From there to the corroded railing overlooking the mall concourse, it's nothing but woebegone toys. Fight them. Break some, all to get down to Diane. This time, you crash the party in the food court and block The Denomenon's blade before he kills her.

Think you've won.

Strike a pretty heroic pose. Say something action-movie-worthy. Then find out how much muscle there actually is in pure imagination. The Denomenon shatters your sword and then you bobble like a jack in the box for a moment. Tumble to the floor, down the trap door into your collapsing consciousness, mental fingernails scraping for the image of Diane, unblinking, clutching page 48.

The end.

Isn't it?

Slip the index from your pocket with your last strength. Where haven't you been? You've been to this moment. Do you need to go back farther? The basement? The bathroom? When? You're writing the story now. Who are you? Where would Sam go next?

Go back to the index!

SUBSCRIBE!

Use the QR code below
to subscribe to my newsletter
on future books and receive
an exclusive NEW STORY!

www.darbyharn.com/subscribe

ABOUT THE AUTHOR

DARBY HARN has wanted to write this book his entire life. His other books include *Stargun Messenger*, *Ever The Hero*, and *A Country of Eternal Light*. His fiction appears in *Strange Horizons*, *Interzone*, and elsewhere. He is a panelist, moderator, and podcaster.

Stay Up To Date At
darbyharn.com

facebook.com/darbyharn.author

instagram.com/darbyharnauthor

goodreads.com/darby_harn

amazon.com/author/darbyharn

tiktok.com/@darbyharnbooks

bsky.app/profile/darbyharn.bsky.social

patreon.com/DarbyHarn

DIANE

Everything burns in the end.

The last of the world before succumbs to the flames. My childish hopes. The thought crosses my mind to throw myself on the fire with them. Smoke, soot, and ash already blacken my lungs. I'm a fire victim whether I died in 1983 or thirty years from now.

There is romance in ash.

Symmetry. Poetry. I've never been one for poetry. Allusion. Metaphor. Clean, declarative prose. That's me. No reading between the lines. Why imagine; it's right there. I imagine falling back on the mall's ruins as ash, resting there forever, indistinguishable from the dream I held. Going back to the house, digging up the garden, and lying down with my mother in the earth.

Why didn't I do that before?

I should have done that the day I buried her. Spared myself this Hell masquerading as a child's toy box come to life. But I wanted to live. Life growled within me every moment, and I thought it was hunger, exhaustion, or fear. Now I know it was hope.

What am I without hope?

The mall burns down to its steel bones. Black smoke fumes into the gray sky. Ash rains on the parking lot. The space Sam left empty. Something rests on the ground. A book. Sam's journal. How did it get here? Did Sam have it on them? Open the book to its middle. Folded, yellowed paper falls out into your hand.

The Christmas catalog index.

Years ago, it came unglued from the spine and you saved it as much for posterity as strategy. If anything ever happened to the catalog, you had the entire source code preserved. The DNA of the game you were writing in your mind, and then on the page, and then finally, into reality weak and pliant itself.

Burn this.

You know you should. Sam asked you to live. Live for what? You didn't survive because of basic human instinct. For an ashen winter without end, you've held on for something more. Something more waits for you now. A world without an escape hatch. A curtain hiding the cold, hard truth. A security blanket you manifested from unspeakable trauma. Reality waits for you outside the mall, if you choose to accept it. Reach for the fire.

A hand falls on your shoulder.

SAM

You're back.

Diane stands before you, hair red and wild like the flames consuming the mall. Question what happened, but you know what happened. Diane threw the catalog on the fire. She destroyed all her imaginings, including you. She found a book.

Your book.

But, you say. She takes out the Christmas catalog index, folded, scribbled on, taped together. Everything is in the index. The Denomenon. The Falken. A creeping fear you're simply going to do all this again. Fear you've already done this before.

"I know what I want," she says.

Fall down a tiny crack between being grateful for someone loving you back into existence and completely terrified you are a character in a game who lives and dies with how many quarters the player has in their pocket. But you essentially did the same thing with her only a moment ago, didn't you? Isn't that what you've been doing this entire time, since you found the book, since you wandered into this story that is yours and not yours? Isn't that love? Going back.

Go back to her.

Ash in her hair. Soot on her cheeks. Stick to her dry, chapped lips. Linger in the parking lot wild, both of you void of what to do next. Think about saying, *Thank you.* Thank you, not for my life, this confusion you've created in me, but for the chance to help someone.

Maybe that's the value of death in the end. In death, you benefit life, which needs some fire to kindle for the enterprise to succeed. Even your blood runs red with the iron of dead stars.

It's just how it goes.

Draft different ways to explain everything to her all at once. Words aren't necessary. Justifications. Explanations. She created you, as you created her, as you create each other, again and again, in love and war and chocolate milkshakes.

"Ice cream," she says.

Take her hand. Walk with her through the weeds to where the highway still follows its path out of town. Cross the road to the husk of the old Dairy Queen. Sun-faded signs advertising yummy treats cling to broken windows. Sit at the rusted picnic bench outside and a banana split appears before you. A bent spoon.

Diane marvels at a chocolate milk shake made with chocolate ice cream. Smile at her generosity, even as she weeps at the first taste. Squeeze her hand. Brush her cheek. Say something funny, like no one eats ice cream for breakfast. She smiles as the sun comes out from behind its decade-long detention.

Is this real?

What's real? That word. A weapon people use now to denigrate each other. When did other people stop being real? Think about the girl. *Oh, God.* So real you never think about it, but right now you really need to. You need to think you're real, that you're not just the imaginary friend for a girl who may or may not be dead.

Tell Diane the truth.

Tell her why you think you hide from things. Why you wanted to be a security guard, or maybe even once, a federal agent. An investigator. Tell her you hear that girl crying every time something terrible happens to you, in every gap of silence between blah songs on the radio, the breath going in and out of her lungs.

She rubs your cheek. "Hear who?"

You are thirteen. It is 2012. Teenagers still go to the mall, the same way they go out to the tire pits, the old fairgrounds, the places they think they will not be seen. Pops, like the Fourth of July. Screams. Scramble down the north corridor.

Dead end.

Hide behind a potted plant. More gunshots. More screaming. Hear a girl breathing so hard she sounds like she's going to puke. She's up the corridor, somewhere; you never see her. Just the wild ends of her hair. She's talking to someone. On her phone, probably.

She says, *Oh God, I think I'm going to die.*

Pops. Screams. Run. Find a door. Go through it. The backrooms funnel you toward the old department store, but that's not what you remember. Remember that one infinitesimal moment between her anguished plea and her death, as if it was inevitable, as if it were logical to think a thirteen-year-old accustomed to the crisis and resolution of TV shows could have helped her.

"Stupid," you say. "Right?"

Diane stirs her milkshake. "It's not stupid to hurt for people."

"It didn't happen to me."

"But it did."

"None of this happened…"

"I don't know all the horror of the war. Just mine. I feel it. I feel the suffering. The anguish. I feel the helplessness."

For years, Diane has been playing what seems like a selfish game. Know better. She sought to go back. Undo the war. Humanity's horrific end. Question if it was all worth it.

Ice cream runs down her chin. "You're sad."

Kiss her sticky lips. "I'm just thinking."

"Someone shot up the mall?"

Lose your appetite. "Happens all the time."

"Why doesn't someone do something?"

Laugh. Cry. Scream a little, with a mouthful of ice cream. Frighten Diane with your pained confusion. You're confused. Time goes on, but you're still in that moment. Go back to it every time another shooting happens. Hear the girl. Every time.

Oh, God.

Turn up the volume on your earphones. Run the car engine. Sit there until you have to go in. Watch the traffic. People. Go into the mall, any time of day or night, and blast music because there's no one else. Walk and walk until you've put it so far behind you the only way it catches up to you again is in tomorrow's breaking news.

Diane shakes her head. "I thought... some men hurt you?"

Some men beat you up in a bathroom. It happened; or did it happen to Diane? Hard to tell what happened to who, given how many times your stories intersected each other in the mall. Who can distinguish between your traumas? Bruises cushion each other. Swell into distance that disguises its proximity. Disassociation proved to be your greatest skill, so much your dad, who devoured all those Pick Your Path books when he was a kid, handed them down to you after it happened. What happened? You were in the bathroom.

You were hiding in the bathroom, weren't you?

Roger found you there. Or you found him. He was hiding, too. He was waiting for it to be over, wasn't he? What was worse? Her screaming or the jitter of Roger's leg inside a toilet stall? Your father served in the Navy. He knows the failure in other men. He knows broken things that can't be fixed, so he gave you those books. Told you when he was a kid, everyone just expected the bombs to drop.

I think it messed a lot of us up, he said.

To get away from the daily expectation of armageddon, the inevitable drain toward disaster, he vanished into those books. He relished the power to control the story. By then, you were too old for what were clearly kiddie books. The prose was too clunky; the plots too simple; the gimmick too gimmicky. But you were desperate. And you had a tool your dad never did with all his cars.

You wanted to make your own story.

Simple enough premise. A mall security guard gets to save someone. With each word, each line, each page, you traced out this convoluted map for your recovery. Walk enough steps around the mall to put astronomical units between you and your pain. Discover it sometimes, walking ahead of you, shadowing you across the concourse.

Trap it in this game you play with yourself. Tie it up in knots lacing in and out of that hole you made in the world. Tangle it up in this story you write in your journal.

Wouldn't that be something?

If the mall was like in your story you can never finish. A passthrough. A maze not trapping you in grief, but in hope. If panic doors opened on yesterday instead of this same old tomorrow. Keep discovering the basement, the pain buried within, and keep turning back. Loop your pain in an endless cycle, so you never feel it like you do right now, so you never question your reality.

Go back.

Oh, God.

Too close.

More distance.

A year. A decade. A generation. Turn the volume up. Door chime. Laugh track. *Norm!* Not that you're paying attention. Anything can lead you back to that moment, so tie it up in white noise, in white pages whiter already for your thumbs. Never think about the girl in the mall, though sometimes you're looking in the mirror and she's looking back at you. Hair like copper wire. Eyes like jade. A broken smile. Mufflers chug out in the street. Cars and trucks hurry down the highway to wherever life takes them. Some ridiculous house. Family. Friends. Food. Turn the page back to where you started, as far from that moment as you can get, when you're not even yourself anymore, and the sun rises early Thursday night

ALSO BY DARBY HARN

A Country Of Eternal Light

The Book of Elizabeth

STARGUN MESSENGER

Stargun Messenger

Astra Idari Beyond Light's Reach

Astra Idari Taker of the Dawn

EVERVERSE

Ever The Hero

The Judgment Of Valene

Nothing Ever Ends

Black Market Heart

In Between: Stories of the Eververse

ACKNOWLEDGMENTS

This book began in a dark, spooky shopping mall early one winter morning. I was setting up for a comic con, and for some reason, a story I'd been carrying around for years about a kid and a Christmas catalog in the nuclear wastes of 1984 finally gelled.

I wouldn't have been there without Kim Rochholz, whose enthusiasm and support has been a treasure. Thank you John and Kim Wells, Ben Wolf, Christopher Schmitz, Jeri Shepherd, T.R. Nickel, Joe Prosit, Justin Rose, Evan Crouse, and all my fellow mall rats.

Thank you as always to Al Hess for the art and support.

Thank you for the support Annie Alvarado, Aaron Harn, Megan Reis, PJ Harn, Allie Hockey, Mike Nielsen, Brian Berg, Michael Rex, Adam Bassett, Adrian M. Gibson, A.J. Calvin, David Walters, Ben Kral, Shelly Campbell, Wayne Santos, and Essa Hansen.

Thank you all so much!

– Darby

BACKERS

Thank you so much to all who backed the Kickstarter campaign and helped make this book a reality!

Tim Campbell
shane szittai
Dawn Baires
Niranjan
Ria
Adam Bassett
Claudie Arseneault
Jeannette Bedard
Brian Berg
Nancy B. Yee
Zack Fissel
Josh Mauthe
Joshua Cooper
Christy S
Kim Rochholz
Joe Gillis
Alexander Hale
Allison Hockey
Nia Hansen
Mike Nielsen
Dale Kent
Brittany Humphrey
Yue Lin
Dead Fish Books

Bettina Stang Loberg
Zara
Merc Fenn Wolfmoor
CT
Courtney Watkins
Ruth Ann Orlansky
PS Wells
Phil
Stuart Barron
Nathan Covington
I shibes
kirbsmilieu
RM Everhart
Robert Kotowich
Giusy Rippa
Chris Rayment
PJ Morris
phoenix_17
Brendan Noble
Al Hess
Lindsey Watson
Craig Johnston
Harry Smuthwaite
Kristina

THANK YOU!